Drew knocked o̶

"Mom? You in there?"

No answer.

Drew turned the knob and pushed the door open wide. He and Linda stepped into the room. One of them gasped but I wasn't sure which one. The rest of us hurried into horror.

Madeline Forsyth was on her back on her bed, a black-and-white checkered scarf pulled tight around her neck. One hand was dipped in a puddle of blood on the bed and the other hand hung over the side, dripping blood from what looked like wounds on her palm. Her grey face and vacant eyes told the rest of the story: she was way dead.

Berkley Prime Crime titles by Paige Shelton

FARM FRESH MURDER
FRUIT OF ALL EVIL

Fruit of all Evil

PAIGE SHELTON

BERKLEY PRIME CRIME, NEW YORK

THE BERKLEY PUBLISHING GROUP
Published by the Penguin Group
Penguin Group (USA) Inc.
375 Hudson Street, New York, New York 10014, USA
Penguin Group (Canada), 90 Eglinton Avenue East, Suite 700, Toronto, Ontario M4P 2Y3, Canada
(a division of Pearson Penguin Canada Inc.)
Penguin Books Ltd., 80 Strand, London WC2R 0RL, England
Penguin Group Ireland, 25 St. Stephen's Green, Dublin 2, Ireland (a division of Penguin Books Ltd.)
Penguin Group (Australia), 250 Camberwell Road, Camberwell, Victoria 3124, Australia
(a division of Pearson Australia Group Pty. Ltd.)
Penguin Books India Pvt. Ltd., 11 Community Centre, Panchsheel Park, New Delhi—110 017, India
Penguin Group (NZ), 67 Apollo Drive, Rosedale, North Shore 0632, New Zealand
(a division of Pearson New Zealand Ltd.)
Penguin Books (South Africa) (Pty.) Ltd., 24 Sturdee Avenue, Rosebank, Johannesburg 2196,
South Africa

Penguin Books Ltd., Registered Offices: 80 Strand, London WC2R 0RL, England

This is a work of fiction. Names, characters, places, and incidents either are the product of the author's imagination or are used fictitiously, and any resemblance to actual persons, living or dead, business establishments, events, or locales is entirely coincidental. The publisher does not have any control over and does not assume any responsibility for author or third-party websites or their content.

PUBLISHER'S NOTE: The recipes contained in this book are to be followed exactly as written. The publisher is not responsible for your specific health or allergy needs that may require medical supervision. The publisher is not responsible for any adverse reactions to the recipes contained in this book.

FRUIT OF ALL EVIL

A Berkley Prime Crime Book / published by arrangement with the author

PRINTING HISTORY
Berkley Prime Crime mass-market edition / March 2011

Copyright © 2011 by Paige Shelton-Ferrell.
Cover illustration by Dan Craig.
Interior text design by Kristin del Rosario.

ISBN: 978-0-425-24022-9

BERKLEY® PRIME CRIME
Berkley Prime Crime Books are published by The Berkley Publishing Group,
a division of Penguin Group (USA) Inc.,
375 Hudson Street, New York, New York 10014.
BERKLEY® PRIME CRIME and the PRIME CRIME logo are trademarks of Penguin Group (USA) Inc.

PRINTED IN THE UNITED STATES OF AMERICA

10 9 8 7 6 5 4 3 2 1

For Charlie

Acknowledgments

Thank you from the bottom of my heart to:

My agent, Jessica Faust, for being nothing less than extraordinary. My editor, Michelle Vega, whose vision is in tune with mine—I am so fortunate. Dan Craig, Berkley cover artist, who has twice now made me cry happy tears. Kristin del Rosario, interior designer—the roosters are the best. Publicists Megan Schwartz and Kaitlyn Kennedy for spreading the word.

Paula Brog for her unbridled enthusiasm and her promotional expertise, but mostly for her friendship. Jacquelyn Orton, Kourtney Heintz, and Rob Kvidt for doing everything in their power to make sure the whole world knows about my books.

Patrick Baschnagel for his military expertise. I hope the liberties I took with military procedures and rules are forgiven. All mistakes are solely mine.

Heidi Baschnagel for her wisdom and sense of humor.

Marilyn Peterson for the Peach Delight recipe and the amazing letter I will keep forever.

Sisters-in-law, Astrid Ferrell, Carole Garcia, Katherine Ferrell, and Francis McCorkel, for their enthusiasm and wealth of knowledge. Oh, and for one day saying, "Lavender is like sage, but with class."

Krista Diez, for reading and offering such smart guidance.

Wendy Leigh, Anne Hollman, and everyone at The King's English Book Shoppe. Your support of local authors is phenomenal.

My cousin Lisa Light and her friend Adrienne Burgoyne, for knowing what needed to be done and doing it.

Chris Martin at Fat Spike Lavender Company, for answering questions and making sure Ian's cookie recipe had the right flower.

My parents, Chuck and Beverly Shelton. They tell everyone about their daughter's books. They've always been my biggest cheerleaders. That's pretty terrific.

My husband, Charlie, and my son, Tyler. I love you, and you supply me with amazing stories every day!

One

Visions of strung-together cherry tomatoes danced in my head; corn kernels tossed in celebration and then strewn across a dirt floor. Then, a gigantic pumpkin carved into the shape of Cinderella's carriage, but with seeds mistakenly left inside. And finally, I'm in my favorite overalls that have been mysteriously Bedazzled.

It was a waking nightmare.

But that was just a state of horror taking over. I couldn't believe what I had agreed to do. A wedding? What was I thinking? Why had I said yes so quickly?

I'd had plenty of practice, of course. Twice in front of the justice of the peace made me an old pro at commitments of the heart, temporary though they might have been. But this time it was going to be with a pastor and a walk down an aisle; something old, something new, something borrowed, something blue, something different—for me at least, and something that was going to require a farmers' market theme.

The only good news: it wasn't my wedding. Phew!

Instead, I'd agreed to be my good friend, Linda McMahon's, twice-divorced maid/matron of honor (we'd simplified the title and decided to call me her "Number One") when she married Superman look-alike Drew Forsyth. In five short days.

The nuptials were on the fast track because of a surprise, but not the old-fashioned kind. Though I'd only recently learned exactly what Drew's job was, I'd always guessed it was something mysterious and important. When I'd first met him, he and Linda never quite answered the question "What does Drew do for a living?" But as time went on and we became closer, and Drew seemed to be a more permanent part of Linda's life, I learned that Super Drew was in the *military* (said in hushed tones). For a while, that was all I knew, but about a month ago I'd learned that he was part of a "military special operations" group. I still didn't have the specifics, but I was terribly impressed. It was only within the last twenty-four hours that Linda had confided in me that Drew was a Navy SEAL. My level of impressed shot even higher.

It wasn't so much that Drew's job was a secret; it was that what he did when he was performing his job was usually a top top top secret. People who did those sorts of things just didn't go about sharing the details of their duties, so it was easier to keep everything about it close to the flak jacket, so to speak.

Drew had been called to duty, which for the rest of us meant Drew would be leaving for some time to go places we couldn't know about, to do things we couldn't know about. He'd been preparing Linda for his certain departure, but it still was a surprise when the call came.

And when it did, it solidified for Drew that he didn't want to leave without first making Linda his wife. She agreed.

Yes, it was very romantic and the stuff of movies with heart-wrenching symphony music, but five days wasn't a lot of time to pull off a wedding.

Their "I do's" could have been handled easily with a quick trip to the justice of the peace—I knew the address by heart—but Linda wanted a real wedding, with guests and all the trimmings. Considering the short amount of time available to plan and prepare, the ceremony wasn't expected to be lavish by any means. But as her Number One, I was responsible for helping make her dream day . . . well, dreamy.

Of course, the ceremony would take place at Bailey's, the farmers' market where we both worked. And the other vendors would help, so it might not be too terrible. But still, being in charge of someone else's "happiest day of her life" is a big job; one I wasn't so sure I'd be able to handle successfully.

I hadn't even been in my fraternal twin sister's wedding. Allison and her husband, Tom Reynolds, had, in deference to our hippie parents, gotten married on a South Carolina beach as the sun rose over the ocean horizon. We'd gathered together, but no one had to do anything beforehand—like plan things, decorate, or help pick out dresses and the like.

I was ill-equipped for such duty. When Linda told me she wanted all food, flowers, and other decorations for the wedding to come from Bailey's, my first thought was *Shoot, I don't even know what she means by "other decorations."*

It had been only one day since I told Linda I'd be honored to stand up with her, and it hadn't been a lie—I *was* honored. But when I really thought about what the job entailed, I realized I was in over my head. Cowardly, I wished for an out, something like the appearance of Linda's long-lost best friend, but it didn't seem likely to happen. I was committed; and truthfully, I would never ditch my duty, my friend in her time of need. Adding to my desire not to let her down was the fact that she was all that was left of her family. Her parents had died when she was a teenager, and she was an only child. We, the Bailey's vendors, were her family now, and none of us would let her down.

So, after spending the night tossing and turning, I did what I normally do in times of extreme crisis: I called my sister Allison and begged for help. I asked her to stop by my stall this morning and offer me words of wisdom. She picked the perfect time—I wasn't busy, but Linda, her stall right next to mine, was helping a customer, so she wouldn't overhear as I vented my concerns.

"Becca, make a list. For instance, I've already decided on an area of the market that will be perfect for the ceremony. Just let me know how many people will be there. Work with Abner on flowers, Stella on a cake, and so on. One thing at a time," Allison said.

Allison is the manager of Bailey's. She took the job ten years ago and has turned the market into one of the top markets in South Carolina. I usually tell people that she's turned it into one of the best on the East Coast, but I have no statistics to back up such a claim.

Bailey's is one of the bigger markets in South Carolina, located outside the town of Monson. Its long, U-shaped design could be seen a good distance down the state highway it was located on. Until recently, a large green and white painted sign announced its location. But the owners had just put up a lighted sign with programmable features that made us all feel uncomfortably modern. Market people didn't usually see much use for lighted signs that could display different things at the touch of a keypad, but we'd get used to it.

I made and sold berry jams and preserves, and worked with many other vendors who made and/or sold many other products. Linda dressed like a character from Laura Ingalls Wilder books, and for seven years had sold homemade fruit pies from the stall next to mine. From the moment we met at Bailey's, we knew we'd be friends.

"Actually, Linda wants me to talk to both Stella *and* Mamma Maria about cake, and maybe some mini pie ideas, or something," I said. Mamma Maria was the one exception to Linda's "Bailey's Vendors Only for the Wedding" rule. Mamma worked down the road at the Smithfield Farmers' Market. She baked piled-high cream pies that melted on your tongue and made your eyes roll back in your head out of sheer pleasure. She was built just like her pies—stacked—and she was dating Bailey's peach vendor, Carl Monroe. We'd all become pretty good friends.

"There you go. Talk to Stella and Mamma. This could be fun. You can ask for samples. You'll get to taste test." Allison smiled.

"Good point," I said as I chewed at my bottom lip.

Allison laughed. "Becca, tell Linda you're a little freaked because you want to do everything right and you want to make sure you accomplish her vision. Be sure you understand exactly what she wants. Everyone here will take good care of her and Drew. You really don't need to worry. You'll have it easier than most . . . what did you call yourself, Number Ones?"

"That's okay to say to a bride? That I'm a little freaked? Aren't I supposed to be the nonfreaked one?"

"Well, you know how to handle it so she'll understand."

"Do you know who she's marrying?" I asked, my voice high-pitched.

"Of course. Drew Forsyth."

"Yeah, well, he's pretty darn amazing on his own, but that's not what I'm talking about. I mean, do you know *who* she's marrying?"

"Linda told me he's in the military," Allison said quietly. "He does secret things, which is pretty impressive." I'd leave it to Linda to tell Allison Drew's job title. "But I don't know more than that." Allison shook her head, her long, dark ponytail swinging slightly. I would never have either long or dark hair. Allison's tall, dark looks are from our father and are the yin to the short stature and blonde hair yang I received from our mother.

"Drew is the son of Madeline Forsyth."

"Okay. Well, the name is familiar, but I can't pinpoint where I've heard it before."

I was stunned that I knew something my sister didn't. "Madeline Forsyth is a banker . . ."

That was all I had to say.

"Oh, my goodness," Allison said. "Is she . . . is she . . . ?"

"Yes, she's in charge of all horror, if you know what I mean." Central Savings and Loan, led by Madeline Forsyth (nicknamed For-*scythe* as a result of her ability to cut someone down just like the wickedly sharp mowing instrument), had been on a foreclosure bender lately. Just in the last week, I'd heard of two farms that she herself had served papers on.

Because one of the farms that Central had recently taken was Simonsen Orchards, a place that I'd become very familiar with the previous fall, I'd paid extra attention to the bank's activities. Matt Simonsen had been murdered behind a Bailey's stall. It took some crack police work and some of my own nosiness to figure out who the killer was. I had mostly recovered from the injuries I sustained as I tried to run from the killer, who was now, fortunately, behind bars—forever or a hundred and twenty years, whichever came first.

The day I heard that Simonsen Orchards had been foreclosed upon had been both weird and sad. Those of us who made our livings off our farm-grown or homemade products were always sad when we heard about someone losing their land, but it was extra hard to hear that Simonsen Orchards had gone from one of the top-producing peach orchards in the region to deeply in debt because of the murder.

"Oh, dear. Madeline Forsyth. I can't believe I didn't make the connection. That's . . ." Allison muttered.

"Awful, terrible, a cruel twist of fate, what?"

"A challenge," Allison said sternly. "Look, you're

supposed to be there for Linda and Drew. What Drew's mother does and who she is don't matter."

"I've met her, Allison. She's tall and loud, both literally and figuratively, and will crush me if I don't help make her son's wedding just perfect. According to Linda, she's having a hard enough time accepting the fact that her son is marrying a pie baker who works at a farmers' market; if I ruin the wedding, she might just foreclose on all of us."

Allison smiled patiently. "That might be a somewhat dramatic take on it, but I do feel sorry for Linda."

"Yeah. Me, too."

"Linda, yoo-hoo!" A voice sounded from behind Allison. She turned sharply, and I peered around her.

"Well, speak of the devil," I said.

Moving at the speed of a type A personality on caffeine, Madeline Forsyth approached. She was at least seventy years old but didn't look a day over plastic surgery. She was tall, thin, and immaculately dressed in a beige Chanel suit with gold-rimmed black buttons. Dust on the market floor flew from the falls of her expensive pumps, but she didn't seem to notice. She was focused on her soon-to-be daughter-in-law.

Linda's attention was pulled away from her customer and to the approaching storm. The customer, a young woman in denim shorts and a flower print shirt, read the situation quickly.

She smiled at Linda and said, "I'll come back for the pie when I'm done shopping." And then she scurried away.

Linda put on a patient smile and said, "Madeline, how nice to see you."

"Uh-huh," Madeline said as she stopped in front of Linda's stall. She stood just far enough away so that her suit wouldn't come in contact with Linda's display table. "Do you not have time to answer your phone?"

"Uh, well . . ." Linda said as she reached into her pioneer dress pocket. She pulled out her phone and looked at it. "It doesn't say I've missed a call."

"Well, you have. I've tried to reach you at least a dozen times in the last hour."

"Really? We'd better double-check the number you've got for me."

Madeline waved her hand. "We'll do that later. For now, I'm here to let you know about dinner tonight."

"Dinner?"

"Yes. When I spoke to Drew earlier, he said that he'd neglected to tell you about the dinner this evening."

"I wasn't aware of a dinner this evening, but maybe he just hasn't gotten around to telling me yet."

Madeline *tsk*ed. "Drew not giving early notice for a dinner? Surely, I raised him better than that."

Fleetingly, I wondered what I would do in such a confrontational situation. Considering the fact that I'm twice divorced, I thought I'd probably just call a lawyer.

Linda, however, was more patient and polite than I would have been, so she just smiled, nodded, and remained silent. Madeline was sure to continue speaking.

"Anyway, the dinner is at my house this evening. I've invited some of Drew's cousins—one will be his best man at this hurried wedding thing that we're having. I want you to meet them before you join the family."

"That would be lovely. I look forward to it. What can I bring?" Linda kept her cool.

"Nothing, of course. I have a cook who does his own shopping." I guessed this was her way of saying that she'd never buy groceries from Bailey's.

"That will be fine," Linda said.

"It will be early. I have work to do this evening. Be at my house at five o'clock."

"Of course."

Madeline did a three-point turn in her pumps and faced me.

"Becca Robins, right? You're the maid of honor?"

"Yes," I said, as though someone had punched me in the gut. Why was she speaking to me?

"You're invited, too," she said regrettably. "Bring a date."

"Thanks," I said. My eyes were wide, and I was unsure what to do with my hands.

Madeline marched her way back down the aisle, toward Bailey's exit. I watched as my friends and market mates observed the powerful woman leave us all in her wake. Barry Drake, of Barry Good Corn, thumbed his overalls and sniffed; Herb and Don, the Herb Boys, flanked their stall and gave Madeline the stink-eye; Abner Justen leaned on his wildflower display table and looked cranky; Jeanine Baker, the egg lady, crossed her arms and looked scared; Allison, still in front of my stall, looked interested and focused; and, last but not least, my very adorable boyfriend, Ian Cartwright, stepped out of his yard artwork stall and caught my eye. He gave me a semi-amused wink.

He knew he'd just been invited to dinner, too.

There was a lot of spite in the aisles of Bailey's that afternoon. Though they might not have known until that moment that Linda was going to marry into the For*sythe* family, everyone knew exactly who Madeline Forsyth was, and no one liked her one bit.

The thing was, though, someone must have taken their dislike to a whole new level, because the Chanel suit and expensive pumps tornado that blew through Bailey's was the last time anyone saw Madeline Forsyth alive.

Two

Linda and I talked briefly before she left Bailey's for the day.
I didn't tell her about my conversation with Allison because I figured she had enough on her plate. She did her
best not to show how much Madeline's whirlwind visit
bothered her, but I knew it had. Otherwise, she never
would have left the market early on a busy Friday afternoon. She packed up her truck and her remaining pies,
and went to get ready for dinner. I promised I'd be there
on time.

In between my own customers and per Allison's sug-
gestion, I made a list. I also talked to other vendors. I'd
be taste testing cake samples from Stella and a peach dish
and some banana cream mini pies from Mamma Maria
the next morning. Abner took his assignment as flower
arranger in stride, but I caught it when the corner of his

mouth twitched like he just might smile. He was pleased to have been asked even if he didn't do "pleased."

The biggest surprise of the day was when Herb and Don, of Herb and Don's Herbs, stopped by my stall.

They were both life and business partners, and had had a stall at Bailey's for about three years. Herb was short, bald, and adorable; Don was tall with a head of curly auburn hair, and as close to a male model as I'd ever known. Apparently, when he wasn't working with herbs, Don was in the weight room that filled their entire basement. He'd been gifted with a chiseled face and swore he hadn't resorted to plastic surgery to get that perfect nose.

Don was literally pulling Herb by his arm.

"Becca," Don said, "you just have to use Herb."

"Use him for what?"

"The music at the wedding ceremony, of course. He plays the violin beautifully. You won't regret it," Don said, still holding tight to Herb.

"Really? You do?" I asked. If he really did play, I was more than thrilled. Allison had been right—Linda would be well taken care of.

Herb looked sheepish, his bald head blushing slightly.

"Oh, don't be modest," I said. "If you can play, you've got the job. Do you know that tune they play when brides walk down the aisle?"

"The Wedding March?" Herb asked, his eyebrows rising to his nonexistent hairline.

"Yes, that's the one," I said. I'd never paid attention to the name of the tune, but it did make sense.

"Of course," he said confidently. Don let go of his arm.

"Terrific. Okay, today's Friday, the wedding will be

Wednesday. We'll have a rehearsal early Tuesday morning. Bring your violin."

Herb looked at Don and then back at me. "Don't you want to hear me play beforehand? To make sure, you know, that I can play?"

"It's either you or something I download off the Internet and put on my iPod. Will you be better than that?"

"Uh, yes, I think so."

"Great. The job is yours."

I wasn't being lazy. I knew that if Don said Herb could play beautifully, he could play beautifully. First of all, Don wouldn't lie about such a thing, and second, no one would offer to do something that would risk Linda's wedding. Again, I noted to myself how right Allison had been. This was probably going to be the easiest wedding to plan in the history of all weddings.

I hadn't written "music" on my list quite yet, but as Herb and Don walked away, I added the word just so I could feel the satisfaction of putting a check mark by it.

"How's it going?"

"Hey, you," I said as I smiled and put down the paper and pencil.

Ian Cartwright, ten years my junior, was my adorable boyfriend, although Allison said he was more exotic than adorable. He was about five-feet-ten, thin but muscled; he had a total of eight tattoos on his body, my favorite one being the sun on the back of his right hand. He wore his long, dark hair pulled back in a ponytail most of the time, and his dark eyes still made me swoon, even after dating him for seven months.

Unfortunately, our otherwise perfect relationship had hit a small snag. Ian wanted me to travel with him back to his home in Iowa to meet his family. When he first asked me, my answer had been a firm "Uhhhh," but the look on my face must have given away my true feelings.

I'd tried to explain to him a number of times that having gone through two divorces made me wary not only of marriage but also of the normal steps one takes on the way to being married, like meeting the family.

I'd tried to explain that though I felt more for him than I'd ever felt for anyone else, our relationship was still new enough that I wasn't sure I was ready to take such a big step.

He said he understood, but I knew he didn't, really. We were still together, but I could feel the strain between us. I didn't want that strain, but I also didn't want to do something that felt like the wrong thing to do, like meet a family I wasn't ready to meet. I hadn't given him a firm answer yet, but said I would soon. I knew he was becoming increasingly impatient.

"I did something," he said with a genuine smile.

I smiled back. There was no strain at the moment, and that was good.

"What did you do?"

Ian rubbed a finger under his nose. "Well, you might not be pleased."

I continued to smile, ignoring the small thread of dread building in my chest. Uh-oh, surely he hadn't invited his family here?

"Okay, tell me," I said.

"You know that coffee shop we love—Maytabee's?"

"Sure. Great coffee."

"And pastries," Ian added.

"Uh-huh."

"Well, the manager of the one by my apartment is also the owner. She's from Monson, but she has four other locations in Charleston."

"She sounds successful," I said. I had no idea what he was leading up to, but the dread was disappearing.

"Anyway, I took some of your strawberry jam to her a week ago."

"You did? Why?"

"To see if she might be interested in selling it in her stores."

My mouth dropped open. "Really? What did she say?"

"She wants you to do a presentation to her other managers. She loved the jam, but she likes to let her managers have a say in the products they carry."

"Wow, Ian, that was unbelievably . . . helpful of you."

Ian laughed. "I wondered if you'd have that reaction. You don't know quite what to make of it, do you? You don't like people messing with your business, but you realize this might be a good opportunity. Don't worry, you'll catch up soon enough."

I nodded slowly. Then I did catch up, and realized how kind it had been for Ian to talk to the owner of Maytabee's. I'd been wanting to find ways to expand my business, and this was a perfect start. "Ian, thank you. You're right." I leaned over the display table and kissed him quickly, in front of the entire farmers' market world.

"You're very welcome, but unfortunately there's some bad news to go along with my great and fantastic news. She just called, and she'd like you to do the presentation Monday morning, when her other managers will be in town for their monthly meeting. What with the wedding announcement yesterday, I think your next few days, Monday included, have become very full."

"True." I put my hands on my hips. I'd already decided I wouldn't have much time to work at the market over the next week. Because I'd already committed myself to not working full-time, I thought I could probably fit in a quick presentation. "I'll make it work. Hey, you want to come to the presentation with me?"

"Sure. Let me know what I can do to help you prepare. I'm good with PowerPoint." Ian smiled. In fact, he was good with anything that had anything to do with computers.

"That's a deal. I'd appreciate it." We smiled at each other, and though I knew he didn't want me to know he was still perturbed about my continued indecision about visiting his family, I saw it in his eyes. "So, how about dinner tonight? You available?"

"I am. Thanks for the invite. I presume we're going to Madeline Forsyth's?"

"Yes. How about that show she put on?" I asked.

"She's . . . interesting."

"Poor Linda."

"I agree."

We made arrangements to meet at Ian's apartment at about four thirty. I'd promised Linda I wouldn't be late. We estimated that it would take about fifteen minutes to get to Madeline's from Ian's, so four thirty would make us slightly early.

Of course, had we known Madeline's fate, we probably wouldn't have been overly concerned about being on time.

Three

My farm was west of Monson. There were lots of farms, some small and some big, west of Monson. The countryside east of Monson was populated with bigger, more commercial farms as well as big houses on large lots. The people in the big houses hired people to take care of their land/lawns. The country east of Monson was where the big money was, so it was no surprise that that was where Madeline Forsyth lived.

Ian lived in Monson, his studio and apartment in the garage of one of the cleverest old men I'd ever met. George McKinney couldn't see well, but he could tell a story better than anyone I knew—that was if the story was full of blood and violence. I drove into Monson, dropped my dog and favorite "person" in the world, Hobbit, off with George, and Ian and I took his truck to Madeline's house. Our trucks were both about twenty years old, but mine was bright orange and his, a dark navy blue. When we wanted to look respectable, we took his more understated vehicle.

"Boy, Madeline Forsyth is something else, isn't she?" I repeated part of our earlier conversation as I twisted the dial on the truck's radio.

"Yeah," Ian said. "She made an impression. Did you talk to Linda about it?"

"Just a little before she left. She checked and double-checked her phone. She couldn't understand why Madeline said she'd called when there seemed to be no way she had."

"Did Linda talk to Drew about it?"

"Yep. He said he knew nothing about the dinner. Nothing at all. He knew one of his cousins—the one who will be his best man, apparently—was in town from Spartanburg. He told her that if other cousins were attending the dinner, it was a surprise to him."

"Why do you suppose Madeline made it such a big deal?"

"Probably just to make a scene and cause more heartburn for Linda," I answered.

"That's too bad."

"This could be an interesting evening," I said.

Hesitantly, Ian reached over and grabbed my fingers with his tattooed hand. I looked down at the sun that I'd looked at and held on to probably almost a million times by now. I knew where every tattoo on his body was located and what they were. A couple of weeks earlier, before he asked me to go to Iowa with him, his reach wouldn't have been so hesitant.

"You know, unlike Linda's circumstances," he said, a

smile in his voice, "my family is very middle-class, very normal, and thrilled that you and I are dating."

"You might have mentioned that once or twice."

"Oh, when? The times I ask if you'll come to Iowa with me to meet them?"

"Yeah."

"Anything new on that front?"

"Still thinking," I said. My throat tightened around the words. I was on the verge of being downright rude, and he deserved better than that. "Just give me a little longer, Ian. I'm sorry."

He smiled patiently, his dark eyes framed in the shallowest twenty-five-year-old laugh lines. His black ponytail was smooth and perfect, and he'd put a casual sports jacket on over his normal T-shirt and jeans. I found him fetching, and when he pulled my fingers to his lips, I almost gave in and said I'd go anywhere with him, but a big lump of commitment phobia clogged my throat and kept me from speaking.

"No hurry," he lied as he lowered both our hands to the middle of the truck's bench seat.

He might not have meant it, but telling me not to hurry was the only response that wouldn't make me defensive or angry. He knew me well.

It wasn't that I didn't care for him more than I'd ever cared for either of my two ex-husbands. I was head-over-heels in love with the man who held my hand. But I'd had a version, lesser though it might have been, of this feeling often enough in my life that some time had to pass before I recognized it as valid and lasting. Before I met someone's family, I wanted to be sure my feelings were one hundred percent real. I still needed some time, which was a lousy thing to tell him, I knew. Ian, however, claimed he was already certain how he felt, and a by-product of his feelings was that he wanted me to meet his family.

Fortunately, the conversation had to be further delayed because Ian was turning onto Madeline Forsyth's circular driveway. A tall fountain artistically moved water in the middle of the circle, and a large redbrick mansion sat on the far side of the driveway.

Ian, being an artist of yard art things, was more interested in the fountain than in the house.

"I bet I could re-create that entire thing in metal," he said.

"That would be amazing."

The fountain consisted of three simple concrete bowls and a spout that sprayed water in the shape of an umbrella into the top small bowl. From there the water flowed over edges into the middle, mid-sized bowl, and then into the bottom large bowl. The effect gave the impression of a layered wedding cake.

"I wonder if Ms. Forsyth would mind if I came out later and inspected her fountain." There was a smile of sarcasm in his voice, but I knew he'd like the opportunity.

"I bet she wouldn't mind. Or we could do it and not tell her."

Ian pulled his truck to the side of the house where Drew's gray Honda and two other sedans with South Carolina license plates were lined up at forty-degree angles. He picked an open space and continued the pattern. Linda's truck wasn't anywhere to be seen, so I assumed that Drew had picked her up.

"Okay, what can I carry?" Ian asked as he turned off the ignition.

"I think I got it," I said, lifting a huge basket from the truck's floor, where my feet had been keeping it stable. I'd filled the basket with lots of my homemade preserves and jams, some of my famous strawberry as well as other fruits. I'd stocked my freezer with barely enough to get me through the winter months. People liked my preserves and jams, but the unexpected winter demand had caught me off guard. And if I got the okay to sell product at Maytabee's, I'd have to bump up storage and production even more, to be prepared for next winter.

"I don't think you've given me as much jam as is in that basket," Ian said as he peered at the gift.

"I didn't need to get you to like me. Madeline Forsyth is another story altogether. I had to bring out the big guns. I even snuck in some of my hidden reserve of pumpkin preserves."

"I shouldn't be so easy, should I?"

"Nah, I like easy."

Ian hurried around to the passenger side and helped me and my basket out.

I grew amazing strawberries, if I said so myself, but I also grew pumpkins. Pumpkins were an easy crop and gave me the main ingredient for my pumpkin preserves, which were heavenly—if I said so myself. The process for making the pumpkin preserves was labor intensive, though, so I didn't make very much.

Almost everyone who worked at Bailey's purchased (or traded for) the pumpkin preserves for holiday gifts. I'd had a big run on those last December, but I'd kept a dozen or so jars hidden away for emergencies.

If Madeline Forsyth didn't like me after tasting the contents of the gift basket, nothing would work.

"Becca, Ian! I'm so glad you're here!" Linda said as she stood in the open doorway.

"The basket is almost bigger than you. Do you want me to carry it?" Ian asked.

"I'm good, thanks."

We made our way toward the door. I always had to take a second glance at Linda when she wasn't in her market getup. And tonight was no exception. She looked nothing like the woman who worked at Bailey's, wore pioneer clothing, and sold the most amazing fruit pies in South Carolina.

"You look so grown-up," I said as I reached around the basket and hugged her.

"Drastic times call for drastic measures." She laughed.

She wore a simple sleeveless black dress and girl shoes with heels. The farm and market life didn't have much use for such frivolity, but outside the market Linda pulled it off like a pro. Her short blonde curls weren't hidden under a bonnet, but bounced freely and framed her high cheekbones perfectly.

"Ian, long time, no see," she joked as she hugged him, too.

"You look great, Linda."

"Thanks. You two, too. Come on in. I'm still standing and all my hair is on my head even though Madeline is late to her own party."

"She's not here?" I looked around the entryway. The floor was patterned marble and bordered by two walnut stairways that probably led to paradise.

"No, not yet. Levi—the cook—said she left earlier this afternoon. She promised to be back on time, but I suppose it's okay is that she's not here yet. I've had the cousins to myself for a good half hour. It's given me some time to get to know them."

"Well, she has a lovely house," I said.

"Yes. I bet that amazing basket is for her."

"Definitely."

Linda took the basket and placed it on a table next to the front door. She peered at the contents and said, "Thanks, Becca. This is a very kind gift—she'll appreciate it. She's a battle axe, sure, but she really does have a soft spot. It's rare and unusual to see it, but this is the sort of gift that might bring it out."

"That's the plan," I said.

"Come on in and meet everyone. Levi will watch the food and we'll eat soon, even if Madeline doesn't show."

She tried to make light of Madeline's tardiness, but I knew it bothered her. I didn't think she was worried about her future mother-in-law, but she might feel she was being slighted yet again.

It was a good thing that she and Drew loved each other so much, because Madeline had done her best to fill their relationship with obstacles and strain. Linda insisted that they were handling it, but I often wondered.

I couldn't quite grasp Drew's relationship with his mother. I only knew what Linda told me. At times I thought it was strained, at times nonexistent, and then, at times, I thought they might get along okay. I didn't want to cause more stress for Linda, so I never pushed her too hard for more information. Besides, it was none of my business.

Ian and I shared a raised-eyebrow glance before we followed Linda down a short hall. We had spoken about my concern for Linda, and he supported that concern. We both knew how important it was to never mettle in any couple's relationship even if a friend was involved.

As Linda's Number One, I was going to have to be extra careful. Biting my lip or the insides of my cheeks to keep from speaking was not in my natural skill set. But I'd have to learn.

The hall opened to a large, plush family room that was occupied by Drew and his cousins. The room was furnished with two big couches and lots of well-placed, comfortable-looking chairs. There was a huge television set attached to the wall above the fireplace. Everything was in muted beiges and browns, except for a few purple pillows on the couches. I didn't know what I'd expected, but I was surprised that a room in Madeline's house felt so comfortable.

"Becca, Ian," Drew said as he caught sight of us. "I didn't hear the door. Sorry."

"Linda beat us to the punch. She had it open before we could knock," I replied as I returned Drew's hug.

I liked Drew a lot, but there were moments when I was almost too much in awe of him to completely trust him. When I first met him, I was taken with how perfect he seemed to be. Later, as I learned more about him, I was more and more impressed. But how could one person be put together so perfectly? My concerns had been for naught, because he'd never been anything less than what he appeared to be. But there was always that question in the back of my mind: *Is he for real?*

"Well, welcome. Come on in and meet some of my family."

As we approached, Drew began the introductions.

"Guys, this is Becca Robins, Linda's friend, maid of

honor, and stall neighbor at Bailey's, and Ian Cartwright, who also works at Bailey's—makes incredible yard art."

Friendly greetings were exchanged all around. The cousins looked to be somewhere in their thirties. None of them were as stunning as Drew, but they were still a good-looking bunch.

Alan Cummings, the offspring of Madeline's youngest sister Mary-Margaret, was a blond version of Drew, though he was less buff.

"Maid of honor?" he asked as we shook hands.

"That's me. Best man?"

"That's me. Nice to meet you."

The other three cousins were siblings, the offspring of Madeline's older sister, Serena. Sally, Mid (so nicknamed because he was the middle one), and Shawn were all dark but didn't look like Drew at all. Sally was petite and round with big hair and lots of makeup. Mid was tall and skinny, and his round glasses and short, disheveled hair reminded me of an English professor I had in college. Shawn was tall like Mid, but he wasn't as thin, and though he was the youngest of the three, he had a receding hairline that made him look older—until he smiled. He was one of those people who transformed into young and playful when they smiled. I liked him immediately.

Linda and Drew had dressed up for the occasion, but the cousins were almost as casual as Ian and I were. I wore some recently purchased slacks, a light blue blouse, and flats. I rarely wore shoes that didn't require socks, so the flats were the most uncomfortable part of my getup.

For a few minutes, the room was filled with chatter and general small talk. I learned that Alan was from Spartanburg and that he was "in between things" at the moment. I was about to ask him more questions when Sally diverted my attention.

"So . . . Becca, right?"

"Yes."

"Tell me how you got into the farmers' market business." Sally inspected me closely. We were both short and could look in each other's eyes without either of us having to strain our neck. But she was so close that I had to repress an urge to take a step backward.

"I inherited the land, farm, house, and kitchen/barn from my aunt and uncle . . ." I began.

Little did I know that the word *inherited* would cause such a reaction. Sally's eyes widened as the word left my lips.

"Really? How interesting. Your aunt and uncle? Didn't they have any children?"

"No, just nieces—my sister and me. They took care of us both." Talking about these things with Sally was uncomfortable. It seemed too important to her, and I immediately regretted that I hadn't lied about the entire matter.

Admiration seeped from Sally's pores. "Well, good for you. What did you two do to make yourselves so charming to them?" She smiled like it hurt.

I shrugged my shoulders. I was ready for the conversation to end, so I looked around for a distraction. Sally seemed to sense my discomfort.

"Indeed," she said.

"What do you do?" I asked quickly.

"Banking, just like Aunt Madeline," she replied, admiration lining her voice. "I work at Fuller Bank in Columbia."

"Impressive," I said, because I thought that was what

she wanted me to say, but she surprised me. She smiled but also blushed a little.

"Thank you, but I have a lot to learn. Aunt Madeline has been . . . well . . ." She was choking up. I had no idea what to do. I recalled what we'd been discussing, and couldn't think of a thing we'd said that would bring some-one to tears. I froze, and wished for something to save us from the awkward moment. My wish was soon granted.

"Well, everyone, Levi says we'd better come and eat." Linda stood in a wide French doorway that led to the din-ing room.

"Linda, shouldn't we wait for Madeline?" Sally asked after she sniffed away the tears that still shone brightly in her eyes.

Drew spoke up, saving Linda from having to answer.

"You know Madeline." It wasn't the first time I'd heard him call his mother by her first name. "She could be in the middle of something that will keep her busy late into the night. She'd want us to eat. She wouldn't want the food to get cold."

"Did someone try to call her?" Sally asked.

"Yes, we've tried. Like I said, she's probably very busy," Drew replied.

"Well, all right, then. If you think it's the thing to do," she said to Drew.

"I do."

Drew directed traffic through the doorway that led to the dining room. It was as large as my front room, din-ing area, and kitchen combined. The walls were covered in Impressionist-like paintings, but I couldn't be sure if any of them were original. The long table was set with what I would call "special occasion" dishes—white with gold trim—and there were enough goblets and forks to confuse even Miss Manners. Where there weren't dishes or silverware, there was food. Roast beef and seemingly every vegetable on the planet were placed end to end.

"Alan, Becca, we'd like for the two of you to be at either end, please," Drew said. "I'll sit next to Alan, and Linda will sit next to Becca. Ian, you're on Becca's other side. Mid and Shawn are between Ian and me, and Sally will be seated next to Linda. There, clear as mud?"

We took our places, leaving a seat next to Sally and across from Drew empty. Without Madeline there, the table seemed much heavier on one side than on the other. Sally, who was next to Madeline's chair, glanced at its emptiness longingly. Again, she looked like she might start to cry. She was either upset about something or her emotions were always close to the surface.

Drew seemed to be okay with his mother's continued absence, but I'd often wondered at his ability to hide things that must bother him. I was sure his military training had taught him how to handle the worst situations. Had his training helped him deal with his mother, or did he really care for her enough that things—odd and mean things—she did, didn't bother him as much as they bothered the rest of the world?

When Linda had greeted Ian and me at the front door, she'd mentioned that Madeline had a soft spot. I couldn't imagine it, but I also didn't think Linda would say something like that if she didn't mean it. She'd shared with me that she thought Madeline was intentionally attempting to come between Drew and herself. But they had persevered, and here they were getting married despite whatever had occurred. I hoped Madeline would get there soon. I wanted the opportunity to get to know this well-hidden part of the woman whose reputation made her downright horrifying to me.

"Well, friends and family, thank you for coming this evening," Drew said. "I hope you all know how important you are to Linda and me. Let's get this dinner started."

Drew was doing his best to be both gracious and distracting. To me, the nine-hundred-pound elephant in the room, Madeline's empty chair, seemed to throb. But we all played along and passed delicious food around the table and tried to talk about everything but Madeline.

"Ian, what did Drew mean by 'yard art' when he told us what you do for a living?" Sally asked.

"I create fairly large metal sculptures that move and change with the wind."

"Oh, that sounds lovely," Sally said.

"They are amazing," Drew agreed.

"Thank you," Ian said modestly. "I enjoy what I do."

As Ian spoke, I caught a strange look passing between Alan, who was at the other end of the table, and Shawn, whose happy smile was nowhere to be found. Then it was as if Shawn kicked Mid's ankle. Mid looked startled behind his round glasses and then gave his brother a questioning glance.

"Mid, you look like you have a question," Drew said.

"Oh." Mid pushed up his glasses and looked perplexed. "I'm sorry. I think Shawn was concerned I wasn't being polite. The roast beef is delicious." Mid took a big bite and chewed as he smiled. There was something going on between the brothers that would have made Allison want to find a way to ease everyone over the moment.

My social graces weren't as refined, and I just wanted to know more about whatever was causing the strain.

Shawn laughed uncomfortably, his smile returning and working its magic, making him once again seem more youthful. "Actually, Mid, that's not it. You're an artist of sorts. I thought you might want to talk to Ian, who makes his living with art. You seemed too into the roast beef to ask questions."

"Oh," Mid said.

Shawn's tone was unmistakable. He was irritated at his brother for something, and used conversation about Ian's chosen way to make a living to cover up whatever the real problem was.

We were early into the dinner, and it was already an adventure. I couldn't wait for what would come next.

"You're an artist?" Ian said easily. "What kind of art?"

Ian and my sister are very much alike when it comes to the world of social graces. Ian's tone magically brought the atmosphere of the dinner back to cordial. I was slightly disappointed, but couldn't help but think how good it was that he could make up for one of my weaknesses.

"I sculpt," Mid said, as though he was giving up the fight. "I'm not very good at it, but I enjoy it."

"What kind of things do you sculpt?" Ian asked.

"Animals, mostly."

"I'd love to see some of your work."

I glanced at Sally, whose eyes were squinted in doubt. She looked at her brothers as though they were speaking a foreign language. My gut suddenly told me that we were all being fed a line, but why? I glanced at Drew. He seemed interested, but there was no doubt showing on his handsome face. Linda looked just fine, too.

Ian knew something was up, too, and though he had great people skills, I could tell that, like me, he was very curious as to what would happen next.

"I might like showing my work to a real artist," Mid finally said before he put more roast beef into his mouth.

For a moment the room was quiet. I caught Alan staring at Linda. It wasn't a curious stare as much as it was an uncomfortable one. Drew didn't seem to notice it, but I wished he had. I had the urge to nudge Linda under the table and point out what was going on, but instead I said, "Alan, earlier you mentioned that you're in between things at the moment."

"Yes." He blinked and looked in my direction.

"What sort of things?" I asked.

Alan shrugged. "I'm *so* in between, I'm not sure. I've done lots of things, mostly with numbers. I'm a CPA, but a few years back I decided to look for another passion. I haven't found it yet. I wish I had some sort of artistic ability." He nodded toward Ian and Mid. Even though Alan didn't look physically superior like Drew, I wondered if maybe he was also a part of the *military*. It had taken Drew a long time to trust me enough to give me even the slightest of details about what he does, so maybe he and Alan both did the same thing, or the same sort of thing.

"It's hard work, but I do enjoy getting up every day," Ian said, smoothing the atmosphere again.

"Our world at Bailey's is unique," Linda said, changing the subject. "Most of us enjoy what we do, we get to be entrepreneurs, and we work with creative and hard-working people."

"Hmm, maybe Mid and I should look into getting a booth there," Shawn said.

"Oh? For your art or something else?" Ian asked.

"Something else. We own Loder Dairy," Shawn replied.

"*The* Loder Dairy?" I asked, my fork halting in midair.

Shawn laughed lightly. "I think there's only one in South Carolina."

My childhood memories of Loder Dairy were vast, almost all-encompassing—and fond and happy. I hadn't thought about the dairy for years, though. When Allison and I were little, we anticipated the twice-weekly truck that brought us Loder milk, butter, and sometimes special candy treats. I was about to wax nostalgic about Loder Dairy and the happy memories it had given me when Levi flew into the room.

He was dressed all in white, his final layer being a food-stained apron. He had a head of blond bushy curls and the thickest glasses I'd ever seen.

"Mr. Drew, I think we have a problem," he said in a thick Southern accent.

"What is it, Levi?" Drew asked.

"I don't . . . I wonder . . . well, I think something must have happened to the missus."

Four

"What do you mean, Levi?" Drew asked as he put down his knife and fork, placed his napkin on the table, and stood.

"Her car is here," Levi said.

The words he spoke weren't alarming in themselves. In fact, they were quite innocuous. The tone in which he spoke them, however, sent chills down my spine.

"I don't understand," Drew said. "Has my mother returned?"

"That's just it," Levi replied. "I don't think she ever left. I had to go out to the garage—to check the freezer for some more pastries—and her car was still in the garage. The missus is not in the car, not in the garage, and I didn't see her come back into the house."

"Did you see her leave?" I interrupted, thinking I wouldn't have put it past her to return home, sneak into the house, and hide from the party just to make Linda angry.

He shook his head. "I'm not sure. She said she was leaving, but I was so busy I don't know if I actually saw her go."

"Please, everyone, stay seated. I'll check the garage. Excuse me." Drew took long strides out of the room and followed Levi into the kitchen.

For a moment the rest of us remained in our seats. I glanced at Ian, who was staring at the doorway through which Drew had disappeared; Linda held on to the table as though debating whether she should use it to push herself out of the chair; Sally looked to be on the verge of tears again. Alan, Mid, and Shawn all looked concerned, but were deep in their own thoughts. Shawn pushed his glasses up his nose.

I didn't understand any of their reactions. There was probably a reasonable explanation for Madeline's car being in the garage, but these people knew her much better than I did. Perhaps this behavior was something to be concerned about, but at the moment I was more irritated than concerned. Later, I would regret my reaction.

"Well, excuse me, I think I'm going to see what's going on," Linda said as she stood.

"Want me to come?" I asked.

"Sure."

I stood, and followed my friend as she made her way through the large restaurant-type kitchen and out a back door. By the time we were on a walkway headed toward the garage, the rest of the group was behind us. If Linda stopped, we'd bump together like a group of misdirected Keystone Kops.

I caught Ian's gaze, and he mouthed a "be careful."

I didn't understand the need to be careful or wary, but I nodded.

Just as we reached the four-stall garage, the automatic door rolled up, revealing Drew and Levi peering into a newer model silver Mercedes sedan.

"She's not in the car?" Linda asked.

"No," Drew answered. "It doesn't look like it's been driven recently. And the hood is cool."

The garage was huge, but clean and mostly empty. A large freezer—the kind you find in restaurants—took up half of one stall. The Mercedes and a bicycle were the only other items in the huge space.

"Is that the only car she has?" I asked Linda.

"Yes."

"Check the freezer," Sally suggested.

In sync, we all turned to look at her as though we weren't sure we'd heard her correctly. But Drew went to the freezer and pulled the door handle. Once a cloud of icy vapor dissipated, it was clear that there was nothing but food inside the thick walls.

"Well, that's good. She didn't go in there and hit her head, fall down, and die, or anything," Sally said.

"Where's your car, Levi?" I asked.

"Over there." He pointed to an old blue VW Bug that was around the other side of the house. The back of the Bug stuck out from behind a corner of the brick mansion.

I took it upon myself to hurry over and glance in Levi's car. There were a couple of old paperbacks on the front passenger seat, but other than that, it was empty. I rejoined the crowd just as everyone was heading back into the house.

"She must be inside somewhere," Ian said as I merged next to him at the back of the parade of people.

"She's probably fine. Just being difficult, you know. But this is beginning to feel weird," I said quietly. *Something* wasn't right, that much I was beginning to understand.

"I agree. Really, Becca, be careful. Other than Linda and Drew, we don't know these people. And you're right, this is definitely weird."

"Yeah."

We didn't split up to search for Madeline, which is something I would later wonder about. Why didn't we? Were we all feeling the heebie-jeebies that Ian and I had acknowledged? Was there, maybe, a killer among us who wanted people around all the time, so they could confirm an alibi or something? Was there more than one killer?

The mansion was as huge as it seemed, with three floors, long hallways, and big rooms. Madeline had great decorating taste, but it was mostly her fondness for purple that I noticed: purple pillows, random purple walls, upholstery, and so on.

We moved along the halls and through rooms together. Despite the largeness of the spaces, our big search party was crowded and uncomfortable. The only person who said much of anything was Drew, as he called "Mom" or "Madeline" over and over again.

There was never one word of response, not the sound of a television or radio on somewhere. The house was as silent as a tomb.

Finally, on the third floor, in the back corner, as far from the kitchen and dining room as we could get, we approached Madeline's suite.

This was it—the last real spot to search. If she wasn't in there, she wasn't in the house.

Drew looked back as the rest of us watched him expectantly. For the first time since I'd met him at the Fall Equinox Dinner in September, he looked real, vulnerable, and worried, not the squared-away paragon of military perfection he was. He ran his hands through his mussed-up hair, and Linda stepped to his side, taking his hand.

Drew knocked on the door.

"Mom? You in there?"

No answer.

Drew turned the knob and pushed the door open wide. He and Linda stepped into the room. One of them gasped, and the rest of us hurried into horror.

Madeline Forsyth was on her back on her bed, a black-and-white checkered scarf pulled tight around her neck. One hand lay in a puddle of blood on the bed, and the other hand hung over the side, dripping blood from what looked like wounds on her palm. Her gray face and vacant eyes told the rest of the story: she was way dead.

Someone screamed, someone yelled, and someone fainted, but I'm not sure exactly who did what. I had seen Matt Simonsen's dead body last fall, but this was different. I was physically closer to Madeline than I had ever let myself get to Matt, and I was part of the group discovering the body, not part of the group coming in later.

My stomach turned and I got light-headed. Someone took my arm and led me to the side of the room.

"Becca, you okay?" Ian asked.

I looked at his concerned expression, and nodded.

"Take a deep breath."

I did as he instructed, and kept my eyes away from the gruesome scene. It was because I was purposely looking away that I happened to see something on the floor at Ian's feet, next to a chaise.

I suddenly crouched.

"Becca?" Ian crouched with me and held tight to my arm. "Let me get you out of here."

"I'm okay. I just . . . well . . ." I looked around at everyone else. No one was paying me or Ian a bit of attention. Everyone was in a state of shock or panic, or comforting or helping someone else.

"What?"

"Look." I nodded toward the floor.

"Oh. Okay, we'll show the police. Come on."

But that wouldn't do. I needed the object I saw. I had some questions that I wanted answered, and the most efficient way to get those answers was to take the object and inspect it myself.

I reached down, picked up Madeline's cell phone, and put it in my pocket, all without using the tips of my fingers.

To his credit, though Ian did look shocked and displeased, he didn't tell on me.

Five

Officer Sam Brion was the most efficient person I knew. Well, other than my sister, Allison. Sam, as I'd been told to call him during the last murder investigation in Monson, had the crime scene secured and all potential suspects/witnesses separated and readied for interview in record time.

Sam had come to South Carolina from Chicago about a year ago, under circumstances I hadn't yet been able to figure out, but I knew there was something horrible in his past; something that had caused him to flee the big city and move to a place where murder wasn't supposed to be such a common occurrence. All the best-laid plans . . .

I hadn't seen him for a couple weeks, but we became friends when I threw myself into the middle of Matt Simonsen's murder investigation. In fact, Sam'd been the one to save my life by taking down the killer before the killer could take me down.

"Becca," he said without cracking a smile. He was definitely in work mode, his short brown hair slicked back and his uniform crisp and wrinkle-free. His bright blue eyes could sometimes be friendly, but they were professionally icy now.

"Hi, Sam." I'd been assigned to the music room, which held a grand piano and a number of chairs and side tables. The piano was black, and the chairs were mostly beige and light yellow. I was perched on a piano bench that had been upholstered in purple fabric. Sam pulled a beige chair next to the bench and faced me.

"How are you?" he said without a hint that he was friendly and could be a fun guy.

"Not great. You?"

"The days without murder are better than the days with murder."

"I agree." I cleared my throat. I wanted him to quit being so official and just have a conversation, but I knew better. He was the consummate professional when it was required.

Over the last few months, and since he'd saved me from Matt Simonsen's killer, we'd become good enough friends that he always visited me at Bailey's whenever he was shopping, and every once in a while we'd run into each other at barbeques. Even though he and Ian were very different, they seemed to get along well, too.

"Tell me what you did today, in detail, beginning when Madeline Forsyth spoke to Linda McMahon at Bailey's this morning."

"Okay, sure. It went something like this . . ."

And I recounted my day, to the best of my memory and up to the point that we found Madeline's body.

"You all found her body? You were all together?"

"Yes."

"Did you think she might be alive?"

"She looked very dead. Oh, Sam, was . . . is she alive?"

"No, but I'd like for you to explain what you mean by 'she looked very dead,'" Sam said, still stone-cold serious.

"A scarf was wrapped around her neck. Her face was gray and swollen, I think. Her eyes were bulging." My stomach turned at the memory.

"What color was the scarf?"

"Black-and-white checkered," I answered without hesitation.

"Anything else you can remember?"

"I think one of her hands was in a puddle of blood on the bed. Is that right? Is that really what I saw?"

"Anything else?" he asked, ignoring my question.

"Well, the other hand was hanging off the bed. There was more than one wound on that hand, right?"

"Why did you notice that?"

"I'm not sure. What were the wounds, Sam? Why was there more than one on the hand? They looked like they were in a line, I think, but I can't be sure."

"They were identical punctures that formed a straight line," he said, sharing more than I bet he did with anyone else. "Do you know of anything that could do that?"

I shrugged. "A comb with really sharp teeth?"

He nodded thoughtfully. "Tell me what happened at dinner. What was discussed?"

Sam took notes in his small tan notebook as I replayed the dinner conversation. For the moment I left out my personal observations about Drew's cousins. It wasn't fair to judge them. I'd only just met them, and who knew what was behind their behavior?

"That it?" he asked when I finished.

"What do you think? Have you talked to the others? Do you think someone there was the killer?" I asked.

"I'm not going to tell you what I think, Becca. This is a murder investigation. One of the rules in the Police Handbook is that we're not to reveal everything we think or know until we solve the case." He didn't smile.

"I know. I was just curious."

"I know. How about you? You have anything else to add? What do you think—did someone you ate with seem murderous in any way?"

Again, I didn't want to judge, but maybe Sam did need to know about any behavior that might not have been wholly appropriate.

"We hadn't been eating long before the chef, Levi, came in to tell us he thought something was wrong. Before that, I thought Drew's cousins were somewhat different, but I really hadn't spent much time with them."

"Different how?"

I told Sam about Sally's visible emotions, Alan's lack of a job, Shawn's supposedly kicking Mid under the table, but, admittedly, none of it seemed like a killer's behavior.

"Those are good things to note," Sam said. "I'll see if I can understand what might have been going on. Ms. McNeil, Sally, is certainly the most distraught of everyone we've talked to. Perhaps she's just highly emotional."

"How are Drew and Linda?"

"As fine as they can be, I suppose. Drew is upset, but he's pretty practiced at being stoic. I think Linda just wants to make sure Drew's okay," Sam said as he peered at me. "Becca, do you think either Linda or Drew had something to do with Madeline's murder?"

"Of course not!"

"I knew you'd answer like that. I'd like for you to step back a bit—back from your friendships with them. Do you think there's any way either of them could have killed Madeline?"

No, I didn't think either of them had it in them to kill Madeline, but I was almost sure that they both might have spent moments wishing Madeline wasn't around any longer.

Finally I said, "No, Sam, I really don't think so. Neither of them . . . well, they're just both so . . . terrific, you know?"

Sam nodded. "I need to ask you a question, and you need to know how important it is for you to answer it one hundred percent correctly. What time did Linda leave Bailey's?"

My stomach somersaulted. Linda had left Bailey's early. I thought back to when I was helping her load the extra pies in her truck. She hadn't been too upset, just distracted.

"I guess she left about one o'clock, maybe one-thirty," I said. I left out *which would have given her plenty of time to kill Madeline.*

"Thank you, Becca," Sam said, seemingly relieved at my answer.

"You sound like I got the answer right."

"That's when she said she left, and though I can't rule her out at the moment—I can't rule anyone out—I didn't want her to have lied about the time she left." Not only had Sam become a friend to me, but to most of my friends, too. He knew Linda and Drew, and from what I'd observed, he and Drew seemed to see the world the same way. They had lots in common, and Drew's profession impressed Sam, just like it did the rest of us.

"Good, then, I guess."

"Yes. Okay, anything else?" Sam closed the notebook and stood as though he was certain we were through.

Apparently, when I looked·up at him, something terrible showed on my face, because his face fell and he sat down again.

"What is it, Becca?" he asked.

Once I'd put Madeline's phone in my pocket, I couldn't figure out the best way to take it out and put it back. I had wanted to. I knew that taking it had been an impulsive and bad (putting it lightly) idea. And illegal, I was sure. But everything from that moment on had happened so quickly that I hadn't had a chance to undo my mistake. I still had it in my pocket.

"Sam," I began.

The look in his blue eyes shifted. He was still serious, but was now preparing to be angry.

"Becca, what is it?"

"Well, it was an impulse. I couldn't help myself."

"Becca. What. Did. You. Do?"

I sighed.

"Madeline's cell phone is in my pocket."

"What? Where did you get her phone?"

"It was in her bedroom, next to the chaise. I just reached down, picked it up—careful not to touch it with my fingertips—and put it in my pocket. I still haven't touched it. It's still there."

Sam sat back in the chair and inspected me, his eyes

going from ice to fire. For a long time he didn't say anything.

"Why did you take the phone?"

I shrugged but didn't answer. I planned to use that answer in a minute.

"Becca?"

"What?"

"I'm trying to figure out if I should arrest you now or wait until you call to ask another question pertinent to the case that will be none of your business."

"Oh, I promise I'm not going to investigate this murder, Sam. I'm very sorry that Madeline was killed, but I have every confidence that you can handle this one by yourself. You don't have to arrest me."

There, I made him smile. Well, not really, but at least the corner of his mouth twitched.

"Stand up. Let's get it out of there," Sam said as he stood up.

I stood and reached for my pocket.

"No, stop! Let me do it." Sam pulled latex gloves out of his back pocket. Even those seemed to be well folded and wrinkle-free. He snapped both gloves in place and stepped forward.

"You're going to reach into my pocket? That seems a bit intrusive, doesn't it?" I said, attempting to make him smile again.

He didn't say anything, but looked down at me with controlled patience. The slacks weren't tight, so it was easy to pull at the seam and reach into the pocket. He maneuvered his fingers into the space, pinched the phone, and plucked it from the pocket—all without brushing my body in any way. However, his eyes did shift again, to something strange that made me want to look away. But he recovered and blinked them to normal as he stepped back.

"Very impressive," I said.

"Becca, did you take anything else that might be considered evidence?" Sam asked, no humor anywhere.

"No."

"Good. Now, it's my job to tell you not to leave town during the investigation."

"Am I a suspect?"

"You are a potential witness. And the fact that you took the victim's phone makes you look suspicious and a bit crazy, but I wouldn't give you the full title of suspect. Just yet."

"Got it."

Sam still held the phone pinched between his gloved thumb and forefinger.

"You're free to go, now," he said.

"Uh, well, . . ."

"What?"

"Then . . ." I was pushing my luck, but I couldn't leave without at least trying.

"What is it, Becca?"

"Well, is there any chance you'd look at the phone's call log and tell me if Madeline called Linda?"

"No."

"Please, Sam, just a quick look. I just want to know if Madeline called Linda at any time today. And, and, well, if she didn't, I might have some information that could maybe potentially be important to the case." This was my only bargaining chip, weak though it might have been. Sam, being a police officer, didn't bargain for such things. But we were friends—I hoped that would help.

"Really?" he said doubtfully. "What information?"

I was stretching his patience, and he was abnormally patient with me, even in the worst of circumstances. But I couldn't help myself.

"Explain the information." He still held the phone.

"When Madeline stopped by Bailey's today to tell Linda about the dinner, she commented that she'd called Linda a number of times. Linda's phone didn't show the calls. It might not mean a thing, Sam, but it might. It's the reason I took the phone. I needed to know—though I'm not sure why—I just did. I didn't look at the phone because . . . well, because I realized how stupid I'd been to take it, I guess. What would it hurt? Just take a quick glance. You have the gloves on," I added quickly. "Please."

Sam took a deep breath and with his gloved fingers opened the phone. I moved to his side and glanced down at the small screen as he pushed the call button and a log immediately appeared.

Madeline had made a number of phone calls on the last day of her life. Sam scrolled down the list too quickly for me to digest much of anything, but I did catch three high points:

1. The name Linda didn't appear anywhere on the log of the day's calls. Of course, Madeline might not have attached Linda's name to her number, and there were quite a few numbers without names listed. Plus, I didn't know Linda's number by heart. She was on my speed dial, and when she called me, my screen just showed her name.

2. The name Jeanine Baker, the egg lady from Bailey's, did appear on the call log. I wondered if Sam noticed

it and remembered who she was, but I didn't say anything. He'd figure it out soon enough, and I couldn't imagine that Jeanine was guilty of anything except making up conspiracy theories. However, I didn't think that she and Madeline moved in the same circle, and it was odd that Madeline had called her. I made a mental note to ask Jeanine for the details.

3. And finally, there was a number I recognized immediately. I wasn't good at hiding much of anything, so I was proud of myself for not gasping as I saw my boyfriend Ian's number move up the screen as Sam scrolled down. Again, Sam would eventually figure that Madeline Forsyth had called Ian on the day she died, but since a name wasn't attached to this number, he might not think it strange that I didn't point it out to him. Even though Ian's number was also programmed into my phone, it had an unusual pattern that was made up mostly of 4s and 5s. I had memorized his number the first time he told it to me.

But why would Madeline Forsyth have called Ian?

"No Linda listed," Sam said as he carefully snapped the phone shut. "I'll look up the other numbers and let you know."

"You'll let me know?" I tried not to sound like I was thinking about Ian.

"Yeah, I'll give you a call. I'll have to have more conversations with Linda anyway. I'll let her know first."

"Thanks, Sam." I tried to sound sincere, but I couldn't make room in my thoughts for anything other than my curiosity as to why Madeline had called Ian. I didn't even know the two of them knew each other.

"Anything else I can do for you?" Sam asked. I caught the sarcasm this time.

"No, I'm good. Really, thanks. I'll talk to you soon."

"Becca, are you okay?" he asked, no sarcasm.

"Oh, I'm . . . I'll be fine." I smiled and tried to sweep away the questions in my mind. "You know that Madeline had lots of enemies, don't you?"

"I'm aware of who she was and what she did. We have many avenues to explore."

I nodded.

"Take care, Becca," Sam said. He nodded, looked away, and left the room. There wasn't any need for me to be there either, so I followed him down the front hall and out the door.

We'd been at Madeline's house for almost three hours, and though it was dark outside except for some yard lighting, the fresh air was delicious. I took in big pulls as I stood on the wide front porch. I didn't know where the other party guests had gone, but Ian was sitting on the open tailgate of his truck.

Officer Vivienne Norton crossed the other side of the yard. She looked at me with surprise. We'd gotten to know each other during the Simonsen murder case, and she was the burliest woman (maybe man, too) I'd ever met. I saw surprise in her eyes as she realized that I was in the middle of another horrible event. Her eyes hardened as she waved—was I the killer this time? I waved back and then stepped off the porch toward Ian.

"Some dinner," I said.

"Yeah, that was rough. You okay? Did you give Sam—I mean Officer Brion—the phone?"

"Yes." I hopped up on the tailgate next to him.

"Good. I bet he wasn't happy that you had it."

"Thanks for not telling him."

"No problem. I knew you'd confess."

"Yeah."

The temperature was perfect, cool and warm at the same time. The air was fresh and clean, and as I looked up at the first twinklings of stars, for probably the millionth time in my life, I was grateful I didn't live in a big city.

"Who do you suppose did that to her?" I asked.

"I have no idea."

"Have you talked to anyone else?" I asked.

"No, everyone else left. Except for you and me, everyone was taken down to the police station."

"Really? You saw them? Linda, too?"

"Yep. Sam talked to me out here. He told me that everyone said you and I were the last ones to arrive and we were always in view of someone. But everyone else has some explaining to do, apparently."

"Oh, gosh. Poor Linda! I hope she's okay."

"I hope she has a good attorney," Ian said.

The thought that my best friend, mild-mannered, pioneer-dressing pie baker Linda McMahon, could have committed a murder dug a pit in my stomach.

"Do you think someone else at the party was the killer?"

"I don't have any idea. No one acted too strange—well, like they'd just taken someone's life, at least. They're an interesting bunch."

"Yeah, I wish we'd had a little more time with them. Did Sam tell you anything else?" I asked.

"No."

A sudden chill shook my limbs.

"You cold?" Ian reached for the jacket he'd removed and put in the bed of the truck.

"No, just . . ."

"I know. Too strange, huh? Come on, let's get out of here." Ian hopped off the tailgate and reached as though he was going to help me do the same.

"Hang on, Ian . . ."

"What is it?"

I hesitated, because the fact that Madeline Forsyth had called Ian was probably none of my business.

But I couldn't help myself.

"I have a question."

"Yes?"

"Madeline Forsyth called you today," I said, no question to my voice, as I looked into his dark eyes. I loved those dark eyes and everything else attached to them. I had to know why the murder victim had called my boyfriend on the day she died.

Ian smiled.

"I've been caught, huh?" he said quietly.

"I don't know. Have you?"

"Yep." Ian looked away and back at the house. His smile faded. "Come on, let's get out of here, and I'll tell you all about my affair with Madeline Forsyth."

six

As Ian's truck ticked off the miles, I began to fight a good dose of delayed-reaction willies. Mostly deep in our own thoughts, we were quiet for the trip back through town. We bypassed his apartment and my dog, and then headed out the other side of Monson, more toward my farm. I was curious about Ian and Madeline, of course, but I was fairly certain they hadn't had *that* kind of an affair.

Madeline Forsyth had been murdered, and we'd seen the body. And we just might have sat at the dinner table with the killer or killers—two potential suspects being my friend and her fiancé. Oddly, the farther we traveled from Madeline's house, the more real the murder became.

I was grateful when we hit the open fields on the other side of town and suddenly I felt like I could breathe again. I knew Ian felt the same. I heard him take a deep breath, too.

"I know," I said. "Too much, huh?"

"Lots to process. I hope they catch whoever did it quickly."

"Me, too."

A moment later Ian turned onto a road I was very familiar with; I had grown up with my sister and hippie parents on this road, most commonly known as "the road right before the state highway." When I was a kid, we had to have a box in the town post office because our address didn't seem to be easy to understand. Rural Route 6 was mostly dirt with a few big rocks thrown in here and there, meant to wreak havoc on nice vehicles and new tires. The hidden road suited my parents just fine; they loved living out in the country with as few visitors as possible. They were making up for it now as they traveled the country in an RV, experiencing as much of America as they could before they passed on to the next realm—hippie parents didn't ever die, they just packed up and hitched a ride to their next journey. I wasn't sure I believed the same things they did, but there was something comforting in their beliefs.

"Ian? Where are we going?" I asked. The turn onto the familiar path erased the image of Madeline's body from of my mind.

"You'll see." Ian maneuvered his truck over a rough patch like he'd done it a time or two before.

When the road suddenly smoothed, I peered out the windshield and into the gloom.

"The road, it's been paved?" I said.

"From here on out for a while."

"I haven't been down this way in a long time."

"I know. Your family moved into town when you were fourteen, right?"

"You knew I lived out here?"

"Yeah. Allison and I discussed it. She's the one who told me about this area."

"Why?"

"You'll see, but first we'll stop here briefly. Take a look if you'd like."

Though I hadn't lived on Rural Route 6 for about twenty years, I had driven out this way now and then, but the last time had been over five years earlier. Ian pulled to the side of the road, and I peered at the house of my childhood. I wasn't all that sentimental, but I loved seeing that the small house had been well taken care of. I couldn't see very well because of the darkness, but the porch light was on, illuminating some big-bellied flower pots here and there on the tiny front lawn.

"My parents wanted us to grow up in the 'wilderness,'" I said. "They loved it out here and managed to save a bunch of money. This house, along with the land, didn't cost them much at all. When it was time for high school, we moved into town. There they became business-savvy and bought a bunch of rental properties. They never worried about money."

"Did you miss the country?"

"I dunno, probably. Allison and I had a great time no matter where we were, but I suppose I must have missed it, because that's where I ended up again. You know, it must be an evening for memories—this is where we lived when we got the deliveries from the Loder Dairy that we were talking about at dinner. Funny how stuff like that happens, huh?"

"Synchronization," Ian said.

There was a light on in the front window of the house,

and though I didn't feel a strong connection to the building, I liked the warm feeling that emanated from the window.

"Ready?" Ian asked.

"Yes, but only if you're going to tell me about this affair with Madeline Forsyth."

"Ah, yes, the affair." Ian pulled the truck back onto the road. "Well, it was pretty wild, really."

"Uh-huh."

"We're almost there. Hang on a minute."

A few seconds later, Ian pulled the truck to the side of the road again.

"Here we are," he said as he put the truck into Park and got out. He reached behind the driver's seat for a flashlight and came around to open my door.

"Where are we?" I asked.

He turned and looked out at a long stretch of land that I could barely see by the milky light from the rising moon. From where we were, the land looked rough, and a small shack that sat in the middle of it looked even rougher.

"This is my affair with Madeline Forsyth."

"Okay." I got out of the truck, and we walked to the edge of the property.

"Supposedly this land is going into foreclosure. Allison sent me out here long before that happened, by the way. I was attempting to purchase it when the owner got the foreclosure notice from Madeline . . . well, from Central Savings and Loan. Madeline was . . . well, she was being difficult about the entire thing. The owner, Bud Morris, is an old guy who doesn't need to be dealing with any of this. He claims there's no way his land could be in foreclosure, but Madeline hadn't been returning his calls. I intervened recently, and I had left her a message. When I saw her at Bailey's this morning, I actually wondered if she was there to see me. Her path directly to Linda told me otherwise, of course. When I realized we'd be having dinner with her, I thought I might approach her then—even if it would be bad manners. Then she called this afternoon, but I was too busy to answer the phone. She left a brief 'call me back' message, which is why you saw my number on her phone." Ian paused. "I think it's good I came along, or Bud might have been scared out of his home."

"Wait, what? Start over. You want to buy this property, work this land, live in that terrible shack?"

"Yep."

"Why?" I wished for daylight. In the darkness, the soil seemed rocky and not fertile; the shack leaned enough that a good sneeze would be the end of it.

"One word: lavender."

"Lavender?"

"Yes."

"Ian, really, start over. Start from the beginning."

He smiled and reached out his hand. "Come with me."

I took his hand. "Does Bud live in that shack?"

"Yes."

"Will he shoot at us for trespassing?"

"No. His hearing isn't all that great."

"Lead the way."

The land was rough and kind of rocky, but maybe not as rocky as I originally thought. I didn't want to voice my doubts, but I still couldn't understand why this was a good decision.

After we'd walked about thirty yards, we reached a small lift of land.

"There, now you can see the whole thing." Ian swept the flashlight in a circle. "Well, sort of. Clearly, we'll have to come back when the sun's up."

I looked around. The land and shack were positioned nicely amid rolling hills, but my impression still wasn't of fertile, healthy dirt.

"Lavender?" I said. "I don't know a thing about it. Oh, except that it's purple." The mention of the color made me think of Madeline's decorating taste, but I put those thoughts to the back of my mind again.

Ian laughed. "Yes, you're correct. Would you like a quick lesson?"

"Yes."

"It's one of the most useful herbs. It can be dried, it can be used in cooking—I make a mean lavender cookie—but I'm going to grow it and mostly create oils, essential oils. I'm going to tear down the shack and build a better house and a workshop for my sculptures and for a place to create the essential oils. I'll be able to do both."

"What are the oils used for?"

"Some people just like the lavender scent. There are other possible uses—including insect bites, acne, headaches, and scars. Hey, I only play a doctor on TV, though," Ian joked. "I know there's a market for the oils, but what people use them for will be up to them."

"That all sounds fantastic, Ian, but I have to ask about growing conditions. I can't see so great right now, but when we first stopped, it looked like the land was kind of rocky."

"It's not too rocky. The land just hadn't been worked. Lavender plants thrive in warm, well-drained gritty soil and full sun. This land is ideal. Someone told me that lavender's like sage—but with class." Ian pointed the flashlight toward the ground at our feet.

"That changes everything." For a long moment, I mulled over what he'd said. "Then I think this could be very awesome!"

"Good," Ian said, "I hoped you'd like the idea. Are you mad I didn't talk to you about it before?"

"No, not at all," I replied, but I did wonder if my non-answer about visiting his family had been part of the reason he'd kept the secret.

"I'm committed to staying in South Carolina, Becca." What Ian was really saying was that he was committed to me, to us.

"Ian," I began, but he stopped me by putting a finger on my lips.

"We'll talk about it later. I don't mean to pressure you, really. I was going to bring you out here next week if I could get Bud's situation straightened out."

"Well, I can tell you this much. Even if you do get this property, build a big house and workshop, and grow some lavender, I'm still going to call you my boyfriend, and I'll probably spend a night or two here with you if I'm invited and if I can bring Hobbit," I said.

I felt Ian lean toward me. He was coming in for a kiss, and I could tell it was going to be a good one. Our kisses had been strained lately, and this one was going to make up for all that, this one was going to propel us back into the "us" that was wonderful and perfect. But his phone buzzed, killing the potential romantic scene.

After a moment's hesitation, he pulled it from his pocket and looked at the ID.

"Sam," he said as he flipped open the phone. "Hello, Officer Brion. Yes, Madeline Forsyth did call me today. I didn't return the call yet. Yes, sort of, we were in the middle of a potential business transaction. No, it didn't occur to me to tell you about that until about twenty minutes ago, but I thought I'd call you tomorrow to let you know. Yes, of course I can meet you at the station tonight. I'm on my way." Ian snapped the phone shut.

"Dang," I said. "Sam wants you to go to the station?"

"I wish I'd remembered to tell him that she'd called me. When he questioned me, I didn't mention Bud's bank issue. I hadn't talked to Madeline yet, so it didn't occur to me that it might be important. I guess I'll have to go clear my name."

"So unless you get arrested, we'll get to resume that . . . well, whatever that was about to be, later?"

"Absolutely." Ian took my hand, and we made our way over the land that might someday be covered in purple.

"Lavender?" I said as Ian opened the truck door for me.

"Yep, lavender."

"Seems like a pretty good plan," I said.

"I think so, too."

Seven

The old brick building that housed Monson's small but ef-
ficient group of police officers was full of activity during
normal business hours, but not so much during the evening. Apparently, the mayor had an office in the building,
as did a few attorneys and some other local government
officials, but no one was working this night except the
police.

Ian and I made our way up a small flight of stairs and
past an unmanned receptionist's desk. The frosted glass
top half of the door we opened had one word on it: Police.

Inside, we found a flurry of activity. The back glass-
walled offices were empty and dark, but the group of
desks in the open area were occupied by officers at work.
Vivienne Norton and her muscles were on the phone. She
was taking notes of some sort. Drew's cousin Sally sat
next to Officer Norton's desk; she looked tired and up-

set. Though not up to Vivienne's standards, another burly officer, Officer Sanford—I'd come to know him during the last Monson murder case, too—was shuffling some papers as Shawn and Mid sat across from him. Sam was standing with his hands on his hips as he looked at something on his desk. He looked up as the door shut behind us, and signaled in our direction.

We made our way, all the while gathering glances from Drew's cousins.

"Ian, Becca," Sam said. "Ian, have a seat. Becca, would you either wait over there"—he pointed to a couple of chairs on the far side of the station—"or outside? We have only one interview room, and it's occupied. I need to have as much privacy as possible with Ian. Grab some coffee if you'd like."

"Sure, of course." I nodded at Ian, and he winked at me with the eye that Sam couldn't see.

"Thanks," Sam said.

I'd had the coffee here once before, and probably still had the damaged taste buds to show for it, so I headed toward the empty chairs, content to wait without a beverage. But something—something that felt magnetic—caused me to veer at the last second.

I made my way to the door Ian and I had just come through, put my hand on the knob, turned around to see if anyone was watching me leave—no one seemed to care in the least what I was doing—went out to the hallway, and hurried the opposite direction of the building's front doors.

So the interview room was occupied, was it? And just who were they interviewing? Linda? Drew? The blond cousin, Alan? The cook? Was there someone the police actually thought was the killer? Or were the rooms and spaces available just being used as efficiently as possible? I had to know.

When the police arrested my friend Abner for Matt Simonsen's murder, I'd visited him in one of the small, cagelike cells that were at the back of the building. On the way to the cells, I'd walked through the area with the officers' desks, and down a hallway that led past the interview room and some bathrooms. I wondered if there was another way to access that back room. I scurried into an unlit area of the hallway, hoping for some place that offered a short cut or something.

The first door I came to had the lettering Law Offices, but nothing else. It was locked. The second door was labeled Janitor. It wasn't locked, but it wasn't any sort of short cut—it was a small closet full of mops, buckets, and cleaning supplies. There were no other doors, but there was one other possible option: at the end of the hall was a large window.

No, I told myself. *What am I thinking? That I'm going to go out a window, use my Spidey skills and hope that there's another window I can go in through?*

Ridiculous.

I turned and resigned myself to waiting for Ian in the truck. Maybe I could get some rest.

But as I passed the janitor's closet again, I stopped and turned.

The window really was big—the kind common in an older government building. It had lots of glass, and the wood frame was in need of a good sanding and staining. If—a big if—I could get it open, I could look outside to see how close another window was, and gauge the possibility of actually making my way to it. Shoot, what would it hurt to look?

The window was as old as the building, and not built for security. It was just a simple window that lifted open when the swivel lock wasn't in place. I stepped up on my tip-toes, turned the lock, and pulled gently on the bottom of the wooden frame.

As it slid up, the old wood traveled on rusted metal sliders, screaming like a herd of hungry zombies.

"Lovely," I muttered. For a moment, I stood still and listened to my own breathing. Surely, someone was going to come out of the police station, gun drawn, and discover my antics. But no one did.

I didn't dare open the window much more than I already had, but the space was enough for me to lean out if I bent over. There were no bars or cage security over the window like the ones I'd noticed on the building's lower-level windows.

I threaded my head and shoulders out the open space and looked to the left. There was most definitely another window, and it wasn't far away—and it seemed to be in the exact area that I estimated was where I wanted to be. The only issue was getting there. A good sized brick ledge, fitting the rest of the old architecture, jutted out from the building and led perfectly from one window to the other one. A quaint courtyard was below me; lit with only a couple of small lights; I could see chairs and a picnic table circled by a narrow walking path.

At that point, my common sense flew right out the open window. Most people who recognized they were two stories above the ground with only a ledge to take them from one window to the other, would probably choose to leave the ledge-walking to professionals. But at that moment, it seemed like a simple and not-too-dangerous proposition.

Plus, despite my insistence that I knew Linda couldn't be a killer, one thought, one question kept running through my mind—where had she gone today after leaving Bailey's? I couldn't stop it from nagging at me. I needed to know if Linda was the one in the interrogation room. I needed to know if she was a main suspect. I needed to know if I was so wrong about my friend. If Linda was a killer then I had to question everything I thought I knew about my instincts. Walking on a building ledge suddenly seemed like a small price to pay to ease my mind.

But I couldn't go out headfirst. I took off my new flats, put them in my pockets, and rethreaded myself out the window, this time letting my feet lead the way. Halfway through, I twisted and somehow got my toes onto the ledge. I maneuvered the rest of my body out the window, and holding on to the frame, I managed to stand up. But I was facing the building, which wasn't the way they did it in the movies.

Still holding on to the frame, I slowly turned around and was pleased I'd managed to get my back to the brick building. This perspective on the world, however, brought my common sense back with the force of a kick in the gut.

What was I doing? Two stories might as well have been a hundred. If I fell, I would land in a small grass courtyard. If I didn't die, I would surely be horribly injured or maimed.

This was stupid. I stepped back toward the window I'd come through. I was going inside, then out to Ian's truck. There was still time to save myself—from myself.

But just before my fingers reached the open space, the window slammed shut. The sound echoed through the courtyard, and then everything became horribly silent. I froze in shock for an instant. Three or four thousand fast heartbeats later, I looked at the closed window and said, "Really?"

I was pretty well balanced, but panic was beginning to cause cool drops of perspiration to bead on my back. I had to get inside that building, and quickly.

I took another side step and grabbed the window frame. But it wouldn't budge. At all. Even a little bit. Because of my angle, and the darkness both outside and inside the building, I couldn't see the lock. The window had gone up so easily the first time—I couldn't help but think that it had been locked again. Had someone seen what I was doing and then locked me out?

I thought about pounding on the window. Someone would eventually hear and help, but I really hated getting caught doing things I wasn't supposed to be doing. A new resolve swept through me and wiped away the panic. I was going to try the other window and see if it opened before I gave in and gave up.

Being able to move along the ledge made me grateful for my small feet, but there wasn't much else that was good about it.

Long seconds passed before my side steps took me to the next window. This one was frosted, so I had no idea what was behind it, except that there were clearly no lights on.

I grabbed the bottom sash, gritted my teeth, and sent a silent prayer out to the universe that it wasn't locked.

It wasn't. In fact, apparently it had recently been oiled.

It was the first time I'd experienced a window "flying" open. The speed caused an air suck, and I was pulled through the opening. Fortunately, the floor wasn't that far down. I know I made some sort of *umph* sound when I landed, but it wasn't loud.

It was dark in the room, but the light from the court-yard illuminated just enough to let me know exactly where I was: the men's bathroom. It could have been worse—it could have been occupied.

I was so happy to be off the ledge and so impressed with my newly learned skills that I didn't care much about what someone would think if they saw me exiting the men's bathroom, or how I was going to appear in the police station from a place no one saw me go to in the first place. I put on my shoes and started to make my way back to where I'd started.

But as I reached the door, I heard a male voice moving in my direction. The person attached to the voice either was going to come in here or move on to the cell room.

I turned to examine the bathroom. There really was no other place to hide, no choices other than where everyone hides when they're hiding in a bathroom. I hurried into one of the two stalls, shut the door, locked it (glad I didn't need a purse strap to keep this one closed), and stood on the toilet. Along with all the adrenaline, there was a good dose of humiliation running through my system. I was hiding in the men's bathroom at the police station. A new low.

Sure enough, the person came through the door and switched on the light. He was talking on his cell phone as he went about his business, and fortunately he didn't attempt to open the stall door.

Once I thought I might not be discovered, I focused on

who the person was. It didn't take long, because it was a voice I'd heard often enough. I was getting to know Drew Forsyth far too well.

"Yes, okay, I can talk better now," he said. "I know. I did the best I could. I hope it was good enough."

He said uh-huh a number of times before wrapping up the conversation by saying, "Enough was enough, you're right." Pause. "I don't care, just make it look good. We'll talk later." He snapped the phone shut.

I told myself that he could have been talking about any number of things, not necessarily about participating in his mother's murder. Nonetheless, I didn't like the sound of it.

He washed his hands, turned off the light, and left the room. I hurried off my perch, grabbed a paper towel and stuck it in my pocket, and hoped the hallway was clear.

Once out of the bathroom, I took a deep cleansing breath and gave myself a silent pep talk. *So far, so good. No one saw, so if I don't act guilty, no one will know what I've been up to.*

While trying to look casual, I hurried to the back room where the cells were located. I was greeted by one lone prisoner—Linda. This was worse than if she'd been in the interrogation room!

"Becca?" she said from her seat as I stood in the doorway.

"Oh, Linda, they arrested you?" I asked as I walked toward her. She was in the same cell that my friend Abner had been in six months earlier. I was beginning to wonder if it was used exclusively for Bailey's vendors.

"No, of course not. They separated us when we got here, that's all. This is where they put me." She stood and walked out of the cell. "The most comfortable seat was in there."

"Oh, Linda, how are you?" I hugged her, relieved that she was still a free woman.

"I'm okay. Terrible dinner party, though, huh?" She gave a strained smile.

"I'm so sorry about Madeline."

"Me, too. Really. Though she was a tough cookie, she was Drew's mother and my future mother-in-law. And what a horrible way for anyone to go. It's hard for me to believe that anyone deserves that."

"How's Drew?" I asked.

"I think he's okay. He seems to be handling things all right. It's in his makeup to be the 'strong one.' He'll probably have some sort of delayed reaction, but we'll see." She smiled again, but her eyes were watery and sad. I felt terrible for her. "But to be honest with you, Becca, I just don't know. Drew and his mother haven't had much of a relationship over the last ten years or so—I know this is upsetting to him, but whether he'll be sad she's gone or sad he didn't get the relationship where he wanted it to be, I don't know. I don't want to burden you with all that now." She paused and looked over my shoulder. "What are you doing in here?"

"I had to use the bathroom," I lied. I wanted her to burden me with more, but now probably wasn't the time.

Linda nodded. "I bet Sam won't be pleased you stopped by to say hi to me. You'd better get back."

"Probably. But are you okay, really?"

"I'm fine. Shook up, but fine. Oh, Becca, of course we're postponing the wedding until Drew gets back from active duty," she said.

Just that morning, I'd wished for some sort of miracle to get me out of being in the wedding, but now my heart sank. This wasn't the type of miracle I was shooting for, and even though Madeline being killed should trump wedding plans, I knew postponing the event would break Linda's heart. On the other hand, if his phone call was any indication that Drew was involved in the murder, Linda shouldn't ever marry him. I wasn't ready to jump to those conclusions, though.

"Linda, I'm so sorry. He still has to go—*on his mission or active duty or whatever* . . . ?" I whispered.

"Yes. We were only able to talk before the police arrived, but it was the first thing he wanted to tell me—that he was going to have to go, no matter what. Drew is committed to what he does. I think the only way he could be stopped would be if he was arrested for the murder, but that's not a possibility. He'll do what he thinks is the right thing to do."

"Oh," I said, because I wasn't sure what else to say. Had Linda wondered the same things I was now wondering? How could Drew possibly handle leaving at this time? Was the fact that he was leaving just good timing? Was he headed out of town, probably to another country, just in time to pull off a murder, ditch his bride, and disappear beyond potential prosecution? I hated thinking these sorts of things about Drew Forsyth, but I couldn't ignore obvious possibilities. I wondered if Sam would let Drew leave. Did the Monson police have enough power to keep someone from *military duty*?

She saw the question in my eyes and said, "I know he couldn't have killed her because he was with me. I was upset about Madeline's 'show' at Bailey's this morning. Drew came over, and we . . . well . . . anyway."

"I get it," I said. I was relieved if she and Drew had spent the afternoon together. Linda's fair skin gave away their activities every time. Whenever she and Drew spent time together, I could discern the details by the shade of red her cheeks took on. Linda's blush told me two things: One, I didn't think she was lying about being with Drew. And two, they'd had a great time. I deduced a third detail—their good time hadn't occurred in the process of committing a murder. I wanted to believe her.

What if the murder was solved quickly? Drew was scheduled to leave a week from today, Friday. Could Sam and his officers figure out who the killer was in that short amount of time? It all depended on the evidence, and I didn't know what evidence they had. Sam would find a way to detain Drew if he thought it necessary.

As these thoughts collided in my mind, a nugget of a plan began to take shape. What if—just what if—the crime was solved in a few days? Maybe—just maybe— Linda and Drew could still get married before he left. I knew the way to the justice of the peace. I could drive them there. It was probably a silly idea, but Linda's blush reinforced how much the two of them wanted to be together, and how just this morning it had been of the utmost importance that they marry before Drew left.

I wasn't going to voice my thoughts to Linda. At the moment they were more like pulses of thought that weren't fully formed anyway. Plus, they were probably the result of the guilt I felt over my lack of excitement over being asked to be her Number One.

"Linda, take a deep breath. Good. One more. Good. Sam will solve this quickly. All will be well."

"I hope so. I appreciate your optimism." Linda laughed awkwardly and wiped away a stray tear. "Hey, speaking of Sam, you need to get out of here before he finds you talking to me. He was pretty clear on wanting us all separated."

I quickly hugged her again. "Call me tomorrow or later tonight if you need to talk."

"Thanks, Becca."

I left Linda and made my way down the empty hall. I'd told Sam I wasn't going to investigate Madeline's murder, but my mind was changing. Even though I was confident that the blush on her cheeks gave me accurate information, I still wasn't one hundred percent sure that Drew wasn't involved in the murder. I didn't *know* Linda wasn't, either, but I held onto my doubt. Sam was great at his job, but there were plenty of things I could look into without getting in his way. If the murder was solved before Drew left, he and Linda could go on with their lives, and I wouldn't have to worry about my friend marrying a killer.

I passed the restrooms on my left. On my right was the interview room. I couldn't resist, so I stopped and put my ear to the door. I could hear voices, but the only distinguishing feature I could make out was that there was one male voice and one female voice. Other than that, I heard nothing. I didn't think I needed to be caught in such a pose, so I moved along.

The door to the station, where everyone else was, was closed as well. I pulled the paper towel out of my pocket, opened the door, and made my way through as I wiped my hands on the towel.

Sally, Mid and Officer Sanford were still in the room, but Shawn, Drew and Officer Norton were nowhere to be seen. I deduced that the female voice I'd heard in the interview room must have been Officer Norton, but I didn't know who was attached to the male voice. Ian was still sitting across from Sam. His eyes flashed surprise, but only briefly. He knew that showing surprise wasn't wise. He'd be in cahoots with me even if he wasn't sure exactly what he was in cahoots about.

Sam, though, was keenly observant of everyone and everything. He turned and looked at me with one eyebrow high. Suddenly he was angry.

"Becca, what were you doing? How did you get back there?" he asked.

"Using the restroom." I threw the paper towel in a gray metal garbage can next to an unoccupied desk.

"I didn't see you walk past. Why didn't you just use the restroom in the hallway?"

I shrugged and continued walking. I was sure I'd have to discuss this further with him. He was a police officer, after all, but he was pretty busy at the moment. I walked purposefully and innocently past them.

"I'll be out in the truck, Ian," I said.

He nodded.

I kept walking and didn't look at anyone else. Before I knew it, I was in the hallway and no one was chasing me. I hurried toward the stairway but skidded to a waxed-linoleum stop and turned around.

I'd almost forgotten! And I had to know. I ran to the end of the dark hall and tried to pull up the window. It didn't budge. I stood on my tip-toes and looked at the lock. My face burned in guilty fear when I saw that the lock was securely back in place. Someone had seen what I was doing and had locked me out—left me to stand on the ledge.

Or had they locked me out with the hope that I'd fall off the ledge and onto the hard ground of the courtyard?

Who? The killer?

Oh, yes, I was most definitely back in the detective business.

Eight

As Ian got in the truck, before he could ask me any questions, I asked him about his interview with Sam.

"Sam believed that Madeline and I hadn't spoken and that I hadn't reached her yet. I didn't save her message, but it was a quick one. She just said to call her back. When I told him why we'd been in contact, he was interested more in Bud Morris's situation than in me. At the moment, I think he has a lot of potential suspects, and bank customers are probably high on his list."

"What about Drew or Linda or anyone else at the party?"

"As suspects?"

"Yes."

"He didn't share anything with me, but he did ask me again about everyone's behavior at dinner. I told him the same things I told him when he talked to me at Madeline's. I said that aside from Drew and Linda, I thought they were an unusual bunch, but what bunch isn't? We didn't spend enough time together to know much about any of them."

"Yeah, I thought the same thing. They're odd, but not in a murderous way."

"Whatever that is," Ian said.

"Good point. We never really know for sure, do we?"

"The good news is that apparently both our alibis are airtight."

"That's good news."

"You want to tell me why you came out of the back hallway?" Ian asked after a beat.

"Oh, that?"

"Yes."

"Well, I won't go into detail how I got there, just in case you're ever forced to testify against me for some reason or another"—I smiled—"but I made my way back to the holding cells and the interview room. I couldn't hear what was being said in the interview room, but Linda was in an unlocked holding cell and I talked to her a minute. In no particular order, the wedding's off, Drew's still leaving, and I think I believe her when she says that she and Drew were together the entire afternoon until the dinner, and they couldn't have killed Madeline." I didn't want to tell Ian about the window because he'd be both annoyed and concerned, and he'd be very concerned if I told him how it had been locked again.

"I'm sorry about the wedding, but I understand. I'm perplexed that Drew is still leaving, but I suspect that's only because he hasn't processed everything totally. Give him a day or two, and he might rethink that—but considering what he does, I don't know if he'll be given the option. And why do you believe that Linda and Drew were together?"

"The way she blushed," I said.

"Oh. Well, that is pretty fail safe." Ian smiled. "I guess I'm glad they got to spend a fun afternoon together before everything hit the fan."

"It was way better than fun," I said.

"She really, really blushed?"

"Yep."

"Good."

We were both silent a moment. I drummed my fingers on my leg and then finally spoke. "I was going to pick up Hobbit and head home. But my inventory for my short day tomorrow is ready to go. Maybe we could just stay with you tonight and I'll go get the inventory early."

"That sounds like a great idea," Ian said.

We gathered Hobbit from in front of George's fireplace and made a hasty path to Ian's apartment above his studio.

Hobbit had become accustomed to our ways, so after her momentary happy greeting, she managed to ignore us as we forgot about the recent strain in our relationship and the gruesome murder, and worked on turning our own blush factor up to high. We were successful.

We were awake a good hour before the sun rose. Ian had a piece of art to install, so he went in one direction, and after Hobbit and I made sure George had plenty of coffee and eggs, we headed to my farm.

The temperature was perfect again, and I rolled down my window. It wasn't going to be too hot or too cool today. Winters weren't all that terrible in South Carolina, but the warming spring temperatures would bring a big crowd to Bailey's today. By the time we got home, the sun was almost up, and despite all the horribleness of the night before, I felt a big dose of spring fever coming on.

I'd already started my pumpkin seeds, and the plants were sprouting from small peat pots in my kitchen. My pumpkin preserves were becoming so popular that I'd started more pumpkin seeds than ever before. I was close to needing a greenhouse. If I started selling product at Maytabee's, I'd have to invest in one very soon.

I was eager to dig in the dirt, plant the pumpkin sprouts, and watch them grow. And my strawberry plants were in terrific shape. The berries would be ready to pick very soon, and if looks were any indication, I was going to have another delicious crop.

I loaded up my inventory for the short day I'd planned and then took Hobbit for a quick run. When we were done, and as she and I surveyed my land from beside the barn, my fingers tingled with anticipation. Hobbit felt it, too, as she lifted her nose into the air and took a couple of good whiffs. We spent lots of time outside during the growing season, and it was difficult to say which one of us enjoyed it more.

"I know, girl, pretty soon now," I said as I scratched that perfect spot behind her left ear.

She smiled.

The sound of tires on gravel got our attention, and Hobbit put one of her long paws on my foot, both to inform me that we had a visitor and to assure me that she'd let me know if he or she was okay.

The tires were attached to Drew's Honda, but he

wasn't the driver. Instead, the blond, less awesome version of him—his cousin Alan—steered the car down the driveway's slope toward me and Hobbit.

Why was he at my house at this early hour? How did he know where I lived? Was Linda okay?

"It's all right, girl. I know him. Sort of," I said. Hobbit hesitantly pulled her paw off my foot. The tone of my voice wasn't as confident as either she or I would have liked.

Alan parked the Honda and got out. He was dressed in jeans and a golf shirt and flip-flops that snapped at his heels as he made his way toward me.

"Becca, hello. Alan Cummings. Drew's cousin," he said, extending his hand.

"Hi, Alan. I remember. Hey, I'm sorry about your aunt. You okay? And what's up? Where're Drew and Linda?" I fired the questions quickly and then cleared my throat.

"Thank you. Yes, everyone's fine. Sorry I'm here so early. Linda said I should get here before you took off for Bailey's." He was close to me, too close. I didn't like him in my personal space, and I tried to step back nonchalantly. He stepped with me.

"What's up?" I repeated.

"Linda has a horrible migraine, so she's not going in to Bailey's today, but she has some orders that are scheduled to be picked up. She wondered if you'd take care of them for her."

"Of course. Let me back my truck up to your car, and we can load them in the back. How many are there?" I tried to hide my relief. Linda hadn't been arrested and was okay, other than having a headache. I'd call her later to see how she was feeling, and to make sure she was really all right.

"Twelve."

"Wow," I said.

"Yes, wow. Apparently she had most of them baked before . . . well, before everything last night, but she stayed up practically all night finishing them."

"Darn it! I wish I'd thought about that. I could have helped."

Alan smiled. I knew he meant it to be a friendly smile, but it didn't sit right with me. Why did he turn on my inner alarm bells? "We all offered to help, but she insisted on doing everything herself." His tone was almost spiteful.

"Did anyone get arrested last night?" I asked.

Alan's eyebrows rose. "No, I'm pretty sure the police think that one of the bank's customers, someone who was foreclosed on, is the killer. I think that's the angle they're exploring right now."

I nodded, and studied Alan for some sign of . . . something. What was it? Was it that he looked so much like Drew but wasn't Drew? I couldn't put my finger on it.

"Again, I'm so sorry."

"Thank you. I think I'm still in shock over the whole thing."

"I understand. Hey, girl, go over there, please," I said to Hobbit, who obeyed and went to sit on the porch. I got in my truck and adjusted the rearview mirror so that I could watch Alan as I backed toward the Honda.

He was looking toward my strawberry plants until I got close enough that he signaled me to stop.

"Becca, you have some beautiful land," Alan said as I hopped out of the truck and pulled down the tailgate.

"Thanks."

"Any thought of selling it?"

I laughed. "Not even one. I love it here, and I hope I never leave."

"You never know who might offer you the right price," he said, but his voice wasn't friendly.

"The right price doesn't exist," I replied too firmly.

"Sure," Alan said, shrugging.

He opened the Honda's trunk, and we were enveloped with delicious fruity scents.

"Yum. I hope I can manage to hold on to these until the customers come for them. I love Linda's pies," I said as we transferred the boxes to the truck. Before long, the bed of the truck was loaded with Linda's pies and my jams.

"Thanks, Becca," Alan said as he closed the Honda's trunk. "Oh, hey, I saw you in an unexpected place last night."

I froze. Naturally, the moment that I felt most guilty about popped into my mind. Had he seen me on the ledge? He had his hands on his hips but was no longer in my personal space. Had he come to my house to confront me about my spying ways? Was he dangerous? Could I get in my truck and leave before he could do something to me? Would I leave Hobbit with someone dangerous? No.

"Oh, yeah?" I said.

"Yeah, you and Ian were turning onto . . . Harvard, I think that was the street. I'd just left the police station."

"Yes!" I said too enthusiastically. "Yes, Ian lives on Harvard."

"I thought it was you."

"Uh-huh."

"You must have been in Ian's truck last night. I would have remembered yours. It's great. I love the color."

"Thanks," I said, still trying to hide my relief and my odd uncomfortable feelings about him.

He'd complimented my land and my truck. I still didn't trust him, but if he said something outstanding about Hobbit, I might actually have to try to like him—if he didn't give me the willies so much. Why did he set off my radar?

He walked to the driver's side door of Drew's Honda. "Hey, thanks for doing this for Linda. She said she'll call you when she can hold her head up and open her eyes."

"Sure. No problem."

"See you later, Becca." Alan got in the car and drove away.

Hobbit was by my side the second the car was out of sight. She whined and put her paw back on my foot.

"Yeah, I know. I've got to get a grip, huh?" There was something about him that still bothered me. I tried to shrug it off as a feeling that was the result of meeting someone at a dinner party where a dead body was found. But there was *something* more, and Hobbit sensed it, too. She whined again.

"Come on," I said, "I've got to get to work." There was no more time to waste. I made sure Hobbit was taken care of for the morning and took off for Bailey's.

As I drove down the state highway, I wished that there was someone in Drew's family I could talk to, *really* talk to. My relationship with him had been built around two new couples: Drew and Linda, and Ian and me. We'd been getting to know each other, but we were still so newly coupled that we wanted to spend more time as separate couples instead of as one of two couples.

I wanted to better understand Drew and his family dynamics. Had Madeline really had a soft side, as Linda had mentioned? What had Linda meant about Drew and Madeline not having much of a relationship? What did Drew's cousins really think about their aunt? Our dinner had been so brief.

Alan, Shawn, and Mid might be strange, but there could be numerous reasons behind their strangeness. If Allison, the human nature specialist, had taught me anything, it was that you never know what happened in a person's life the second before they came in contact with you. Until you understood what they'd been through, you could never truly understand why they did the things they did in the present.

I thought Sally was the strangest one of the bunch—too emotional and melancholy. None of the rest of her family made much of her behavior, though. I didn't notice anyone roll their eyes or sigh impatiently when she teared up. I also didn't see anyone shocked by her behavior. Was she always like that, or was last night unique? Was she emotional and melancholy because she'd just killed her aunt?

Because of the strange dynamics among the family members the night before, I wasn't ready to think the killer had been a bank customer. I hoped that would be the case, but at this point any information could be helpful.

I could approach any of them under the pretext of curiosity or friendly conversation, but I decided I'd try to talk to Sally first. At the moment, it was her behavior that made me the most curious.

I filed a plan to call her later as I pulled into the U-shaped loading/unloading area of Bailey's and followed tire ruts to the back of my stall. As I parked, I noticed that the market was already getting customers. The beautiful weather and the spreading spring fever would definitely draw a big crowd.

"Can I help you with that?" Allison appeared beside my truck.

"Hey, Sis. Sure, but don't you have something more important and managerial to do?"

"I'm being managerial. Drew called to let me know you were helping Linda. I said I'd come help you."

"I'll take the help."

"I thought maybe I'd hear from you last night." Allison lifted two pies out of the truck. "I talked to Ian this morning. You were at a dinner where someone—Madeline Forsyth!—was found brutally murdered, and you didn't think to fill in your own sister."

"Huh," I said as I stood holding a stack of pies. "It hadn't occurred to me. To call you, that is. So much has happened, and I've been trying hard to pay attention to everything. Sorry about that."

Allison smiled. "Well, first of all, are you okay?"

"Yeah. Seeing Madeline Forsyth's body wasn't the best moment of my life, but I think I'm more worried about Linda than anything else."

"Me, too, but she'll be fine. They'll need some time."

"The wedding's postponed."

"I figured as much."

"Be careful what you wish for," I said.

"True. So, do you want to fill me in on the details now or later?"

I gave her the condensed version, leaving out my escapade on the ledge. I also didn't tell her about taking

Madeline's cell phone. If I'd told her about that, she'd get all big-sisterly on me. Her few extra minutes of life had been used against me often enough that I knew better.

"You don't think Linda or Drew . . .?" she asked when I finished.

"I really don't know for sure but I don't think so. Maybe Sam will give me some more insight, if I push him."

"Sam's a bit too giving of his information with you, but I suppose that's what happens when . . ."

"When what?"

"Never mind. I've got to get to work."

"Thanks for the help."

"You're welcome," she said as she walked away, pulling her cell phone out of her pocket.

"Hi, Becca," a voice said from the front of my stall. I looked up and saw two of my favorite people, whom I liked for more than their phenomenal baking skills. They were holding their own personal versions of heaven, and I was forced to transform back into Linda's Number One, even though the job had been all but eliminated.

Nine

News of Madeline's murder might have been spreading, but apparently Mamma Maria and Stella had been too busy baking to pay attention to the news. When I saw their amazing creations, I didn't want to be the one to tell them about either the murder or the postponement of the wedding, but Allison had left, so I had no choice.

"I'm so sorry," I said as I glanced longingly at Mamma's peach delight and mini banana cream pies, and Stella's cupcakes. "I should have called you last night. You put so much work into these. Honestly, I didn't even think about it. I totally forgot you were bringing samples by this morning."

"Madeline Forsyth was murdered?" Stella asked, ignoring my apology. "Oh, my gosh." Stella was round and beautiful, her cheeks always rosy and dusted with a little flour, and her blue eyes bright and happy. Her husband owned a restaurant and they had two teenagers who didn't act like teenagers, so I enjoyed the whole family.

"I can't believe it," Mamma said. "I didn't know her or even who she was, but what a horrible thing to have happen. And you saw her body?" Mamma wore tight jeans and a low-cut shirt that revealed massive cleavage. Even though she was tall, gorgeous, and physically perfect, I liked her a lot.

"I did." I told them a version of the night's events similar to the version I'd told Allison, but this time, as I spoke, the idea I'd had when talking to Linda the night before began to take a new shape in my mind. I didn't allow myself to think it through, but let it roll off my tongue as I shared it with Stella and Mamma.

"So, what do you think about this? I know that a wedding is probably very inappropriate right now, but Drew is leaving no matter what—he's definitely reporting for duty." I didn't burden them with the fact that if he was arrested he wouldn't be going anywhere but to jail. "I think he *has* to report for duty or something like that. Anyway, I know Sam . . . I mean I know the police will be all over this case, and it could be solved quickly. What if it is solved? In the next few days?"

Stella and Mamma nodded, but they still didn't understand where I was going.

"Well, if it is solved, and the killer isn't either Drew or Linda"—I laughed, but they didn't laugh with me— "well, I was thinking I might kidnap them and take them to the justice of the peace. But why not bring them here instead? That is, if you ladies could handle some last-minute preparations? What do you think—how much time do you need to prepare? One day, two?"

"Do you think Drew will want to get married, have a wedding so soon . . . even if the murder is solved? And Linda, too?" Mamma asked.

I shrugged. "I know, I know, I'm sounding insensitive, but I'm really attempting to be the opposite. Yes, it's horrible what happened to his mother, but originally he and Linda wanted to get married before he left anyway. It was a rush wedding as it was. If the murder gets solved, and if they're willing—then why not? Why not have some happiness? As they say, life goes on, right?"

The more I talked about my idea, the more I liked it. The way I saw it, if Drew and Linda got married before he left they'd both have something good to hold on to—while he was gone. I didn't have either Stella or Mamma convinced, but I thought that might be because they were still recovering from learning about the murder.

"You're much more romantic than I've ever given you credit for, Becca," Stella said.

"I'm not romantic. I'm realistic."

Mamma and Stella looked at each other with raised eyebrows.

"I guess I'm game," Mamma said hesitantly. "The peach delight was for the rehearsal Tuesday morning, so if you have any sort of rehearsal, just let me know. Linda was going to consider the banana cream pies for a wedding-day luncheon dessert, but I don't think we should count on that."

"Probably not"—I looked at the mini pies longingly—"but at this point, let's plan on having the rehearsal." I moved my eyes to the peach delight. "The murder could be solved by Tuesday, and if we rehearse in the morning, we'll be prepared. It's kind of crazy, but it might work just fine."

"This will be a surprise to Linda and Drew?" Mamma asked.

"Yes."

"Will you invite them to the rehearsal?"

"Dunno. We'll play it by ear."

Mamma and Stella looked at each other again. They were warming to the idea, I could tell. Or at least they were becoming less horrified by it.

"I guess I just need a day's notice. I'll bake the cake and have it ready to go, but I won't frost it until I hear from you," Stella said. "You can tell me which kind of cake, and take a look at a sketch I did and let me know if you think it will work okay."

"Great. Thanks, ladies."

"I guess if all the pieces fall into their proper places, it could be very sweet," Stella said.

"Absolutely," I agreed.

"I suppose we should do something with all these samples. Any ideas, Becca?" She smiled.

"Yes, but give me one more second." The early crowd was still light, so I knew I might be able to round up some willing help. I called both Allison and Ian. In an uncanny twist of luck, which made me think it was a sign that my plan was a good one, they were both available. Allison's managerial moment was over for the time being, and Ian was pulling into Bailey's from his early installation.

They both appeared at my stall just as I put a bite of Mamma Maria's peach delight in my mouth. It was like a cobbler, cake, and crisp all in one, and would make a

perfect dessert; it would also be a great rehearsal morning breakfast—fruity comfort food.

"Yum," I said with my mouth too full. I swallowed.
then told Allison and Ian my plan.

They were both hesitant at first, but I bribed them with
some of the peach delight and mini banana cream pies,
and before long they were on board.

"I guess there's nothing wrong with being prepared,
just in case," Allison said after a bite of a pie. "I get what
you're thinking, Becca. If Drew really is leaving, and
their goal was to be married before he left, if the murder
is solved that quickly, and if Drew can get to a good emotional place, then you have a good plan. But there are a lot
of ifs in that equation."

"Yes, I know. Here, try the peach delight."

"This is amazing," Ian said as he dug into his samples.

Mamma laughed as she caught my eye. She saw that
my plan to conquer my sister and boyfriend was working.
"The peach delight will be easy. Sorry about the pies,
but we'll use them for someone else's surprise wedding.
Okay, Stella, I think it's your turn."

I eyed Stella's box of cupcakes.

"Okay, first, I need a man's opinion. Ian, look at this
and tell me what you think." Stella held an open notebook
in front of him.

"Wow, Stella, that's something," he said as he set
down his fork and took the notebook from her.

"What?" I nudged my way to his side. "Oh, wow."
Stella had sketched a wedding cake design.

"I can do the cake in any flavor, or more than one flavor if that's what Linda wants—or you think she might
want, but she was pretty specific about the type of design.

This is just my first sketch. If it doesn't work, I can do more."

It was difficult to pull our eyes away from the notebook. The design was simple, yet very elegant. The round cake had three layers; every layer was covered in white fondant, the bottom layer had navy blue stripes, the middle layer was circled with tiny gold anchors, and the top layer had tiny navy blue dots over it. Instead of a couple on the top, there was a navy blue bow of sorts. Somehow Stella had made the cake look both feminine and masculine at the same time.

"When I talked to Linda, she was very clear that she wanted the anchors and the navy blue. I think Drew's profession might be a bit clearer to me now, but I still get the feeling I'm not supposed to talk about it."

"It's gorgeous, Stella," I said. "This looks like a lot of work, though. Are you sure . . . ?"

"Of course I'm sure." She waved away my concern. "It's for Linda."

"This will be perfect," Ian said, his artistic eyes registering approval.

"Good. Try these now." Stella pointed to the cupcakes. "Decide on a flavor."

We tried white, chocolate, carrot, marbled, and raspberry filled. It wasn't an easy choice, but considering that Linda made fruit pies, we finally decided on the raspberry filled.

It wasn't even eight o'clock in the morning, and we were starting the day on very full stomachs. Once the decisions were made, Stella and Mamma packed up their supplies (but left their remaining samples for us to snack on) and took off to attend to their own businesses.

Mamma would be driving to the Smithfield market, and Stella would probably already have a line at her stall. We were surrounded by the pleasant buzz of a building crowd of shoppers. It was going to be a beautiful day.

I wouldn't say I thought my plan for a surprise wedding was perfect, but at the moment it seemed harmless enough. The wedding, if it occurred, wouldn't be lavish by any standards, but it would be perfect in its own way. The preparations weren't going to be that hard on anyone except Stella, and she seemed fine with it. I attempted to look into the future, hoping to see that it might turn out to be the right thing to do. Of course, it might not to be, but I'd deal with that if necessary.

Allison patted her stomach. "I've got to get to work, for real this time. You need me for anything else?"

"Yeah, I have a question."

"Ask away."

"Can you think of any reason that Madeline Forsyth would have called Jeanine Baker yesterday afternoon?" I asked. Jeanine's stall was down the aisle from mine, but I had yet to see her this morning.

Allison blinked. "That's a strange question, Becca, and frankly, it worries me."

"Why?"

"I have no idea why Madeline would have called Jeanine. You wondering why she did only adds to another issue. Jeanine didn't show up today. I've been trying to reach her all morning. What do you know? How do you know Madeline tried to call her?"

"It's a long story, but I looked at Madeline's phone after we found her body," I said. "Was Jeanine having any financial issues? Did she bank at Central?"

Allison looked away from me. It was a quick maneuver, one she normally pulled off without a hitch. She was always very good at being evasive when she needed to be, but something made her hesitate in her maneuver this time.

"Al?"

"Barry was supposed to pick her up this morning, but she wasn't home. It's very unlike her to not be home, and it's very very unlike her not to let Barry know that she doesn't need to be picked up. And she isn't answering her home phone or her cell phone. I'm really worried now."

My first instinct was to drive to her farm and see if she was okay, but I wasn't in a position to leave Bailey's. I'd promised to take care of Linda's customers, and soon I'd have a decent crowd of my own.

"We'd better call Sam," I said as I pulled out my cell phone.

"Becca?" he answered on the first ring.

"Yeah, Sam. Hey, Jeanine Baker isn't at Bailey's today." Without explaining, he'd realize I'd seen the number on the call list

"That's interesting," he said a few seconds later. "I'm in Bailey's parking lot. I came by to talk to you and to Jeanine. I'll be right in."

"Why do you need to talk to me?"

"I have some questions about your trip on the ledge of my building last night."

"Oh."

"Stay there, Becca. I'll see you in a minute." Sam ended the call.

"What?" Allison said.

"Uh, well . . . Sam's here. He'll check things out," I said guiltily.

"Becca?"

Fortunately, one of Linda's customers had arrived, and my attention was diverted. Allison went to greet Sam as I waited and helped more customers. I wondered if he was going to make good on his constant threat—was I finally going to be arrested?

Ten

My "trip on the ledge of Sam's building" must have been far less important than Jeanine's whereabouts. I didn't see Sam for a long time. He was probably talking to Allison and Barry and whoever else might know more about Jeanine Baker.

Jeanine had had her egg stall ever since I'd started working at Bailey's. She was shorter than me, but very strong. I doubted she'd ever worn a stitch of makeup, her hair was cut boyishly short, and she had one of those faces that made her look like she was somewhere between the ages of fifty and seventy. And her farm fresh eggs were phenomenal—until I'd tried them, I hadn't known the difference "fresh" made when it came to eggs. I didn't purchase eggs from anyone but Jeanine.

Jeanine was also paranoid. About everything and everyone. It was rare that she trusted anyone with anything.

I knew she admired and trusted Allison and Barry of Barry Good Corn, but they seemed to be the only two people she'd relax around. Whenever she and I had a conversation, I sensed that she was on edge and couldn't wait for the conversation to be over. I didn't take it personally; it was just the way Jeanine was. Plus, the entire world trusted Allison. I couldn't fault Jeanine for keying in on my sister's strengths.

I couldn't begin to imagine why Madeline Forsyth would have called her. I could imagine, though, that such a call—no matter the reason—might send Jeanine into some sort of panic. But what would Jeanine do with that panic—run away? Kill Madeline? Surely not the latter.

I didn't know exactly when Jeanine had left Bailey's yesterday, but usually she brought only enough eggs to last part of the market day. She was the sole operator of her farm, and she had to get home to attend to her chickens and prepare for the next day. The care and feeding of livestock wasn't something I dealt with. Where I could use my days off or any extra time here and there to create inventory, farmers with livestock had to stick to a schedule.

Even though I wasn't looking forward to discussing my activities with Sam, I hoped he'd share something about where he thought Jeannine was.

I didn't have much time to ponder, though, because suddenly business picked up and I went into full work mode. A few customers morphed into a nonstop flow of them; some wanting my jams and preserves, and others in search of the pie they'd prepurchased from Linda. I had to give her kudos for getting the pies done. She knew they *loved* her pies. If she hadn't finished them, I'm sure her customers would have understood, but not without having to hide irritation or anger.

"Hey," someone said after a twenty-minute rush.

Ian was suddenly behind me.

"Oh, hey again," I said as I turned.

"I've got to head out for another install, thought I'd let you know."

"Thanks. I hope it goes well."

He squinted. "Becca, you okay?"

"Fine. Why?"

"Let's see, it's been a crazy couple of days. You've seen a dead body, now you're an undercover maid of honor. You have a lot going on. I think we should reschedule the Maytabee's presentation."

"Undercover Number One," I corrected him. "No, let's not reschedule. You said they only meet monthly?"

"Yep."

"Even without a murder and a wedding, next month could be crazier than this month. Bailey's will be really busy. I wasn't going to work on Monday anyway. We might as well keep it scheduled. And thanks again for getting me the 'in.' "

"You're welcome." Ian squinted again.

"What?"

"Becca, you're not going to 'investigate' this, are you? Madeline's murder, I mean. I know how much you care for Linda, and I know you'd like to pull off this surprise wedding. But you know you need to leave the investigating to the police, don't you?"

I wasn't going to lie to Ian, even if I wanted to.

"I'm not going to be stupid," I said. "But I might ask some questions."

"The last time you asked a few questions about a murder, you got pretty beat up. I'm concerned the same will happen again."

He was one hundred percent correct, but that still didn't change my plans.

"How about this?" I began. "How about I keep a good distance from anyone who might be dangerous and leave the real investigating to Sam? I won't do anything . . . well, anything important, without calling him and letting him know. He's at Bailey's right now and wants to talk to me. I'll be up-front with him, too." All this forthrightness made my throat hurt, but I didn't want to lie. In fact, I wanted to do exactly as I said. I hoped I'd be able to stick by my words.

"Promise?" Ian's expression was doubtful.

"Scout's honor." I held up a two-fingered peace sign.

Ian laughed and reached for my raised hand. He put my first two fingers together and raised the third. "Now, cover your pinkie nail with your thumb. That's an appropriate Scout's honor."

"You were a Boy Scout?"

"Yes, but that was long before the tattoos." He smiled.

"I'll be careful, Ian, I promise." I looked up into the dark eyes that could make me do just about anything, with the possible exception of agreeing to meet his family.

"You'd better. I'm going to need help with all that lavender," Ian said. He tipped up my chin and kissed me quickly. "See you tonight?"

"Absolutely," I replied as he turned to walk away. The strain between us was definitely dissipating, but I'd still have to give him an answer soon.

I watched as he and Sam greeted each other in the

aisle. I couldn't hear their conversation, but it seemed to be just simple hellos.

"Sam," I said as he made his way to my stall.

"Becca."

"Did you find Jeanine?"

He shook his head. "Becca, what were you doing on the ledge of my building last night?" It was like him to take ownership of the government building, just like he probably called Monson "my town."

"How did you know?"

We were interrupted by a customer who wanted three jars of blueberry jam. The delay allowed Sam's serious face to relax slightly. I always liked talking to my friend Sam better than to the police officer Sam.

"Really, how did you know?" I said after the customer walked away.

"You just told me."

"What?"

"The night janitor saw an open window. He shut and locked it, then later thought maybe he should let me know about it. I remembered the direction you'd come from when you walked through the station. I guessed."

"You're a good policeman, Sam."

"Becca, putting any illegalities aside, that wasn't a safe maneuver."

"I know. I realized as much when I got out on the ledge. I tried to get back in, but your janitor was too quick, and . . ." I paused.

"And?"

"I guess I wish it hadn't been the janitor who shut the window. I thought that whoever did it might also be the killer. I thought maybe I'd narrowed it down to the dinner guests. Now, it could be anyone." I bit at my bottom lip.

Sam looked at me for a long moment and then said, "Exactly. That's why you should have volunteered the information about someone shutting you out on the ledge. It might have been valuable to the investigation." He sighed. "Becca, I really wish you'd let the police do our jobs."

I nodded. "Okay, I will," I said hesitantly. I'd just told Ian I would be up-front with Sam, but it wasn't going to be easy.

"Did you discover anything on your excursion? And what were you trying to discover in the first place?"

"Originally, I wanted to know if Linda was in the interview room. I wanted to know if she was a prime suspect. I knew you wouldn't let me walk though the station to find out."

"True."

"I made my way into the men's bathroom. From there I went to the cells. I talked to Linda for a minute, and then you saw me come through the station again. That was all." I'd had a moment like this with Sam before—a moment when there was something I knew he should know but I wasn't ready to share quite yet. He—the police, at least—should know what I overheard in the bathroom. Drew's end of the conversation was suspicious, but I wasn't going to make him look guiltier than he might be. There were plenty of other avenues to explore, and I had a plan to find out more about Drew before I told the police. I fought the urges to do what I knew I should do and what I wanted to do—keep quiet. What I wanted, won.

And just like that, I broke my promise to Ian.

"What did you and Linda talk about?"

"How terrible it was that Madeline had been murdered. How awful it all was. How the wedding was postponed. Nothing much beyond that."

"You sure?"

"Yes."

Sam nodded.

"But there is something . . ." I began, thinking I might have something I was willing to share that could be useful to the investigation.

"What?"

"This morning, really early, Drew's cousin Alan came by my house to bring me some of Linda's pies to deliver to her customers. He was . . . well, he was strange."

"In what way?"

"He wanted to know if I'd ever consider selling my land."

Sam thought for a minute. "Okay."

"He was sort of pushy."

"That might not be strange. He might be pushy by nature. Besides, Alan recently sold some land outside Smithfield, and he's looking for some around Monson. He was working with Madeline to find something. He has to invest quickly or pay some sort of tax penalty."

Is this what *in between things at the moment* meant?

"Okay, but still, he was either kind of creepy or it was too early in the morning for me to process normal conversation. He didn't stay long, but it was a minute or two too long, if you know what I mean."

"Noted. Thanks for telling me. See how easy that was?" Sam smiled, cracking his tough image. I liked it when he did that.

"Now, how about you share? Anything you want to tell me?" I smiled.

This time Sam laughed. Any minute now, his slicked-back hair would spring a curl.

"Well, I sent Officer Norton out to Jeanine Baker's farm, but haven't heard back yet. I thought I'd go myself. You want to come along for the ride?"

"Really? On official police business?"

"Tell me you weren't going to go out to her place alone. I figure if you go with me, I can at least attempt to keep you out of trouble."

In fact, I *was* going to check on Jeanine after work.

"Can I have five minutes?" I asked.

"You can have three," Sam said as he looked at his watch.

I still had two of Linda's pies, but they were easily taken care of with a conversation with Herb and Don and a handwritten sign on Linda's stall. I still had plenty of inventory, but didn't have time to pack it into my truck, so I just put it in boxes and set them under the display tables.

I'd gone well over my three minutes when Sam's phone rang.

"Sam Brion," he answered it. "Okay. Yes, sure. On my way." He snapped the phone closed. "Sorry, Becca, gotta go. Can't wait."

"Was that about Jeanine?"

"Gotta go."

"Can I still come? I'll clean the rest of this up later," I said. I didn't want to miss whatever was happening on the other end of the phone conversation.

Sam hesitated, then nodded stiffly. "Come on."

For the first time in all the years I'd worked at Bailey's,

I left my stall unattended without so much as a note letting customers know when I'd be back. The market manager wouldn't be happy, but at least I'd made sure that Linda's pies were in good hands. Fortunately, since the market manager was my fraternal twin sister, I didn't think she'd kick me out of Bailey's for one small infraction.

Or at least I hoped she wouldn't. She did take her job pretty seriously.

Eleven

Much to my hippie parents' disappointment, I'd never ridden in a police car. And my truck could barely go over fifty-five miles per hour, so the high-speed drive to Jeanine Baker's chicken farm in the front passenger seat of Sam's police Charger was an adrenaline rush like I'd never experienced.

Sam kept his eyes on the road. I double-checked my seat belt, held on, and tried not to yell, "*Wheee!*"

"What did Officer Norton find?" I asked.

"It's what she didn't find."

"What?"

"No Jeanine and not very many chickens."

Jeanine might be out, but it was unlikely that she'd taken her chickens with her. I understood Sam's rush.

Jeanine lived closer to Madeline's estate than to my farm, but she wasn't one of the rich people. Her land had been in her family a long time, and the property was small and hidden from the main road, which was only a two-lane state highway.

Sam had turned on his flashing lights but kept the siren off. There wasn't much traffic, and he was extra cautious going through intersections. Even though we were in a hurry because we were worried about a friend, I was having a blast.

In record time he turned onto the narrow dirt road that led to Jeanine's farm. The Charger handled the bumps much better than my old truck would have, and in a few seconds Sam maneuvered the car to a stop in front of Jeanine's house.

"Stay here, Becca," he said in a firm tone. I nodded, knowing I shouldn't argue.

The inside of the car became heavy with quiet once Sam disappeared into Jeanine's house.

The house was old, in need of paint, and there was a crack in one of the front windows. There was a small front yard with mowed grass and no weeds. The patch of green stood out against the drab house and the dirt area behind the fence to the left of it.

Jeanine's house seemed very empty. The long moments ticked by as I waited for Sam to reappear.

Suddenly, a flash of movement appeared to the left of the house and atop an old fence post. I didn't know much about chickens, but I was fairly certain that a rooster had just jumped or flown to the top of the post. The bird had a bright red crest on its head; its body was mostly dark with a splash of orange on its wings.

"Hello, there," I muttered quietly. "Where are all your friends?"

As if to answer my question, another bird, all white, appeared from behind the side of the house and paced the ground underneath the rooster. And then another one appeared. And then a few more. Before long, the entire area was full of chickens.

"I guess that's one mystery solved," I said, and got out of the car just as Sam came out the front door.

"Did you find Jeanine?" I asked.

"No, but we found the chickens."

"Were they hiding?"

"Sort of. There's a coop in the back—some were in there—but there's a whole other area behind the coop. Officer Norton thought the property ended after the coop, so she didn't look any further. The chickens were behind the coop and couldn't get through what looks like an accidental barrier made by some fallen rocks. It was strange."

"Ms. Robins," Officer Norton said as she walked out the front door. She looked embarrassed but was attempting to hide it. "How are you today?"

"Fine, thanks. You?"

"Fine. Excuse me." She continued past us and went to look over the fence into the chicken yard. She put her hands on her hips, and I understood why people call well-muscled arms "guns." She had some of the most amazing guns I'd ever seen.

"She's the one who actually found them," Sam said, "just as I joined her out back."

I nodded. I was the last person to criticize someone for jumping to an assumption. "Can I go in and look around?"

Sam rubbed a finger under his nose. His eyes narrowed as he said, "You can walk around with me. This is not standard procedure, mind you—in fact, it's down-right stupid of me to do—but if you don't touch anything, you can look around. Let me know if you see something I should look at. I'm worried about Jeanine. According to your sister, her behavior today is something she's never done before. She might just be out running errands, but the chickens being loose when we got here bothers me. I'd like to find her. Any ideas that occur to you would be helpful."

The outside of Jeanine's house might need some work, but the inside was just fine. The small front room had a matching chair and couch, done in country blues and reds, that faced a modern flat-screen television. The only messy part of the room was a desk stacked with paper-work and what looked like coin wrappers. I stepped to-ward it for a closer look.

"Don't touch anything, Becca. Just tell me if anything looks curious."

I nodded as I peered at invoices, bills, and coin wrap-pers. Other than the wrappers, the desk looked like a smaller version of my dining table. There was no laptop anywhere, but that wasn't so unusual for someone who had been farming all her life.

From the desk, I could either take a doorway directly to my left, into the kitchen, or the hallway farther to my left, to the rest of the house. First, I went into the kitchen; it had a round antique table and chairs, but everything else in the room was modern: shiny stainless steel appli-ances and a polished wood floor.

The room was clean and tidy, with only a coffeemaker and a toaster on the counters.

"Sam, what am I looking for?"

"Something that doesn't look right."

"That's not very helpful."

"You'll know when you see it. I searched the house. There's no evidence that there was any sort of struggle, no evidence that Jeanine left in a hurry or against her will. Her purse—or bag, whichever—isn't here, so she must have taken it with her. You know Jeanine; you might be able to sense something . . . off."

The hall led directly to a small bathroom. There were bedrooms on each side of the bathroom. One was small and the other was smaller, but they were clean; beds were made, and there was no dust anywhere.

"She's a very clean and neat person," I observed aloud. "But I don't see anything that tells me more than that."

I followed Sam back through the kitchen and out a back door that took us directly to all the chickens.

"Whoa, chickens stink," I said as I reached for my nose.

"Yes, but did you smell it before you came back here?"

"Not so much."

"Me either. That surprised me. I checked the coop; nothing but chickens laying eggs in there," Sam said as he pointed at the wooden structure on the other side of the yard. "The accidental rock wall is behind it. I have no idea how they got back there or who stopped them from coming into the yard, but if it was Jeanine, she's not going to be happy we let them back in."

"Why did you?"

"It didn't look like there was a fence on the other side, and I wondered why the rocks were there."

"Can chickens be herded?" I asked, wondering how in the world someone could get what looked like hundreds of creatures in the yard to go anywhere they didn't want to go.

"I don't know, but I imagine they'll follow food anywhere."

"That's probably true."

"Officer Norton will check the rocks for any sort of evidence, but who knows what that will turn up? Seems like a long shot."

I looked at Sam as he surveyed the chickens without holding his nose. He was looking at the same things I was looking at, but I knew he saw much more than I did. I didn't think it would ever occur to me to consider that the chickens had been put someplace they didn't belong.

"Okay, Sam, what's up? You took me for a high-speed ride in your car. You're letting me walk around a potential crime scene. What's going on? Why are you letting me do this stuff?"

"First, this really isn't a potential crime scene—unless we consider it a potential crime against the chickens— but there isn't anything on the books that I can reference." He smiled. "And they weren't harmed. We're looking for Jeanine. If there'd been signs of a struggle in the house, I wouldn't have let you go in. Second, maybe we were going faster than your truck can go, but I've made police cars go a lot faster, so really we didn't get here at high speed. And finally, like I've told you before, Becca, you have good instincts." He looked purposefully away from me and observed Officer Norton high-stepping her way back through the chicken yard. She held a black container high and mumbled mean words to the noisy birds that clucked and pecked around her. "Besides, you'd have come out here later today on your own. Am I right?"

"Yeth." I said, still holding my nose.

"Saved you the trouble. Come on, Officer Norton's got this handled. I'll get you back to Bailey's. I don't think Jeanine's come to any harm, but I'd sure like to know where she is."

I looked around one more time as I followed Sam back through the kitchen and the living room, then out the front door. As I stood in front of the small house, I focused on my gut, my instincts. But nothing happened. I had nothing I could share with Sam.

Suddenly, a sound came from down the dirt road in front of the house. Sam and I hurried to the edge of the lawn, Sam motioning me to stay behind him. We both hoped the sound was attached to Jeanine's van and that she was returning to her house.

But it wasn't Jeanine. Instead, for the second time that day, I saw Drew's Honda making its way toward me, stirring up a dust cloud and griming the hood.

"Sam, that's Drew's car."

The Honda pulled to a slow stop and Sam approached it. Once the dust cleared, the driver's window was rolled down.

"Officer Brion?" Alan said. "Becca?"

"Yes, Mr. Cummings. Can I help you with something?" Sam asked.

"Uh . . ." Clearly, Alan was unsure what to say next. There was nothing wrong with driving down a dirt road and minding your own business, but it was strange that he'd picked this particular dirt road. "Well, I came out to talk to Jeanine Baker."

"Really? About what?" Sam asked as I crossed my

arms in front of myself. This was too weird for my comfort.

"I wanted to talk to her about buying her land."

I couldn't restrain myself. "That doesn't seem likely."

Sam's look told me I'd probably just ruined his desire to take me anywhere again.

"Mr. Cummings, did you have an appointment to talk to Jeanine?" Sam asked.

"No, I was just stopping by," he said, sounding too innocent.

"When's the last time you saw her?"

"Uh, well, actually, we haven't met in person."

"Do you know where else she might be?"

"Doesn't she work with you at Bailey's, Becca?"

I nodded. Finally, my instincts were kicking in, and they were telling me how much I didn't like this guy. Jeanine would never sell this land. It had been in her family forever.

"Yes, she does work there, but she's not here. We're not exactly sure where she is, but if you hear from her, would you give me a call?" Sam said.

I didn't tell him that she hadn't shown up at Bailey's today.

"Sure. I hope she's all right."

"We do, too."

"Okay, well, I suppose I'll be on my way, then."

Alan did a U-turn and left in another cloud of dust.

"Sam, that was strange."

"Maybe."

"Maybe? He stopped at my house today, and now at Jeanine's. Both places he inquired about land for sale.

Mine isn't, and I know Jeanine would never in a million years sell hers."

"Maybe."

"Maybe?"

"Becca, we need evidence. Honestly, though it is a coincidence, I didn't see anything wrong with what you said that Alan said to you. And if Jeanine was planning on selling her land—which you don't know for sure she wasn't—there's nothing strange about him driving by and talking to her about it. Coincidences."

But I just *knew* something wasn't right. "Originally, you were looking for Jeanine to find out why she was on Madeline's call list, right?"

"Yes."

"Why would Madeline Forsyth call Jeanine Baker? They weren't friends. I can't think of two more different people. There must have been some banking issue."

"Maybe," Sam said as he looked down the road. Alan had disappeared.

An idea occurred to me. "Sam, we've got to go through the papers on her desk. *Maybe* she has something there that could tell us more."

He hesitated, but only briefly. "Let's go."

Upon closer look, it was obvious that the multiple stacks on Jeanine's desk were organized. There was one stack for bills, one for invoices for her customers, one for junk that she probably wasn't ready to throw away yet, and then, of course, the coin wrappers.

There were the normal utility bills and two credit card bills, both of which revealed that Jeanine kept low-to-nothing balances. There didn't seem to be any statements for liens or mortgages on her land or house. The invoices didn't shed much light either. Jeanine had a number of customers, mostly small grocery stores that she delivered fresh eggs to on a regular basis. This, along with her Bailey's business, probably made for a good living. We had to open the drawers to find the bank statements, which were organized and filed by month.

I would never want someone to know how much money I had in my accounts, so I felt guilty for even peering at one of the statements, but it seemed important, especially since the envelopes they were stored in had Madeline's bank, Central Savings and Loan's, logo on them.

"It's such a small town that they probably knew each other, though not very well," I said as I unfolded a statement.

"Well, judging by Jeanine's balance, I'm sure that Madeline at least knew who she was," Sam added.

The statement showed that Jeanine had lots of money in her checking account. So much that I wondered if maybe she'd just decided to drive off, retire, and leave the chickens to fend for themselves. Her most recent statement showed a balance in the mid-six figures.

"I'll have to check with the bank to see if she's withdrawn any money," Sam said, echoing my thoughts.

"There's lots of money in eggs," I declared as I looked closer, my guilt replaced by surprise and curiosity. Chickens might stink, but Jeanine had made a comfortable living from the creatures.

"According to what we've found, she doesn't have many expenses, and you said her land has been in her family for some time. This is probably her life's accumulation."

"Not a bad showing."

We searched the rest of the drawers but found nothing that told us anything important about Jeanine.

"But why was Madeline trying to call her?" I asked as we replaced everything we'd removed and then closed the drawers.

"We'll have to hope we find Jeanine or she comes home so we can ask. Come on, let's get you back to Bailey's."

I knew one person who might help. Allison might know more about Jeanine's financial situation, but getting her to share would be next to impossible.

As I thought about the best way to approach my sister, something sauntered down the hallway toward us, greeting us with a high-pitched howl and a hiss that made the hair on the back of my neck stand on end.

Twelve

"Hello, there," Sam said to the unfriendly cat. "Are we invad-ing your space?"

His soothing voice calmed the black cat to something slightly more sociable. The fur on its back relaxed, and its green eyes went from suspiciously slanted to wide and blinking. It meowed again, but more with curiosity than with anger.

"I think we've been found," he said. He smiled at me and then back at the cat.

"You like cats?" I asked.

"I like animals. Come on, I don't think we're going to learn much more from the papers. I'll talk to someone at the bank."

I listened to what he said but I watched the cat, who looked back and forth at the two of us. It was up to something.

"Sam, I think it's trying to tell us something." I crouched. "What's up? Are you trying to tell us something about Jeanine?"

"Uh, Becca, I'm not sure we speak the same language," Sam said.

I looked up at him. "Well, not technically, but Hobbit and I communicate very well. Maybe . . ."

I didn't get a chance to finish my thought before the cat darted into the kitchen.

"I guess that's the end of the communication," Sam said.

I stood. "Sam, is the back door closed and locked?"

"No, the screen door is closed but not locked. It was like that when we got here."

"Do you think the cat can get out? And isn't it a bad idea for a cat to mix with all those chickens?"

I'm sure he and I shared the same vision of flying feathers and splattering chicken blood. As far as I knew, cats and birds didn't get along. I suspected the cat took us for the fools we were, and used our presence to escape to some easy hunting.

"Damn," Sam said before he ran into the kitchen. Sure enough, the screen door was open just enough for the beast to escape.

I followed Sam into the smelly chicken yard. The cat was in the middle of the noisy chickens. It was licking a paw.

"Hey, come here," Sam said in an official tone.

I couldn't help but laugh. "I don't think cats follow police commands."

He rolled his eyes. "Here, kitty, kitty."

It was either the tone of his voice or his words that

made the cat stand on all fours again and paste an evil look on its face.

"Uh-oh. That doesn't look good," I said. "Sam, I think we'd better get it before it . . ."

"How do you suggest we do that?"

"I don't know. Come on, cat . . . kitty, come here," I pleaded. I've always been a dog person, though I have nothing against cats. Until today. When I was little, we always had cats, but they were outside animals, meant to keep down the rodent population on our farm. My current barn was modernized enough that a rodent never so much as darkened its door. Plus, when I needed such help, Hobbit was a pretty good mouser in her own right. I might have wrangled a cat or two in my day, but not when there was so much temptation all around. The cat was bound to choose chasing a chicken over listening to our pleadings.

"What's going on?" Officer Norton appeared from behind the coop. She carried the black container I'd seen her with earlier.

"We're trying to get the cat back into the house," Sam said.

"Do you want me to shoot at it? Scare it back in?" she asked as she put down the container and placed her hand on her gun.

"No!" Sam and I exclaimed together.

"Hey," I said, watching Officer Norton reluctantly move her hand away from her gun, "let's move in together. It will run some way, and the one who's closest can grab it." I wanted to leave the cat and the chickens to figure it out for themselves, but if Jeanine came back to a bunch of dead fowl, I'd feel horrible for having contributed to the bloodbath.

The three of us looked at the paths we'd have to take to close in on the cat. There were no choices other than walking through at least some chicken poop.

Sam muttered something under his breath that I couldn't make out.

"Let's step together," I said. "Ready?"

We stepped toward the cat, who looked around at the three of us as if it knew the jig was about up.

There was nothing pleasant about walking through the chickens and their yard. It was mushy, and we disturbed the chickens enough that I thought a couple pecked at my ankles, but I was so focused on the cat that I couldn't be sure.

The cat looked at me, at Sam, and then at Officer Norton. We were getting closer, and it sat back on its haunches as if preparing to take off.

"Get ready," Sam said, and he bent over a bit more.

Suddenly, the cat took flight and ran toward Officer Norton. Fur flew from her fingers as the cat made it past her and ran straight into the coop.

"Damn," she muttered.

"Sam, the cat's in the coop!" I yelled, sounding like a panicked line from a Dr. Seuss book.

He looked at me and grumbled something before turning to Officer Norton. "Vivienne, you go to that end of the coop, I'll go to the other. We'll scare it enough that it'll have to leave from one end. If it's yours, catch it this time. That's an order."

"Yes, sir."

I followed Sam, walking on my toes to avoid both chickens and chicken poop. He stopped at the entrance—or was it the exit?—of the coop and crouched down.

"Vivienne, do you see anything?" he asked through the opening.

As I glanced over his shoulder, I saw Officer Norton peering in the other end.

"No."

"You in there, cat?" Sam asked. I thought he might be over liking animals.

The cat meowed from somewhere in the darkness of the coop.

"Come on out, then," he said, exaggerating a patience he surely didn't feel.

I didn't want to laugh, but my cheeks suddenly stretched tight and I could feel a giggle begin in my throat. Sam's back was to me, so if I could keep it quiet he'd never know. Unfortunately, a *huff*-like noise escaped my mouth.

Sam turned and peered over his shoulder. "You think this is funny?" He wasn't amused.

"I'm sorry. Nerves," I lied. Truthfully, I thought the whole ordeal was hilarious, but I knew I had to get a grip. I cleared my throat.

Sam turned his attention back to the coop. "Come out right now, dammit."

I had to bite the insides of my cheeks.

Suddenly, I saw two glimmers of light.

"Sam, I think I see its eyes."

"Yes, I think you do. Come on, kitty, come on. That's it."

The cat was creeping toward Sam, but it was creeping in a way that made me think it might pounce. I didn't think Sam needed help, so I didn't voice my opinion.

Besides, I was wrong; it wasn't preparing to pounce, it was preparing to run again, really fast.

Suddenly, the cat took off in a sprint right at Sam. He held out his hands like he was going to catch a football. The cat's speed was alarming, however, so instead of making the reception, Sam's fingers grazed the speedy creature as it ran right through his open hands and directly into my arms.

I held tightly to the animal as I tried not to topple from the laughter that had taken over and couldn't have been controlled even if I wanted to.

Sam was flat on his back, covered in chicken poop. It was even in his perfectly groomed hair. To make matters worse, Officer Norton and her guns had come around the coop to join us. She didn't want to laugh, I could tell, but in a few moments all three of us fell into fits of uncontrollable hilarity.

As we let the moment happen, the cat purred contentedly in my arms.

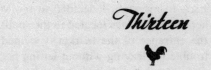

Thirteen

Once we regained our composure, we got Sam out of the chicken yard and the cat back in the house, and locked the back door before we left Jeanine's. We didn't know where she'd gone, but at least we'd found her chickens and her cat.

I hoped she hadn't met with harm or run away because she'd killed Madeline Forsyth, but I couldn't make either of those concerns fit with what I knew about her. She wasn't a killer. But still, where was she? Sam would continue to search, and before he dropped me at Bailey's, he promised he'd let me know if he found her.

As I stood outside of Bailey's and watched him drive away, I thought again about Alan showing up at Jeanine's. No matter what Sam said, Alan's surprise appearances bothered me. I wanted to know more about him. I pulled out my cell phone, called the Fuller Bank in Columbia and asked for Sally McNeil. They told me she wasn't in, but they'd be happy to give her a message. I left my name and number, hoping I'd hear from her quickly; something told me the best and safest person to ask about Drew's family was Sally.

Before I went back to my stall, I decided to try to catch my sister in her office that was located in the small brick building at the entrance of the market. I wanted to see if I was in trouble for leaving without letting her know, and I had a favor to ask her. Surprisingly, she was there and I wasn't in trouble, but my luck ran out when I asked for the favor.

"Becca, I can't do that," Allison said firmly. "Plus, it would be wrong for Sarah to give such information."

"One call, one question, that's all I'm asking," I said as I made another try.

She was sitting behind her desk, and I sat in a chair across from her. As my sister, she'd do almost anything for me, but as the manager of Bailey's, she was a stickler for not breaking laws or invading others' privacy. It was, at times, very annoying.

I'd asked her to call a friend and find out what that friend knew about Jeanine and her potential issue or issues with the bank. We'd gone to high school with Sarah Nelson, who worked at Central Savings and Loan. Last I'd heard, she was a vice president of something there. She and I hadn't been close, but Allison, senior class president, had gotten along with everyone in our class. I knew that if she just called Sarah and worked her charms, Sarah might tell her everything we wanted to know about Madeline and Jeanine's relationship.

"Al, I'm worried about Jeanine. I don't think she killed Madeline Forsyth, but I think we all need to know where she is—or why Madeline called her. Maybe Sarah could shed some light."

Allison took a deep breath and studied me intensely. "Close the door, Becca."

I froze for a moment. Was she giving in that easily? I'd thought I'd have to try at least a few more times.

"Becca, the door, please," Allison said.

I did as she asked and sat down again, this time on the edge of my seat.

"I'm not going to call the bank for you."

I deflated and sat back in the chair. "Why did you want me to close the door?"

"I'm going to tell you something I shouldn't."

I wanted to cheer, but I just nodded. I couldn't remember one other time in our lives that she had uttered those words. She never told anyone, including me, something she shouldn't be telling them.

"Listen, this goes against everything I believe in. I don't break confidences—that's why I haven't told Sam, and believe me, if I should be telling anyone, it should be the police. Jeanine told me what she told me only because I promised to keep it to myself."

"I understand. I won't tell Sam either," I said, but I wasn't sure that's the response she was looking for. "I won't tell anyone, Allison."

"Yesterday, right after Madeline blew through here, Jeanine came and talked to me." Allison's brown eyes locked on my blue ones. "She was angry. Angry at Madeline, and she wondered if there was any way I could prevent Madeline from ever coming into Bailey's again. Keep in mind, *this was right after Madeline blew through here.*"

"Okay, Jeanine didn't want Madeline here because she made a scene, and that made Jeanine uncomfortable?" We all knew how paranoid Jeanine was; her asking Allison to ban Madeline from Bailey's seemed like a normal Jeanine reaction.

"No." Allison paused and swallowed. We must have been getting to the part she was supposed to keep to herself. "Because of the correspondence Jeanine had just received from Madeline: a foreclosure notice from Central Savings and Loan."

"What? Really? But, that doesn't seem . . . Al, I saw her account balances. She has enough money to buy at least two more small farms."

"I know . . . well, I don't know how much money she has. You saw her bank statements?"

"Yes, when I went with Sam. It seemed prudent at the time, but go on."

"I know she doesn't owe money on her farm. According to what she said, she has never had any sort of mortgage. She just pays yearly property taxes."

"Then why the foreclosure notice? Some misunderstanding?"

"Jeanine didn't know, but she told me she'd left at least ten messages for Madeline. Actually, I offered to call Sarah Nelson for her—maybe someone other than Madeline could help. She refused, said she wanted to talk to Madeline and no one else, and she was going to do it that day, no matter what."

"Oh? Oh. But according to what I saw, it looked like

Madeline did try to call her back. Maybe they resolved whatever the issue was. Or maybe not."

"Maybe not is right. It doesn't look good does it? I know I should tell Sam, but I keep thinking Jeanine will call or show up, and we can get it cleared up. She was so adamant that she didn't want me to say a word to anyone about it. I shouldn't be telling you."

The police would want this information, but I still didn't think Jeanine was a killer. There must have been some mistake regarding the foreclosure notice. Jeanine was a rich woman, or at least extra-comfortable. I doubted that she would have killed over anything, let alone a paperwork mistake. There had to be something else. Someone else.

I said, "Don't tell Sam, not yet. He'd like to talk to Jeanine, but that's based on Madeline's phone list. If Jeanine had been home when Officer Norton stopped by, all of this would probably be cleared up. Now, Sam's more curious than anything. Let's not make Jeanine look guiltier than she already does. Sam's got other things he can look at. Plus, he's going to talk to the bank. Maybe he'll figure it out from that end."

"I'll think about it," Allison said, "but no promises." This was eating at her. Most of the time Allison saw the world and its issues in black-and-white; there were no gray areas. She knew the right thing to do, knew the correct answer, knew the appropriate response. This was the first time I'd seen her unsure what to do next.

A knock suddenly boomed on her office door, launching me off the chair.

Allison smiled. "You feel guilty, too. See, it isn't good to keep secrets, is it?"

Allison had to assist with some sort of crate delivery problem, solidifying my belief that while she might be better at almost everything than I was, it was vastly more fun to sell jams and preserves than deal with delivery issues.

Despite what she had said, I thought it was just fine to keep a secret or two. It was necessary sometimes. I wouldn't tell Sam—or anyone—what Allison had told me, but not because I wanted to investigate it on my own. I wouldn't risk the chance of Allison not wanting to ever share with me again.

As I thought about Jeanine, I threaded my way through the smallish crowd left at Bailey's and toward my stall. Usually, late afternoons were quiet, and the best time to visit with other vendors, or relax and wait for the few customers left to finish their shopping. I waved at Herb and Don as I passed their stall.

"Becca, you're here?" Herb asked as he lifted a small rack display from his table.

"I'm here. Were you looking for me?"

"Only to tell you that someone else was looking for you," Herb continued.

"Who?"

Herb bit at his bottom lip. "Darn it. Don, what did that guy say his name was—the one who was looking for Becca?"

Don duplicated Herb's lip biting. "Give me a minute."

"He was blond, good looking, nice enough guy," Herb said as he thought.

"Was his name Alan?" I asked, taking a pretty sure guess.

"That's it! And, he didn't really want to talk to you as

much as he wondered if you'd ever talked about selling your property. I told him I didn't think so. Do you? Are you selling?"

"Never, not in a million years." I bit back the other choice words I had for Alan. I thought about what Sam had said. Alan hadn't done anything wrong, that was true, but he was certainly irritating. "When did he come by?"

"Gosh, late morning, I think," Herb said. He looked at Don, who nodded confirmation.

That was right after I left with Sam.

"Did he say anything else?" I asked.

"Well, he asked if we'd seen Jeanine, which we hadn't. He also asked about other properties up for sale. I couldn't help him at all."

"Did he, by chance, leave any contact information?"

"No."

"Thanks for letting me know."

"Sure. And Allison stopped by to tell me about the ambush wedding. I'll be prepared if you need me. How are Linda and Drew?" Herb asked.

"Ambush, huh? Well, we're shooting for a pleasant surprise. I think Linda and Drew are hanging in there, but I haven't talked to them today."

"Give them our condolences, and let me know if you need any help with anything."

I continued down the long aisle, visiting with other vendors or helping some of them load their trucks and vans. Speaking of pleasant surprises, I had one when I saw that my stall had been completely cleared, all my items packed in the back of my truck.

It had been a long two days, and I wanted to get home to Hobbit and write down some notes about what had happened. I pulled out my cell phone to call Ian and see if he wanted to come over for dinner, but the phone rang before I could push Ian's speed dial button.

The number had a South Carolina area code, but it was unfamiliar.

"Becca Robins," I answered.

"Becca, this is Sally McNeil," the voice drawled.

"Sally, hi. Thanks for calling me back."

"Certainly. What can I do for you?" She sniffed. Was she crying?

"Sally, do you have a few minutes? I'd love to ask . . . well, I'd love to talk to you some more." I hadn't prepared a good reason or good lie. Hopefully she wouldn't push the matter.

"Right now?"

"Sure, unless you're busy."

"No, darlin', I'm not busy, and I'd love to talk to you, but not over the phone. Can you meet me tomorrow morning?"

"In Columbia?"

"Oh, no, darlin', I'm still in Monson. I want to wait until the police figure out Auntie's . . . murder before I go home. I'm stayin' at the Monson Inn, and I have an appointment for a pedicure tomorrow mornin' at the salon next door—Hard as Nails, I think it's called. How 'bout you meet me there at nine o'clock and I'll call them and get you an appointment? I find there's nothin' better'n a little socializin' while I get my toes done. What do you say?"

I had never had a pedicure before, and I thought about what I'd have to do to the calluses on the bottoms of my feet to prepare them to be seen by a professional. I didn't want to have a pedicure, but Sally had a point; she would probably be relaxed and willing to gossip, and that was ideal.

"Uh, sure, that sounds like fun."

"All right, then. See you tomorrow."

"Looking forward to it."

I hung up and thought about where I could pick up a pumice stone on my way home.

Fourteen

🐓

"What did you tell her?" Ian asked. *He and I sat were sitting* on George's couch. George faced us from his old leather high-backed chair, and Hobbit was curled up at his feet. I was decidedly Hobbit's favorite human, but when Ian was around, she felt the need to split her time between the two of us. And when George was present, she gave him her full attention, especially when we were in George's house.

The room was the kind where you half expected the smell of pipe smoke to be combined with the scent of worn leather. In the winter, when George lit the wood in the fireplace, it was heavenly.

We were invited to dinner at George's, so instead of going home to Hobbit and staying there, I picked her up and we made our way back to town.

"I agreed to go," I said. "I could use a pedicure, I suppose."

I'd unloaded my leftover inventory from my truck but hadn't taken the time to find a pumice stone. My feet would have to be fine the way they were, though I wondered how many thirty-five-year-old nail salon customers hadn't had a pedicure before. Maybe I'd win a prize or something.

As dinner cooked, we "lounged" in the best part of George's old French Tudor house. Full and inviting bookshelves surrounded us. There was a painting above the fireplace of George in his younger days, when he had dark hair and a tall, trim body. He was still trim, but the years had taken some of his height and turned his hair steely gray. Even with thick glasses he couldn't see well, and though he could still work his way around a kitchen, many times Ian would read to him from one of the thousands of murder mysteries on the shelves. Hobbit and I had become an eager part of the story time audience.

"So," George interjected, "tell me about this young man, Drew Forsyth, and his relationship with his mother." George, though saddened that someone had died, had been excited to talk about a real-life murder mystery; thus the dinner invitation. Once Ian told him we'd been part of the group to discover the body, George insisted on hearing the details.

"Oh, well"—I sat up straighter—"Drew's an amazing guy, really. He's kind, he's handsome, and he loves Linda very much. He's *in the military,* which both impresses me and makes me watch my manners when I'm around him. I'm not sure about his relationship with his mother, but I'm determined to understand it better. Linda said that Madeline had a soft spot, and I never heard Drew say one thing bad about his mom. Linda was often frustrated by something Madeline had done, but to be honest with you, I can't think of one specific thing Linda told me. I wish I'd asked her more questions when she was frustrated, but I just tried to be supportive and not add to Madeline's terrible reputation."

"Do you think Drew could have killed his mother? To clear the path for his new wife, maybe?" George asked.

I hesitated. I still hadn't told anyone what I'd overheard in the men's bathroom at the police station. After Linda told me that she and Drew had been together all afternoon, I thought I would talk to Drew myself. I felt I owed him that, at least. I didn't want Drew Forsyth to be a killer, but I had to acknowledge that his profession might give him a trained advantage in that area. The longer I kept the secret to myself, the more I wondered about his involvement. "The thought crossed my mind, but I don't have much to go on. I can't begin to tell you how much I hope he isn't. Beyond the fact that he's Linda's fiancé, he's supposedly reporting for active duty next week. This has to get solved quickly."

"He's still going?" It was George's turn to sit up straighter.

"Yes," I replied.

"Hmm. That seems . . . somehow wrong, doesn't it?"

I gulped a swig of the heavily creamed tea that George had handed me when I came in the back door. "Maybe, but I'm not sure how it works. I get the impression that he can't delay his departure." Still careful about what I said about Drew's profession, I continued. "George, I'm pretty sure he's part of some special operations group. When he's called to duty, I think . . . well, I think important things are involved." I could only imagine.

"Oh, I know a little about the military world," George said. "I understand if Drew doesn't want to request a hardship discharge to leave the military permanently, but there are such things as emergency leaves. I'm sure his commander would understand. In fact, I would be surprised if Drew wasn't ordered to take some extra time. I don't understand why he wouldn't want to, Becca. I think that needs further exploration."

"I agree. I know Sam is looking at it more closely, but I think I can ask Drew myself. As well as I *don't* know him, I understand something about him that's difficult to explain. If, as I hope, he isn't the killer, he's got an amazing sense of loyalty. He would never want to fall short of doing his duty. Does that make sense?"

"Yes, but I still hope the police are looking closer. And I hope he isn't the killer, too." George tapped a fingertip at his chin. "But someone is, so tell me more about his family, the cousins you and Ian met." George sat back and crossed his legs.

"Okay. Well, Shawn, Mid, Sally, and Alan. I wish I knew more about them than I do. Hopefully, Sally will tell me more during the pedicure. My first impression was that . . . well, that Sally is an emotional wreck, Alan is annoying, and Shawn and Mid had perhaps had a discussion or an argument earlier in the day. They were silently communicating things to each other and to Alan. Did you see that, Ian?"

"Yes, but I don't know that I'd put much into it. They're

a family, and families create their communication patterns. Maybe that's the way they normally behave."

"What about Alan? Did he bug you as much as he bugged me?"

"I don't think so."

"Tell me why he bugged you, Becca. Give me the details," George said.

"It was more than the dinner. I ran into him today, too." I hadn't yet told Ian about my day, so I replayed the events for them both. Even though the pie delivery was legitimate, I made sure to emphasize how Alan's appearances seemed wrong somehow, as though he was trying to be sneaky but wasn't good at it, but I wasn't sure they agreed. However, they both enjoyed the adventure with the cat at Jeanine's house.

"Well, coincidentally, I'm making my famous quiche Jeanine for dinner tonight. Does Sam think she had something to do with Madeline's murder?" George asked when he stopped laughing about the cat's escape from the chicken coop. Once George had been introduced to Jeanine's fresh eggs, he refused to purchase eggs anywhere else. He had also become a quiche expert, his quiche Jeanine (quiche Lorraine) becoming everyone's favorite.

"He doesn't know what to think at this point. Her behavior is odd, more odd than normal even for Jeanine. I know he'd like to talk to her, and I think he's concerned about her. I know I am." Keeping my earlier promise, I didn't tell them what Allison had shared with me about the foreclosure letter.

"Plus, and I hate to be too graphic . . ." Ian said.

"Oh, please do," George requested seriously.

"Well, Jeanine might be strong but she's little. I have no idea how she could have handled Madeline and done what was done to her."

"Gracious, you didn't tell me what was done to her. Don't leave anything out."

Between the two of us, we told George about the state in which we'd found Madeline. The scarf around her neck, the wounds on her hands, the blood, the position her body was in, and the gruesome details of her gray skin and bulging eyes. It didn't make for good predinner conversation, but George insisted, and we indulged him.

"I knew Madeline. A little," George said when we finished. "I bank at Central, as so many of us do. There aren't many choices in Monson, and Central has always been the biggest bank around. Plus, years ago, when they got into the mortgages, it was so nice to do business locally. When everyone seemed to have money, and mortgages were both easy to get and easy to give, Madeline was sort of a local superstar. But over the last few years I know she's done some pretty vicious things. She was a businesswoman first and foremost—oh, I'm not trying to defend her, but I do think her reputation was partly because of the times we're in. I don't know if Jeanine had any sort of money difficulties"—I kept my expression neutral—"but when their livelihood is threatened, some people have been known to do desperate things . . ."

"Go on," I prompted him to continue.

George tapped at his chin again, and his eyes grew

bigger behind his glasses. "Madeline was killed in her home, in her bedroom, in the middle of the day. Becca, dear, that doesn't sound like the actions of a mere customer, someone Madeline knew impersonally and had angered. In fact, the place she was killed and the way she was killed sound very *personal*, indeed."

"So, you think it was someone she knew well, a family member?"

"If I were an investigator, which clearly I'm not, that's where I'd be looking most closely. I don't think a customer would have sought her out at her home. I think a customer would have done the crime at or around the bank."

I thought George made some good points. I hoped even more that Sally would shed some light on her family's dynamics.

"Another question, Becca, dear," George said as he folded his hands on his lap.

"Yes?"

"What about Linda?"

"What about her?"

"You know what I'm asking. Do you think Linda could have killed Madeline? Lord knows she had plenty of good reasons. From what you've said, Linda's future mother-in-law was not making the relationship easy."

"No, I don't think Linda killed Madeline. I don't think Linda killed anyone." I didn't mean to sound so emphatic. Ian put his hand on my knee. "Sorry, George, but Linda doesn't have that in her."

"I understand your loyalty, but Ian told me that Linda left Bailey's shortly after Madeline caused the scene. Do you know where she went?"

I hesitated and looked at Ian, who kept his face expressionless.

"Linda said that she and Drew were together all afternoon."

George was silent for a long, thoughtful moment before he said, "I don't suppose someone else can vouch for them?"

"Not that I know of." I didn't want to share details about Linda's bright blushing with George.

"*Hmm.* Well, the good news is that Sam Brion is a topnotch police officer. Perhaps he and his cohort will move quickly and solve the crime so you can fulfill your duty as . . . what did Ian tell me you were calling yourself? As a Number One or something."

I smiled. George had changed the tone of the conversation and purposely avoided emphatically pointing out Linda and Drew's weak alibis because he was a gentleman first and foremost. He didn't want to risk hurting my feelings or Ian's feelings by showing how clear it was that Linda and Drew should probably both be considered prime suspects in the murder of Madeline Forsyth. I appreciated his effort.

"Well, I do believe it's time for dinner and some lively discussion about you two and your trip to Iowa." George stood and, with Hobbit by his side, made his way to the kitchen. Even though it was probably rude, Ian and I had frozen in place on the couch. Fortunately, Ian figured out what to say next.

"I, uh, mentioned that I was inviting you to visit my family. I might have mentioned that you hadn't agreed to go quite yet. Sorry about that awkward moment."

"It wasn't so bad—more surprising than awkward."

"Come on, let's have dinner and save the inevitable and uncomfortable conversation about why you still can't decide to come meet my family for later, much later." Ian stood and held out his hand. I looked at the sun tattoo that was perfectly centered on the back of his hand.

I felt awful. At that moment, I wanted to tell him I'd go with him—go with him anywhere. I adored him and couldn't believe I was risking the possibility of losing him, but I just couldn't say yes yet. Borrowing a line from my parents, I needed it to "be real, be totally real" before I said yes.

"Ian . . ." I said as I took his hand.

"Nope, not now. Later."

Though George's eyesight was almost gone, his hearing was more acute than mine. He spoke from the kitchen. "Nonsense. Becca, life is short; enjoy it completely while you can. And love is rare."

Ian smiled but shook his head and mouthed, "Later."

We ate dinner, laughed at George's stories about his adventures when courting his wife, who was engaged to another man when they met. George was bound and determined to marry her, no matter that he would have to break into her father's house, steal her fiancé's car, and beg her sister to lie to the entire family just so he could spend some time alone with the woman of his dreams and convince her that he was the man for her. His escapades landed him in jail for two days, but when he was released, Marylou was waiting for him. They eloped and enjoyed fifty-six years of marital bliss, and eventually Marylou's family welcomed them both back into the fold. The jilted fiancé held a grudge all his life.

The evening ended with what George called one of his "nuggets."

"True love is hard to find, Becca. Don't be one of those fools who can't see it right in front of their eyes. Hang on tight to the good stuff."

Fifteen

"How's the temperature?" the young girl asked. She was seated on a very small stool facing me. She reminded me of Pippi Longstocking, with two bright red braids, though they didn't stick straight out from her head.

I dipped my feet into the swirling warm water and said, "Great. Perfect, actually."

There was a method to entering a salon and moving toward the pedicure chairs/feet tubs. I was able to take my shoes off discreetly, sit and turn in the chair, and then submerge my feet without feeling like they were on display. No one gawked, not even Sally. No one pointed or rolled their eyes. I watched my pedicurist's face for some sign of distaste, and when I didn't see anything unusual, I realized I was being too paranoid about the whole thing. I decided to relax and enjoy the fabulous sensation of the warm water pulsing and swirling around my feet.

"Would you like a cocktail, Becca?" Sally asked from the chair next to me. Her pedicurist, dark and exotic, was named Orchid.

"No, thanks," I replied. It was not too long after nine in the morning, and I didn't want to insult her by pointing that out.

"Fine. Yes, Orchid, I'd like a Bloody Mary, please."

A cloak of sadness hung over Sally. She wasn't attempting to hide her feelings or make anyone think she was ready to be over her aunt's death. Her face was puffy and her eyes were red. Though those things could have been because she'd been drinking, I suspected there hadn't been many moments since Madeline's death when she hadn't been crying.

Of course, I felt terrible for her loss, but the way she wore her emotions so boldly also made me uncomfortable, and I remained aware that even though she was emotional, she still might have had something to do with Madeline's death. I couldn't buy into her tears without remaining on my almost pretty toes.

Pippi—actually, her name was Hallie—tapped on one of my ankles. I looked at her, wide-eyed. A wave of recognition passed over her face. She realized I'd never done this before. Suddenly, she became the master and I became the student; she liked it that way and so did I. She held my ankle and lifted my right foot onto a ledge above the bath. I decided to trust her.

"How are you doing, Sally?" I asked.

"Oh, I guess I have good moments and bad moments," she said, her drawl even thicker than before. "Who'm I kiddin'? All my moments are pretty bad right now."

"I'm so sorry. You must have been close to Madeline."

Hallie was working the outer regions of my nails, clipping at them with miniature garden shears. So far, so good on the pain level, but I noted that she was awfully close to potentially drawing blood. I tried not to tense up.

"Darlin', I was closer than close," Sally said as she took the Bloody Mary from Orchid. "Aunt Madeline took care of me, Mid, and Shawn when there was no one else to take care of us. Our mamma was a piece of work, if you'll pardon the expression—she was an S.L.U.T. Instead of caring for her kids, she spent her time carousing and chasing men. Aunt Madeline had no patience for her. We spent more time with Auntie than with our own mamma."

"I'm so sorry to hear that about your mom. It was good that you had Madeline."

"Probably saved our lives, or gave us lives. Who knows how we'd have turned out if Auntie hadn't intervened to raise us with some sort of respectability?"

"She's the reason you went into banking, right?"

Sally swallowed a sip of her drink and then snorted. "She's the reason I did everything. And I should probably tell you now, I'm not quite at the level Madeline is . . . was. I'm just a teller, Becca."

"I couldn't be a teller, Sally. I don't think there's any 'just' about it." It was the truth. I knew my limitations, and working indoors was one thing I hoped I'd never have to do. Plus, numbers weren't my strong suit.

"Thank you, dear." Sally smiled crookedly at me and then put her head against the chair. She closed her eyes and took a deep breath.

I didn't want her to fall asleep quite yet, so I said, "What about Shawn and Mid?"

"What about them?" She rolled her neck and looked at me again.

Hallie was beginning to file my nails, which hurt more than the garden shears had. It felt like the edge of the file was slicing into the skin under the nail. I tried not to wince.

"Did they feel as much love for your aunt as you did?"

Sally seemed to think about it a minute before answering. "Weeell, yes, but she had to work for their love. Theirs wasn't as automatic and grateful as mine was."

My eyebrows rose. I couldn't imagine Madeline working for anyone's love. From what I knew, she didn't seem to care what anyone thought of her, just as long as she got to make the decisions.

"What do you mean?"

"They were more affected by our mother than I was. I don't know, maybe it was a girl/boy thing. I could see what a loser she was, and they just wanted to defend her. I think they resented Auntie's intervening in our lives. Over the years, Shawn and Mid were challenges to her, but she always figured out some way to get them in line— get them to behave or get them to listen to her."

"What methods did she use?"

Sally looked at the ceiling. "I wouldn't say that Madeline was ever one to give the soft sell to anything. At times she was harsh with them to the point it became clear that without her, we might not have a roof over our heads or food on our table. I'm the oldest, but they're only one and two years younger than me. Shawn's the baby. I remember when we were teenagers and one time when they were being particularly mouthy, Auntie took their plates of food away and kicked them out of her house, telling them they had to figure out how to make it home on their own—in the middle of a horrible rainstorm."

"Hmm," I said. I didn't want to pass judgment.

"Yes, it was mean, but she made her point. They hitchhiked home and found our mother with yet another man in her bedroom. It was very ugly." Sally shook her head. "Goodness, that was so long ago, and I don't like talking about it. Besides, it all turned out okay. Auntie eventually gave them the family business, after all."

"The dairy?" I didn't know that Madeline had had anything to do with the Loder diary.

"Yes, she gave them the Loder Dairy about ten years ago."

"How did the rest of the family feel about that?"

"Good question. It was interesting. I think there was some resentment—did Shawn and Mid deserve such a gift? Eventually, I think we all came to the conclusion that she did it to make up for how horribly they'd been treated by our mother. I wouldn't have wanted to run the dairy, so I was okay with it."

"How did Alan feel about it?"

"If I remember correctly, he thought Madeline's desire was to be worshipped, and Shawn and Mid didn't worship her correctly. He thought it was her way of manipulating their feelings."

"Ouch," I said, and I wasn't talking about Hallie's abuses.

"Believe it or not, Alan might have been right, though that's not something I want to admit. I love my brothers, and I loved Madeline more than anyone, but we were all set up to have some less-than-desirable family dynamics."

"Madeline wanted to be worshipped?" My toes curled involuntarily. Hallie straightened them with great skill.

Sally huffed again. "Probably, but it was something you rolled with, you know? Madeline was Madeline. If you loved her, you also worshipped her. You never corrected her, you never pointed out her faults, and you always put yourself in second place."

"Your brothers didn't want to worship her?"

"No. They not only didn't want to, they didn't know how. They didn't know how to go with the flow. Instead, they'd get their hackles up and be bothered and snotty. I tried to tell them how stupid they were being, but they just called me Little Madeline." Sally laughed. "It was actually great fun to see their faces when Madeline told them what she was going to do about the dairy. They were so shocked and humbled. I loved it. I bet she did, too—Alan might have been right, that she gave them something so spectacular to humble them and make them realize she was worth being worshipped."

"Twisted" was the word that came to my mind, but I didn't say it out loud.

"Shall I use the blade?" Hallie asked as she held up an odd-looking implement. I had no idea what she was talking about.

"Let me see." Sally sat forward as she peered at the bottom of one of my feet. "Not bad, Becca. I don't see many calluses, but you should let Hallie go ahead and get rid of what you do have."

I was so pleased that my feet were "not bad" that I nodded agreeably. Hallie held my ankle in the air and began to shave at the bottom of my foot. I saw little bits of skin fly and hit the floor. I wanted to yank my foot free and run out of the place, but I was getting far too much good stuff from Sally to give up now.

"Uh, okay. Anyway, Sally, did Shawn and Mid change once they had the dairy?"

"Totally. Watch out for that last toe, Orchid. Thanks. Yes, they changed totally. Shut up and got to work. The whole thing was a terrible strain on both their marriages, though. Their wives couldn't be convinced to revere Madeline, no matter what she gave them."

"I've been through a divorce or two myself. I know how difficult it can be."

"Oh? Sorry to hear that. I've never had a steady beau of any sort. Maybe someday." She smiled wearily and raised her half-drained glass.

I smiled and nodded. "What about Alan? He married?"

"Nope, never. He's very private, so I don't know if he has a girlfriend . . . or a boyfriend . . . or whatever. You know, we all thought that Drew would never marry. I have to tell you, I was worried about Linda and if she could take the pressure."

"She could have," I said, but I didn't really know. I knew that if I had been in the same situation, I wouldn't have kowtowed to Madeline, but Linda was much more affable and sweet than I was. Plus, she and Drew loved each other so much.

"I guess we'll never know now," Sally said quietly.

"Do you think Linda had something to do with Madeline's murder?" I asked. I tried not to sound defensive, but some must have slipped through.

Sally smiled at me knowingly. Suddenly, I wondered if she was much wiser than I'd given her credit for. "I hope not."

Hallie was now using a square block-type file on the bottom of my feet, and I wished for the blade to come back. The file both hurt and tickled. My legs involuntarily tried to twitch out of her hands, but she had a firm grip on the situation.

"It's hard for me to believe that Alan didn't want the dairy. What does he do, exactly?" I asked between clenched teeth.

"Trust me, he couldn't have cared less about Shawn and Mid getting the dairy—he's always been very happy-go-lucky about life." Sally laughed again and took a long swig of the Bloody Mary. "No one really knows what he does, though. It's a mystery, but we all think that somehow Madeline made it so he'd never have to worry about money."

"That's interesting." The sanding was over, and my leg muscles relaxed. Hallie rinsed my feet in the bath and then gently patted them dry.

"He's my cousin, but I really don't know him all that well. He was always with Drew when Shawn, Mid, and I were with Madeline. Alan's parents weren't psychotic, so he didn't need Madeline as much as we did. He and Drew took piano lessons and Chinese lessons together."

"Did it bother you that they got to do those sorts of things and the three of you didn't?" Hallie had squirted some lotion up and down my calves and she'd begun massaging it in. For a moment I thought I might dump Ian and ask her to be my third spouse.

"Oh, no, we weren't in any shape to practice anything. Madeline had to stay on top of us just to make sure we got through high school without damage to ourselves or anyone else." Sally's eyes teared up again, but she sniffed away the emotions this time.

From Sally's perspective, Madeline sounded sometimes like a saint and other times like a manipulative horror. I was glad she hadn't been a member of my family. Had Linda felt the same way?

"Sally, did Drew and Madeline get along?" I asked.

"I don't know, Becca. They never argued in front of us, but I always wondered how much time they spent together when Drew got older. She never complained when he wanted to go into the military, though I know she wished for Harvard or Yale instead of Navy. Outwardly, she supported him in whatever decisions he made for himself, but I have to say I always wondered what was really going on."

"What about Drew's father?" Hallie's fingers were digging deeper into my calf muscles, and I was beginning to turn into a puddle.

"Winston Forsyth? Well, he died when Drew was a baby. He left Madeline with some money, but most of what she had she either got from her family or made on her own. I don't know much more about him than that. I heard once that he married her so he might get the dairy one day, but that's probably all just old rumor and speculation. She never talked about him to me. She wasn't the sentimental type, of course, and I don't think she spent much time in the past. She was always looking forward—and moving forward, too."

"How did Madeline get control of the dairy in the first place?"

"It was her parents' business. They were the Loders. They left it to her in their will. My mother wasn't going to get a dime from them, that was certain. Alan's mother didn't want anything from them. She's still alive—Aunt Mary-Margaret—and I know Alan's tracking her down to tell her about Madeline, but she's off in New Zealand or somewhere with her husband, Alan's dad, Jack. They're wanderers and haven't had close contact with the extended family for many years, but they stayed home with Alan until he was fully grown. There aren't any issues there that I know of." Sally was beginning to slur her words and keep her eyes closed longer. She was getting her calves and feet massaged too; and that, combined with the Bloody Mary, was relaxing her deeply.

I tried to imagine Madeline's power over her entire family. It sounded as if there wasn't one branch she hadn't been in control of—well, maybe one, but that branch had taken off to New Zealand. Was that what someone had to do to get out of Madeline's grasp? Sally's version of her family life wasn't pretty, and yet it was still sugarcoated because she loved her aunt. I wondered about the reality and how the others truly felt, particularly Alan. He had been the dutiful nephew and a good friend to Drew, and Madeline gave the dairy to the obnoxious cousins. That had to be a blow, but I didn't think Sally had seen it that way.

"What time did you get to Madeline's on Friday?" I asked casually.

"Let me think," she said. "I got there around four. Alan was already there, and then Shawn and Mid arrived. Drew and Linda came shortly after that. Then you and your boyfriend, who's adorable, by the way."

"Thanks," I said, noting that Alan had been at the house before the rest of the guests. Had the cook, Levi, seen him arrive? "Sally, you seemed upset at the dinner. Were you?" I tried to keep my voice casual, but it probably sounded phony.

"Oh, shoot, yes, I suppose I was."

"Do you mind if I ask why?"

"The last time I spoke to Madeline was the day before she was killed. I said something to the effect that she should be happy that Drew had found someone wonderful to marry, no matter how quickly the wedding was to take place. She didn't like what I said. I thought maybe she was missing the dinner because she was mad at me. I didn't want her to be mad at me."

"Oh." I peered at Sally, who seemed about to fall into a deep sleep. I wondered if she might actually feel a sense of freedom now that her all-powerful aunt was dead. Even though she was sad Madeline was gone, I thought that a new world might open up for her now that she didn't have to worship someone and live by that someone's rules.

And that applied to Drew and his other cousins, too. But did one of them want that freedom so much that he or she killed for it? I had no idea.

I decided it was time to succumb to the sheer pleasure of Hallie's calf and foot massage. I put my head back on the chair and thought more about what Sally had said.

When she woke, she wasn't in the mood to talk further. I left the salon with lots more information about Madeline's family, massaged calves and feet, and pretty pink nails.

I still had more questions than answers, but mostly I couldn't wait to show Ian my toes.

Sixteen

"Sam Brion," *Sam said, answering his phone on the first ring.*

I'd called to see if he had anything regarding the investigation that he'd like to share with me. Of course, I couldn't ask him outright for information; I was going to have to do an end run, and the only way I could think of to do it was to pretend I had information I wanted to share with him. I told him about my pedicure with Sally and her insights regarding her family.

Sam spoke to me with lots of *hmm*s and *oh*s, and didn't form any full sentences I could use. After a brief lull in the conversation, I asked, "Sam, since Madeline was killed in her own home and in her own bedroom, do you think the killer was someone who knew her personally? I mean, if it had been someone she foreclosed on, wouldn't they have killed her at the bank?"

He was silent for a moment. I sensed he was thinking, so I didn't interrupt.

"There's something to that, I suppose. The thing you have to be careful of, though, is closing your eyes or mind to other ideas because you're looking for something specific. Profiling is a great tool, but you have to remember it's a tool and not always one hundred percent correct."

"I get that, but do you think there might be something to it?"

"Maybe. The bank customers are giving us more dead ends than we'd like. I've been looking at the family, but the information from Sally makes me think I need to look deeper. There certainly are some strange dynamics."

"Did you find out anything about Jeanine? Has she cashed any big checks or anything?" I asked.

"I don't have that information yet." The tone of his voice told me he did, but I didn't push it.

I was grateful for what he was sharing with me—more than I knew he should share with a civilian. I'd take whatever crumbs he wanted to throw my direction. I tried to come up with something else to keep him talking.

"Okay. So how are the bank customers leading to dead ends?"

"Madeline orchestrated the foreclosure of a number of properties, but not as many as you might think. And some of those who had reason to be angry at her either have left the area or have found another way to make a living. However, I'm hitting some roadblocks at the bank. I'm not getting the cooperation I'd like."

"How do you mean?"

"People are working hard to hide something, but I

can't pinpoint what it is, and I can't be sure it has anything to do with Madeline . . . Well, I'm rambling and telling you far too much, aren't I?"

Shoot, I knew it wouldn't last. "Not at all, Sam. Thanks."

"Thanks for letting me know about Sally. There's a picture of Madeline forming. There are some big pieces still missing, though. I have to go now, but I want you to be careful, Becca. I know you're nosing around, and I don't want you to get stuck in something you can't get out of."

"I won't. I promise I'll call you if I think I'm headed toward anything sticky." I decided not to tell him I was on my way to talk to Linda. I held on to my belief that she wasn't the killer, but even if she was, I held tighter to the fact that she would never hurt me.

"Good. Talk to you soon."

I closed my phone with a sense of satisfaction. Sam was right, there were pieces coming together that might lead to Madeline's killer. I just wished we'd find a couple of the big and important ones.

My trip to Linda's had more to do with being an undercover Number One than it did with questioning her about her possible involvement in Madeline's death. I also had some other questions I thought I should ask her, and I wasn't going to miss the opportunity.

She wasn't expecting me, and I didn't know if she'd recovered from her migraine, but the drive to her very small farm was worth the effort.

Linda's farm was smack-dab in the middle of a neighborhood. She had a cute little house on a double lot. The house was as close to a gingerbread cottage as I'd ever seen, and the large plot of land behind it would be overflowing with her juicy berries by the middle of the summer. Like me, she wasn't sure how she was able to grow delicious, sweet fruit—it just happened.

The cottage was too small for more than one person, so she was planning to move into Drew's house, but they hadn't decided if they were going to keep the farm so she could continue to grow berries, or if they would sell it and she would buy all her berries and focus on baking. I'd heard some amazing things about Drew's kitchen but had yet to see it. As I pulled into her driveway, a small wave of sadness made me hope she kept the picture-book home. She'd lived there as long as I'd known her.

I parked, made my way to the front door, and knocked three times, which was our code. She opened the door quickly.

"Becca, what a great surprise! Come in." She had a scarf over her head and a berry-stained apron in place. She looked fine.

"Three questions first," I said.

"Okay."

"Do you still have a headache?"

"No." She smiled.

"Are you super busy?"

"Uh, not really. I was just finishing up some pies, but they'll be out of the oven in a few minutes."

"Good. Can you come with me when they're out?"

"Where?"

"I didn't say you could ask a question. Do you have time to come with me, get out of the house, for an hour or so?"

Linda thought for a moment. "Yes, I think I can."

"Good. Then I'll come in for a minute."

Linda pulled the pies out of the oven and set them to cool. She offered me a piece of blueberry, and because I was neither stupid nor crazy, I happily accepted and ate it while she cleaned ingredients off her face and hands, and changed into a shirt that wasn't berry stained.

"Thanks for taking care of my customers yesterday, Becca. I was down for the count," she said once we'd climbed into my truck and I steered it toward Monson's small downtown.

"No problem. It's understandable. I'm glad you're better. I know you must still be upset."

She waved away my concrn. "So, where are we going?" she asked.

"You'll see." I cleared my throat. "How are you and Drew doing? You know you can talk to me about anything, Linda. How's he holding up?"

"Oh, fine, I think. He's taking care of the arrangements. Actually . . ."

"What?" I said as I turned down the dial on the old AM radio.

"You know Drew. He always does the right thing, the appropriate thing." She sighed. "Frankly, I think he's too controlled right now. His mother was just murdered, and he's . . . well, he's functioning. He knows what needs to be done, and he's doing it. He won't accept any help from me. I don't know if Alan is helping him or not, but he's staying with Drew. I'm afraid Drew's not taking the time he needs to grieve. Like I told you, he and Madeline hadn't been close for some time, but still, she was his mother."

"Why hadn't they had a relationship?" I asked, hoping

for something specific and filing away the information regarding why Alan was always driving Drew's car.

"I don't know the entire story, but Madeline was Madeline and Drew wanted his own life. When we got together and it seemed to be something that would be permanent, Drew and I thought we should try to make things better between him and his mom. It was rough, and I wonder if it wasn't a mistake. She wasn't making it easy on either of us."

"I'm sorry, Linda."

"Thanks."

"So, is he still reporting for duty?"

"Yes, he is," she said, exasperation in her voice.

"You don't want him to go?"

"Of course not, but not because I want him here for me. I'd already come to terms with the fact that he was going to be leaving. I just think it's bad timing, and frankly, though he might believe he's doing the right thing, I think it's terribly inappropriate." She took another deep breath and laughed. "Well, aren't you sorry you said I could talk to you about anything? I think I needed to get that off my chest."

"Do you feel better?"

"A little, thanks."

"I get what you're saying. Will he change his mind?"

"I don't think so, and . . . well, I suppose he has good reasons."

"What are they?"

"I'd tell you, but I'd have to kill you afterward." Linda forced another laugh.

I looked at her. "Oh, top-secret stuff?"

"Something like that. I guess I need to be more patient about it all if I'm going to marry him."

"I have a deal for you. You can be patient for the rest of the world, but you can always tell me how you really feel. I won't tell anyone, and I won't ever hold it against you. Ever." Linda's eyes were tearing up. "Well, I suppose you can even cry if you really need to."

"I'm so glad you came to get me. Where are we going, anyway?"

I stopped in front of one of the two small women's clothing shops in Monson. This one had nicer things, like dresses. The other one, a block down, was where I usually purchased my overalls, both short and long. The shop we were in front of was Veronica's, and the one down the street was Viola's.

"Well, this is going to seem weird, and might make you mad, especially considering what we were talking about, but I had an idea."

"I'm listening."

"We were going to go dress shopping today for the wedding, right?" She nodded. "Well, I know the chances of the murder being solved before Drew leaves are slim, but what if it does get solved?"

"What if?"

"Let's be prepared." I flicked a small spider off the dashboard. "Let's try on some dresses. If there's time, I'll take you and Drew to the justice of the peace. I know, I know, it's not the ideal wedding, but it's better than nothing. And if it can happen, we don't want to be caught without dresses, do we?"

Linda looked at me a long moment, then turned her attention to Veronica's display. Three mannequins, all with their hands posed on their hips, stood in the window. One wore a blue housedress, another wore a denim dress, and the third was done up in a red sequined number with a headband. A red feather boa completed the ensemble. Linda turned to me and said, "You know, it's rather surprising how sweet you can be."

I grimaced. "You make me want to change my mind. Come on; let's go in before I come to my senses."

Of course, the real plan was to have the surprise wedding at Bailey's, but I wasn't going to tell Linda that much. I already had Ian on the hunt for a rented tuxedo that would fit Alan. Drew would wear his dress uniform, and I knew it was always in a state of readiness. If the wedding could happen, it would happen at Bailey's, just as Linda had originally planned, but I wanted at least some surprise.

Sequins were immediately ruled out. When we told Savannah, the young girl working in the store that day, that taffeta and satin were also ruled out, she exclaimed in a high-pitched voice, "But it's a wedding! You want cotton at a wedding?"

"Or denim," I said with a smile. She didn't think it was funny.

After much debate and many flourishes of all sorts of material, Linda found some suits she liked. They had skirts that fell just below the knees and the jackets were short and simple with two buttons. There was a light cream-colored one that was exactly her size, and three of varied colors that should fit me. I tried the yellow one on first.

I exited the dressing room on my toes, because I'd certainly be wearing some sort of heels for the occasion, and pirouetted.

"Whoa, yellow isn't your color," Linda said. "But I love the suit. Try the purplish one."

"Yes, ma'am." I had no idea yellow wasn't my color. I tip-toed back to the dressing room.

We finally settled on the light lavender-ish suit for me, and I approved wholeheartedly of how she looked in the cream one. She gave a grin of satisfaction in the three-way mirror.

Linda wanted to pay for both suits, but I insisted on getting my own. We confirmed with Savannah that we could return them if the tags were intact. She made sure to add, "And if y'all wear them, we can tell, you know—so don't try to slip one by us."

We promised not to.

The next stop was for some shoes to go with the suits. One good thing about living in a small town was the complete lack of options. Bradford's Shoes would have what we wanted or we'd have to go barefoot, or in our sneakers. Bradford's was able to accommodate us both with shorter-heeled dressy shoes that matched Linda's suit perfectly, and the cream color worked well with the lavender, too. She managed to buy both pairs of shoes before I realized they'd been rung up.

"Then the coffee break we're about to take is on me," I said.

We ventured into The Coffee Stop and loaded up on lattes and cookies. I was reminded of my presentation at Maytabee's and felt a little panic at my lack of preparation. I also hoped the Maytabee's owner didn't catch me in The Coffee Stop. That would be awkward.

"Becca, thank you. This was fun. We'll probably end

up returning the suits and shoes, but this was still fun anyway."

"It was fun," I agreed. And it had been the part of the job as Number One that I'd dreaded the most. Between my painted toes and my new clothes, I was becoming much more girly than I'd ever been.

But I had to get down to business now. There was a chance I'd ruin the good time we'd had, but just as with Sally at the salon, I had to take advantage of the moment.

"Linda, who do you think killed Madeline?" I said between bites of cookie.

She blinked. "Well, if I were to venture a guess, I'd say it was probably someone she foreclosed on, someone who was angry at her." She squirmed. I'd just thrown a wrench into the middle of the carefree fun we'd been having.

"Maybe. Did you know Jeanine Baker is missing?"

"No. Really? Do you think she had something to do with Madeline?" Linda squirmed some more.

I told Linda what I'd done with Madeline's phone. I told her that somehow curiosity had taken away my intelligence and good sense. I told her about not seeing her phone number on the call list despite Madeline's insistence that she'd called Linda numerous times. I told her I saw Ian's number and Jeanine's name. I explained what I knew about Ian's involvement with Madeline, and I told her about my trip with Sam out to Jeanine's farm. I was practicing the same method with her that I'd practiced earlier with Sam. If I shared some things with her, maybe she'd find it easy to share something with me; something she didn't want to share with anyone. It was rotten of me to pull such a maneuver on a friend, but time was ticking by.

"Okay, so for some reason Madeline called Jeanine on the day she was killed, and now Jeanine's missing. I don't think that means Jeanine had something to do with the murder, Becca. Do you? Frankly, I'm worried about Jeanine's safety."

"Me, too, but her disappearance does look kind of fishy," I said.

"Sure. Sort of, but Jeanine is Jeanine. She makes things fishy." Linda's face scrunched up as she thought. "But Jeanine couldn't have done what . . . what was done to Madeline."

"Probably not."

"Their phone calls must have been about bank business. I can't see them being friends," Linda theorized.

"Me either. Anyone else come to mind? Besides a bank customer, I mean. What about the cousins?" I asked over the brim of my latte.

"Oh, Becca, I don't think the family was involved at all," Linda said. "We were all questioned and released that night. Sam told us he'd check our alibis. I know Drew and I were together. No one has been arrested. I'm sure we'd have heard if any of the cousins had been taken into custody."

"Do you know what their alibis are?"

Linda shook her head. "Not really."

"Who was at Madeline's when you got there?"

"Everyone but you and Ian."

That was consistent with what Sally had said.

"You and Drew came together?"

"Yes. We were together, like I told you."

"All afternoon?"

"Yes . . . Becca, you don't think Drew was involved,

do you?" Linda's cheeks were pink, but this time it had nothing to do with blushing.

I didn't say anything for a second, and for the first time in our friendship, I wondered if Linda was about to get angry at me. We were long past most of the things people get angry at each other about. We were both content in our own lives and enjoyed each other's company enough to look past minor irritations.

"No," I finally said, hesitantly. "No, Linda."

"You wonder, though, don't you?"

I put my latte down and reached over the table to put a hand over one of hers. "Listen. No, I don't think Drew killed his mother. But if—this is a big if—if he was involved, I for sure don't want my best friend marrying him."

Ka-boom. So much for wanting to be a good Number One. Talk about a one-eighty. I'd lured her out to shop for wedding things and then thrown a bomb of accusation right into the middle of one of the best friendships I'd ever had.

"I see." Linda pulled her hand out from under mine. "Becca, I appreciate what you're saying to me. I appreciate that you think you're being a good friend, but Drew couldn't have killed his mother. He wouldn't have."

"Good, I'm very glad to hear that." I gulped. Would we be able to move forward from this moment?

Even if I'd damaged our friendship, maybe Linda would make certain that she knew Drew hadn't been involved in Madeline's murder before she married him. If she was telling the truth about him being with her, as her vivid blushing had indicated, I was thrilled. But if she wasn't, maybe my words would make her think twice and she'd come to her senses before it was too late.

"Linda, I'm sorry if I said something that . . . well, it wasn't my intention," I lied. "We were having such a good time. I got carried away with . . . with investigating, I guess. Your happiness is very important to me. Please forgive me if I offended you." I wasn't lying about that.

"No, it's all right." She forced a smile. "But I really need to get home now. Shall we?"

The ride back to her house was quiet and strained. I wanted us to talk further, but nothing I could say sounded right. Unless she fired me from my Number One duties, I'd still be there for her in every way. I was still going to make her wedding the surprise of a lifetime, if Drew wasn't a killer, and if she forgave me.

What I wanted to tell her was that I was doing all I could to rule people out, and this was the only way I could think of to rule Drew out. She claimed he was with her—and she was the only one that I knew of who could dispute that.

I wasn't equipped to deal with the possibility that she had been the killer or had been in on the murder. I didn't accept either of those because I knew her so well and cared for her so much. If she'd been involved, I would be devastated.

Linda seemed less icy by the time I dropped her off, but not back to normal.

As I drove away from her cottage, my phone rang.

This time, Sam was calling me.

Seventeen

"Madeline was strangled," Sam said. **"Asphyxiation, defi-**
nitely. Why?" He'd called me to ask where Sally was
staying. After I told him, I asked him what the official
cause of Madeline's death was.

"I thought as much," I said, noting silently that knowing didn't tell me anything more than I knew. I wasn't sure
what I was hoping for, but if nothing else, Sam hadn't put
up a fight about giving me the information. I was almost
feeling downright official. "What about the blood and the
lines of wounds on her hands? What were those?"

"We're not sure, but we think they're defensive
wounds of some sort. We're working on putting together
a sequence of events, but don't have it yet."

"So someone strangled her with a checkered scarf." I
said it aloud but was talking to myself more than to Sam.

"Scarf? That's right, that's what you thought it was.

No, Becca, that wasn't a scarf, it was a shirt—a T-shirt. I didn't tell you before, but I don't suppose there's any harm in you having that information now."

"A T-shirt?" I couldn't identify what I'd seen around Madeline's neck as being a T-shirt. "Was it Madeline's?"

"We have no idea. It was a size Large, but we don't know if it was a man's or a woman's shirt. We're trying to track down the manufacturer and where it is or was sold. It's actually pretty old, and the only mark it has is the L on the tag. Madeline wasn't a Large, but the shirt looked like it would fit her just fine."

"Someone strangled her with a shirt?" I repeated. Whether it was a T-shirt or a scarf, the person who did the deed had to have been pretty strong to pull off such a maneuver.

"Yes. There were no finger-shaped contusions on her throat or neck. A sleeve was tied to the hem, and then pulled tight to cause the asphyxiation."

I veered my truck to the left, onto a road I hadn't traveled in some time. It was a road that would eventually lead to Columbia, the route that Sally would take when she went home. I hadn't been to Columbia in over a year, and I wasn't going today. I had another destination in mind and it, coincidentally, was on the same road, though not far from town.

"Whoever killed her must have been pretty strong." I voiced what I'd been thinking a moment before. "Sam, that would have to rule out Jeanine Baker. She's strong, very strong, but she's smaller than Madeline, and she couldn't possibly handle all that must have gone on in that room."

"I've thought of that, Becca, but you never know. I'd still like to find her and talk to her."

I nodded, even though he couldn't see me.

"Have you talked to Levi, the cook?" I asked.

"He's the only person who admits to being in the house during the time of the murder, but we don't have any evidence that he was involved. Plus, we don't think he was. He'd worked for her for a long time, and she paid him very well. If you remember, Madeline's room and the kitchen are not only on separate floors, but at opposite ends of that huge house. It's more than conceivable that the murder occurred without Levi hearing much of anything. Someone could have come in through the front door, and Levi wouldn't have seen a thing. If, as he says, he was in the kitchen the whole time, other than going out to the garage in search of pastries, I understand how he might have missed any commotion. He's pretty upset."

"His apron, his clothes were stained. At the time, I thought they were food stains, but they could have been more than that."

"We examined and tested his clothes and apron. There was no blood, human or otherwise."

"No chance he was involved?"

Sam paused, then said, "It isn't wise to totally disregard anyone at this point, but I don't think so."

I sighed. "Anything else on the bank customers?"

"Since the last time we talked? No."

I'd repeated the question with the hope that I'd push some button about Jeanine's foreclosure notice, but my method didn't work. It was time for me to strongly urge Allison to tell Sam what she knew.

"Well, she didn't just kill herself," I said.

"That would be correct."

"Do you have any leads you're following more than the others?"

"Maybe."

Excitement zipped through me. Was it possible that the police were on to something, something I was still grasping to find? "Come on, tell me *that,* please. Do you think you might have this solved quickly?"

"I want to solve any murder quickly, but I'm definitely not going to tell you what we think are the best leads at this point. That would be very irresponsible."

"Yeah, probably."

"Gotta go, Becca."

I closed my phone, slipped it into my pocket, and made my way toward my next destination: Loder Dairy.

I had a sketchy memory of touring it when I was a child. Even though she homeschooled Allison and me, our mother made sure we took the same field trips that other elementary school-age children did. Loder Dairy was always a big one.

I remembered lots of cows, lots of strong scents, lots of mooing, and lots of people in white coats and white shower caps. I also remembered what a shock it was to see where the milk that was delivered to our home originated. It was one thing to look at a picture book about cows and their milk, but it was a totally different thing to see machines hooked up to udders and making plenty of noise as they pulled the milk from the cows. In fact, I had been momentarily traumatized by the whole thing, thinking the cows didn't look like cows but space aliens.

Allison had rolled her eyes at my horror and my mother smiled and held my hand a little tighter.

At the end of the tour, the guide allowed Allison and me to milk a cow by hand. That took away the fear, and I still had a clear memory of the cow turning her head to look at me as I milked her, or attempted to. I was certain that she smiled, which made the whole trip worthwhile. A cow had smiled at me! How many people could say that?

And though Loder Dairy was a Monson-area landmark, it originally gained its stellar reputation because of its ever-present delivery trucks and delivery people. Beginning very early in the morning, the simple white trucks with pictures of a smiling cows on the panels were all over Monson and the surrounding countryside. The drivers were friendly and courteous, and quickly got from their trucks to customers' front porches and back to their trucks again. I hadn't had milk or butter delivered since I was a child.

I stopped my truck across the road in front of the dairy. It was an impressive facility that took up at least a hundred acres. Most of the buildings were white, except for a tall, round, bright blue silo behind one of the smaller buildings.

There was a small number of black-and-white cows in the very green pasture to the east of the buildings. Though the pasture was lush, there was an area right next to a large barn that was well trampled and, from my vantage point, looked muddy.

Visiting Loder Dairy was another way for me to get to know Madeline's family better. Sally had said that Shawn

and Mid had been ungrateful kids but had turned humble
when given the dairy. I couldn't imagine giving something so magnificent to someone I didn't like, even if they
were family.

There was something that sat funny with me about
what Sally had said, and I wondered if Shawn and Mid
would give me their version of how they'd acquired the
farm. Plus, visiting them would give me a good reason to
revisit some childhood memories.

I put my truck in Park, got out, and crossed the road.
There was a gravel driveway that led to a big house with
a wide porch. I followed it to the house and climbed the
porch stairs. I knocked on the door, but no one answered.
I peered in a few windows as I walked along the porch
that stretched around the side of the house, but all the
blinds were shut tight.

The biggest of the dairy's buildings was directly next
to the house. For a few moments I stood on the porch
with my hands on my hips. I could see a good deal of the
property, but I didn't see any people. As I stood there, I
thought about calling out to see if anyone would hear me,
but then I thought again.

Sure, I wanted to talk to Shawn and Mid; I wanted to
know what they had to say about their family history and
the circumstances behind Madeline giving them the dairy.
But I also liked to snoop. From what I could see, no one
would notice if I just took about ten steps and made my
way through a space between the back of the big building
and a whitewashed fence that separated it from the muddy
area between it and the pasture. I didn't have much of a
plan for what I'd do when I made it to the other side of the
building, but at the moment that didn't concern me.

Testing fate, I waited a minute for someone to discover me. When no one appeared from anywhere, I dashed to the hidden space that, unfortunately, wasn't as wide as it had seemed to be from the porch.

Only the cows could see me now, and I wasn't worried about being heard; there was a constant stream of noise: mooing and machinery, some far off, some seemingly close. The fence was simple, posts spaced about five feet apart and two cross slats between each pair of posts. It would be easy for a human to get through the open spaces.

I had to turn sideways so I faced the pasture as I moved along the tight space. When I was halfway to my destination, a calf trotted across the pasture and made her way purposefully my direction. If I was going to get caught sneaking around the dairy, I didn't want it to be when I was in a small space behind a building. I swiped my hand through the air, hoping to send her back the other way. Then, of course, I realized how ridiculous I was being; I doubted she understood my hand waves. I continued side-stepping and ignored the calf—until she ran into the fence, uttered a squeaky moo, and shook her head. Once I knew she hadn't been hurt, I just wanted her to go away.

"Hello. Yes, you caught me. Now I've got to be on my way."

The calf didn't moo again, but she continued to watch me maneuver over what she surely thought was her property.

I made it to the end of the path and stepped into a semi-open space between the big building and another one. There was a door to the big building that I could go through without the rest of the world seeing me.

I craned my neck in every direction but still didn't see anyone. I hurried up a short metal stairway, opened the door, and hurried inside. I closed the door and leaned against it as I looked around. There was a bunch to see.

This was where the cows were hooked to the milking machines. There were four even rows of machines laid out on the concrete floor. The floor was wet, as though it had been recently hosed down. And there were no cows anywhere. Did cows get milked only in the morning? Being the owner of a farm should give one instant knowledge about such things, but since my farm was filled with strawberries and pumpkins, I was at a loss about cows' milking schedules.

My covert operation was still working for me; there were no people anywhere. *So far, so good,* I thought as I descended another small stairway and went to inspect the milking machines. I was fascinated by the alien childhood memory and wondered if they'd make the same impression.

Truthfully, they were wicked. I knew they didn't hurt the animals. Nevertheless, the whole mechanism—the tubes, the things that attached to the teats, even the clear tubs for gathering the milk—looked alien to me; unnatural. I decided my childhood impression was right on target.

But what was most curious was that the first machine I inspected hadn't milked a cow in the recent past, as far as I could tell. The tubes were disconnected and draped over a red metal fence/divider that kept the cows a safe distance from the machines. But it was more than just the tubes; the entire machine was in pieces, a jigsaw puzzle that would be hard to put back together.

In fact, the entire row of machines I was standing in front of was disassembled. Out of the four rows, it looked as if two of them were in working order and two of them weren't. It was hard to tell for sure because the rows went on for a long distance, and I was just short enough that I couldn't see all the way to the ends of them.

Maybe they used only two rows at a time, taking apart and cleaning the other two. It seemed like a sanitary plan, and the building itself looked pretty spotless. I wasn't sure that I was looking for anything specific, but there were no puddles of anything that might cause alarm.

Deciding I'd seen whatever there was to see, I made my way back outside and down the steps. Outside again, I felt very exposed. I glanced in every direction and saw that no one was paying me any attention; no one was anywhere. I couldn't believe my luck. Was I going to be able to trespass and snoop and not be caught?

Though I was feeling brave, smart, and somewhat cocky, I hunched over a little and hurried to the smaller white building that was next on my hunt. There was no stairway on this one, and the door opened just as easily as the first one had.

The smaller building, just like the bigger one, was empty of people but held machinery. It wasn't the kind that was used to milk cows. The scent told me that I was in a room that turned the milk into butter. The air was thick with a sweet, creamy freshness, and I was once again impressed at how clean everything was.

I didn't take a lot of time to inspect the pot-bellied machine that took up most of the space, but I took a quick walk around it just to see if I could figure out how it worked. I couldn't, but I thought I'd discovered the entrance and exit points for the products. The best part of the entire excursion was what I found next. It was something that brought my childhood back in a strong wave of happy memories.

At the end of the machine, on large worktables, were butter stamps that pressed designs into finished butter. The Loder Dairy butter that was delivered to our front porch when I was a child had always had a stamp. The one-pound packages were wrapped in thick, waxy paper. Every time we got a Loder delivery, Allison and I would guess which stamp the butter would have. There were a number of different designs: a cow, a flower, stalks of wheat, a pineapple, and two acorns. Whichever one of us guessed correctly which stamp was on our butter that day got to be the first one to put some of it on her toast. It was great fun, almost something magical, for two little girls who lived in the country and didn't see one moment of television.

The stamps hadn't changed, including their star borders. I remembered that when you felt the design through the waxed paper, you could feel the impressions of the border, but no matter how much you felt and prodded, it was nearly impossible to know the design inside.

I had the sudden urge to steal a stamp, one with a cow on it. It would make a great gift for Allison. I silently debated just how awful such a theft would be.

In the end, I didn't take the stamp. Regretfully, I put it back with the others and walked away from the preparation tables. Perhaps I'd ask Shawn and Mid about the stamps when I was given a proper tour, and see if they'd let me buy one.

My invisibility luck changed as I walked out of the

butter building and toward the large blue silo. Suddenly, three people, all of them in white coats and white shower caps, were walking in my direction. They were still a good fifty feet away, in the middle of a conversation, and didn't notice me right off. I leapt forward and put my back against the silo. As their voices got closer, I moved around to the back of the building. When I was halfway, I was once again facing the pasture. The cows were more interested in eating than in me, though a few of them did look up and twitch their ears before going back to their lazy, crooked chewing. Except my new friend, the little calf that was more curious than any cat I'd ever known.

It hadn't moved far from where I'd last seen it, but when it eyeballed me, it exuberantly, if not skillfully, trotted my direction. It stopped and faced me again from the other side of the fence.

Her calf moos startled some of the other cows. They looked up again, this time with more focus.

"You need to go back to your mother," I said quietly.

She didn't, but mooed back as though she'd like to continue the conversation.

"Sheesh."

There was another white building on the other side of the silo, but its back was right against the fence, and I couldn't tell if there was a door on that side of it. I had no choice but to make my way to the front. I could go back the way I came, but I suspected that the three white coats had gone into the butter building, and I didn't want to give myself up that easily.

Moo.

I was going to have to decide what to do quickly. My

friend was causing enough of a scene that the other cows were becoming more curious, and one was even coming to join the party. Who knew cows communicated so well with each other?

"Troublemaker," I said.

I think the calf laughed, but I didn't stick around long enough to ponder it. Keeping my back tight against the silo, I maneuvered a little further. The calf watched my every move, even craned her neck to evaluate my progress.

It seemed my luck was returning; again there was no one anywhere in sight. The white coats were gone, presumably into the butter barn. I was pleased I hadn't stolen a butter stamp.

I dashed to the front of the next white building and ran through the open double doors. I was in another barn, one that did open on the other side to the pasture. Clarification: one that was already opened to the pasture, but the opening was at an angle I couldn't see from behind the silo.

I'd gone in the open doors in the front, and my new friend was now trotting through the open doors at the back. She seemed very happy to see me.

"Oh, no," I said as I turned to leave the barn the way I came in. But walking directly toward me this time were Shawn and Mid. They weren't in white coats, but in jeans and T-shirts. They weren't looking up, but it wouldn't be long before they noticed me.

Besides the open middle part of the building, there were bales of hay stacked everywhere. The only place to hide was behind a stack. I backed up and went around the first stack I could find. And my friend followed.

Moo?

"Oh, good gracious. Seriously? *Shoo. Shoo.*"

The calf didn't listen, and would surely give up my location quickly. For the briefest of instants, I silently debated whether I should confront Shawn and Mid and tell them I'd explored on my own when no one answered my calls, or hide. Maybe it was the guilt I felt over considering the butter stamp theft, or maybe I was just in sneak-around mode; whatever it was, I chose to hide.

My friend followed me around the stack of bales and watched as I dived into a haystack and hid amid the sharp, irritating pieces of dry straw. In a flurry, I covered myself and then tried to be still. Except for the calf's noise and my pounding heartbeat, no one would be able to hear a thing. At this moment, I realized that confronting the brothers would have been the better choice, but it was too late.

I stood only a small chance of not being found, but that was better than no chance at all. When Shawn and Mid came into the barn, I couldn't focus on their words. I didn't know them well enough to know who was who; both their voices were heated, angry. I couldn't tell if they were mad at each other or about something else. And then the calf distracted them.

"What the . . . ?"

I felt the footsteps more than heard them as the brothers approached the calf.

"Hey, what're you doing in here?"

"Hey, little girl."

I was relieved that the two men weren't angry at the calf. Poor thing just found me too irresistible to ignore.

The calf mooed with expression. I was certain she was

trying to tell them that there was a person hiding in the straw right over there. *Why can't you see her? She's right there—that lump in the hay. Look!* I hoped they didn't speak cow.

"Come on, let's get back out there."

Moo.

"I don't think she wants to go." Whichever one of them said this had a hint of humor in his voice.

"She must be confused or lost or something. Do you suppose she's blind?"

Moooooo.

"No, she's just adventurous. I suppose we could leave her in here, but we shouldn't. Come on, help me carry her back out to the pasture."

In the commotion of wrangling the cow, one of the men kicked the bottom of one of my feet. I sucked in a dusty, straw-scented breath and swiped my legs into an unladylike wide-open position, hoping I was still hidden by straw. I stopped the screech that was making its way up my throat and held on to the gasp of air I'd pulled.

"What was that?"

"What was what?"

"I swear my foot hit something."

"Your imagination. Come on and help me. I don't want to hurt her, and she's squirmy."

If the pause had been a second longer, I would have either passed out from lack of oxygen or ripped a tendon in my groin.

"Yeah, okay, but I'm not done talking to you about the other matter. That cousin of ours can't get away with it. I'm going to make sure of that."

Of course, the last comment got my attention, but I

needed oxygen so desperately that I was beyond caring if I got caught. I pulled my scissored my legs closed and rose from the straw like I was escaping a grave.

I sucked in some clean air and then scurried to the other side of the bales.

Mid and Shawn and the calf were out of sight, and I wished for some more invisibility luck.

Whatever I had left wasn't going to last much longer, I was sure of that. I didn't have time to attempt more cloak-and-dagger maneuvers. I crossed my fingers, and then ran out of the barn and into the open area. If I was going to be caught, it was going to happen soon, but I was focused more on getting out of there quickly than on not being seen.

Unfortunately, I hit a dead end. From this side, there was no way to get around the house without going to the other side of the milking barn. I was going to have to run back through the courtyard for a moment and make my way.

The door to the butter-making barn began to swing open. I couldn't go around the milking barn, and I couldn't run back the way I'd come. In fact, the only real option I had was to cross the open area at its shortest part, and go through the house itself. I wasn't thinking clearly as I ran though the space and then to the back door of the house. Amazingly, it was unlocked; I opened it and made my way in.

I was certain someone—another person in a white lab coat or someone cooking something delightful in the kitchen—would greet me. But no one was inside the house. In fact, there wasn't anything in the house at all. I ran through three empty rooms. They were probably the dining room, the living room, and a den. I didn't stop to look closely at all the nothing but flung myself out the front door, which was unlocked, too, and down the porch steps. I kept to the side of the driveway and ran without looking around to see who might be watching.

I made it to my truck, hopped in, and started the engine. Just as I drove away, I noticed the calf had come to the front of the fence. It must have seen me run down the driveway.

What I didn't notice, though, were the two brothers making their way back into the hay barn. They heard an engine rev, but when they looked around, all they saw was a bright orange truck. They didn't know anyone who drove a bright orange truck, but their cousins did.

Eighteen

"You've come here either to break up or to tell me about your latest adventure," Ian said as he looked up from his laptop. He was sitting on his couch, his legs extended onto the coffee table.

"Why would I be here to break up with you?" I asked as I climbed the last ladder rung into his apartment. I joined him on the couch.

"You've been rolling around in hay," he said as he plucked a piece from my hair. "If you weren't alone, I assume you've come here to tell me about the other guy."

I returned his smile. "No, I'm not here to break up. And I must have missed a few pieces."

"Good news, then. So, what other trouble have you been causing?"

Ian listened patiently as I told him about my visit to Loder Dairy. He didn't interrupt and he didn't chastise, but the look on his face was none too pleased until I told him about the calf. Then it was all he could do not to laugh. I hadn't even considered it funny until I saw Ian's amusement.

"So, what do you think?" I asked when I was finished.

"Let's see—I think that Shawn and Mid would have gladly given you a tour of the dairy, and you wouldn't have had to trespass, and you wouldn't have had to hide. And they might have given you one of the butter stamps, or at least sold you one at a discount. Other than that, I'm not sure I have many thoughts . . . oh, of course, I'd love to have seen you with the calf."

"You're probably right, but then I wouldn't have known what I know."

"Besides what you overheard—which might not mean much of anything—what did you learn that you couldn't have learned on a tour?"

"The empty house."

"They might not have shown you through their empty house, but what good is knowing about it?"

"It's odd that it's empty."

"Not really. They probably both live in their own homes away from the dairy. Or maybe they're in the process of doing some remodeling or painting. Your instincts are great, Becca, but I'm not sure that their house being empty is much of a revelation or a clue."

He was probably right, but there was still something about it that bothered me, though it wasn't strong enough to argue about. Maybe it wasn't the house, or even what I'd overheard. But there was something there that didn't sit right. I wasn't sure what it was, but it might come to me if I gave it enough time, and if I didn't try to think about it so hard.

"I know this is going to push the work on the presentation even later, but I have something else I want to do before we get started. Would you come with me on the next adventure?"

Ian looked at me a moment, then said, "You're inviting me along? This is a big development in our relationship." He closed the laptop. "Shall I change into all-black clothing and search for a ski mask?"

I smiled at his ribbing. "No, I'd just like to go talk to Drew. Since Alan is staying with him, we might be able to talk to him, too. I hope Linda isn't there. I think I upset her today, and I need to ask Drew some questions. In fact, I should have talked to Drew before talking to anyone else, really, but for some reason that's clear only now."

"How did you upset Linda?"

"I said some things that made me sound suspicious of Drew."

"Are you?"

"Sort of."

"Why?"

"That's another long story. Come with me, and you can hear it the same time I share it with Drew."

"Sounds interesting."

"Come on, hang out with me."

"Absolutely."

The plan was that after we talked to Drew, we'd go back to my house and prepare the presentation. Ian gathered his laptop, which he would use to help me create a

PowerPoint presentation, and then do some of his own work. Not only was he an artist, but he had received a degree in mathematics from the University of Missouri. His mathematical mind had been a huge asset to his artistic career. He'd created a computer program that assisted him with his yard sculpture designs. I could look over his shoulder for hours as he worked the program and created some things that shouldn't even be able to stand upright. But with considerations of weight distribution and balance, the program showed him how he could put together sculptures that seemed to defy gravity. He could probably make a mint off the program alone, but he wasn't interested in selling it. He would just continue to use it for his artwork.

We'd talked about moving in together—this wasn't as frightening to me as meeting his family was—but the logistics didn't work. Ian needed his studio and I needed (and didn't see myself ever leaving) my land and my ultramodern kitchen/barn. Plus, there was George. Neither of us could imagine leaving George. I wasn't sure what it would all mean when and if Ian purchased Bud Morris's property for the lavender farm, but I knew that we'd work it out, including taking care of George.

We'll work it out, I thought as I drove us toward Drew's. Not for one moment had I thought of Ian as someone temporary, someone who was just a fling or an affair. Perhaps it was because our relationship had been so easy. We dated and became a couple quickly. It had been a natural transition. Maybe I needed to work harder to appreciate what I had. Or maybe I was just chicken. Decision time regarding the Iowa trip was long past, and Ian was being extra patient.

Drew lived in a nice, but not too nice, house in Monson. He had built his own life, and Linda once told me that he wouldn't accept money from his mother. After discovering his ties to the Loder Dairy, I admired him even more. It would have been easy to live off the fruits of his ancestors' and relatives' labors, but he chose a path he could call his own—one that was not easy.

But I still wasn't one hundred percent sure he hadn't been involved in his mother's death.

The plan was that Linda and Drew would move into Drew's house once they were married. The people who'd lived in Drew's house before he bought it were professional chefs. I'd never seen the amazing kitchen they'd created, but Linda had raved about it the first time she saw it. I teased her about being more in love with the kitchen than with the man who owned it. Apparently, it was something to behold, and I'd been remiss in not stopping by to *ooh* and *ahh*. Since I didn't know another way to ask Drew about what I'd heard in the men's bathroom, I was going to confront him. I should have done it sooner, I knew that now. If I'd talked to Drew first, I might not have had to hurt Linda the way I had. Darned hindsight.

Maybe I could ease into it by asking to look at the kitchen first, I thought as I pulled into Drew's driveway.

The street was tree-lined, and all the houses were similar in their modern-traditional architecture but they were not cookie-cutter designs. The lots were big, giving the houses a good amount of elbow room and large, green front yards. Most of the backyards were fenced off from view with white vinyl posts and slats.

I didn't have the sense that I was on a street with a

bunch of rich people, but with a diverse range of household incomes.

"Nice area," Ian said as he came around to the driver's door and opened it for me.

"I think Linda likes it."

"Even though she won't be able to grow her berries anymore? Or will she? Are the backyards big enough?"

"I don't think so. She's probably going to sell the farm, but she isn't sure. If she does, they're going to look for some other land, or she might purchase the berries and stick with the baking end only. I don't think she knows exactly what she'll do until she has a real taste of what her new life will be like—that is, if that new life really happens."

Ian nodded. "I suppose so."

Ian's dream was to work the land like his family had in Iowa. Giving it up for a push lawnmower didn't fit with his vision, but he'd never criticize. "To each his or her own" was his motto. I didn't doubt that Linda would be able to move easily into her new life. Her favorite part of her business was baking the pies. She enjoyed growing delicious berries, but that wasn't her passion as much as the baking was.

The doorbell *ding-dong*ed pleasantly, and Drew answered a moment later.

"Becca, Ian," he said uncertainly. "Nice to see you. Come in." He wore a white T-shirt and jeans. His hair was wet, as though he'd just showered. He'd probably been working out just before we came over—he worked out a lot.

"Hi, Drew," I said as Ian and I walked in. "No, you

haven't forgotten that we were stopping by. This is a surprise attack." The entryway was roomy and didn't show many signs that a bachelor lived there. I wasn't much into decorating myself, but I predicted that there would be a table against the wall when Linda moved in. Didn't all entryways need tables for keys, bags, and so on? The wood floor was polished and showed no sign of wear. There were no discarded socks or random pairs of shoes, the way there had been in my entryway during my second marriage.

"Ah, very good. Welcome. Can I get you something to drink? You hungry?"

"No thanks," Ian said. He looked at me.

"I'm fine, too, Drew. Thanks, though. We're so sorry about your mom, so sorry. How are you holding up?"

"I'm okay," he said strongly. "I'm making the arrangements for her and getting ready to go. It's a lot, but it's getting done."

I looked at him a long moment. Was he really this strong, or was it something he'd been trained to be?

"Good. Is there anything we can do for you?" I asked.

"No. Well, take care of Linda while I'm gone."

"Consider that done," I said.

Ian added, "Absolutely."

After another long moment, I said, "I'd love to see the kitchen I've heard so much about. Would that be all right?"

"Come on."

Drew led the way down a wide hallway to the back of the house. I didn't see Alan, or hear noises as though someone else was around.

At the end of the hallway was the most amazing place

I'd ever seen. My teasing Linda about her loving Drew for his kitchen might not have been far off. I fell a little in love with him when I saw the room.

"Oh, my gosh," I said as I looked around, kitchen envy spreading through my body.

"Yeah, I know. The previous owners took out the back wall and extended everything about fifteen feet, which made all the difference. I bought the house two years ago, long before I met Linda. I'm glad she got to know me before seeing this"—he waved his arm—"or she might have fallen for me for my kitchen." He'd read my mind.

The room was about double the size of a big kitchen. There were two huge islands in the center, with an aisle between them. Underneath the island tops were dozens of pots and pans, all hanging from hooks screwed into the undersides. I'd seen such things hanging from kitchen ceilings but never underneath islands, and suddenly the idea seemed perfect. There were four double doors, two on the west wall, two on the east wall. I assumed some were freezers and some were refrigerators, but I opened all the doors and peered inside to confirm. I'd been correct, except I hadn't guessed they'd all be extra deep with shelves that pulled out for easy access.

There were a three-tub sink, and a six-burner stove top opposite the sink. And there were four extra-big ovens that would probably be able to bake a total of twenty-four pies at a time.

"Yeah, they overdid it. Apparently, they had the freezers and refrigerators custom made. The company that made them is now producing them for other customers. They've become quite the big deal." Drew laughed. "Linda says it's heavenly."

I looked at this man who adored my friend in ways that you would wish for a friend, and amid my kitchen envy, my heart hurt at what I was about to do, but I had no choice.

"Drew, it's fabulous," I said. Ian looked closely at the design of one of the freezers. His exclamations of admiration were as sincere as mine.

"I think Linda will enjoy it," Drew said.

"I'm certain of it," I replied. I looked around and tried to think of some way to get to my question. I cleared my throat. "Drew, on second thought I'd love a glass of water, if you don't mind." Now I was stalling.

"Sure." Drew pulled out three glasses, filled them with ice and water, and we sat on high stools around one of the islands.

I was still stalling when I said, "Drew, do you really have to leave? Can't you can't put it off, request an emergency leave or something?" I used the words George had used.

"No."

"Why not?" I asked.

Drew smiled patiently. "I just can't, Becca."

"Secret Navy SEAL stuff?" I smiled.

"Something like that."

Clearly, that was as far as that was going.

"Drew, I have a confession," I said.

Drew and Ian looked in my direction.

"Okay."

"I overheard you. In the men's bathroom, the night of your mother's murder. I heard you on your cell phone."

Ian's eyebrows rose, and Drew blinked. I'm sure Ian was surprised at my revelation, and Drew didn't know quite what to make of it. He looked puzzled.

"I don't know. What do you mean, Becca?"

I explained how I sneaked along the ledge and into the men's bathroom, how I hid, and what I heard.

"What did I say?" he asked, seemingly perplexed.

"You said you did the best you could. You hoped it was good enough. Then something about enough being enough and that you didn't care, you just wanted to make it look good."

Ian's leg was next to mine, and it tensed. He wasn't happy with the way I'd decided to handle my confession. Drew's words in the bathroom didn't proclaim his guilt, but they did sound suspicious. If I'd said something earlier, Ian would have urged me to tell Sam.

"Oh, I remember that conversation," Drew finally said. "Huh. Well, that might sound suspicious, having been said on the night of my mother's murder, but I assure you, Becca, it wasn't suspicious in the least."

"What was it about?" I asked boldly. If he didn't tell me, I would let Sam know.

Drew thought a long time. He looked at Ian and he looked at me. He wasn't happy, and we didn't have any weapons if he chose to use a Special Ops skill or two to take us down. I wouldn't go without a fight, and though Ian was substantially smaller than Drew, he wouldn't either. Maybe the two of us could battle the one of him if we had to.

Finally, he spoke. "Becca, I was having a conversation with a comrade, another SEAL. He and I serve together. The conversation was regarding our commanding officer, who's one of the most honorable men you will ever meet. He's been falsely accused of something—my buddy and I know this because he was with us at the time the alleged event supposedly occurred. I can't tell you more than that because, frankly, that's more secret *military stuff*."

"What about 'making it look good?' What did you mean by that?" I wasn't ready to let it go yet.

"I submitted a report regarding the time frame of the incident. When I said I wanted to make it look good— well, I did. I wanted to make sure that my report was clear and explained how my commander couldn't possibly have been where he was accused of being. It had to look good."

I nodded as I listened. His story sounded valid, but how would I know, really?

"Look, Becca, you need to understand something. The mission I'm being sent on is top-secret and can't be compromised. I've explained this to Sam Brion, telling him what I thought he should know, but no more. My mission cannot be compromised even by my mother's death. I have to do what I have to do. If you can't understand that, I'm very sorry. I'm not cold-hearted. I'm sad about my mother, but there's nothing I can do to bring her back. If I don't go, someone else will, and I can't have . . . well, if something happens to them, I couldn't live with that. Do you understand?"

"You're going because you don't want someone else to get hurt." As I said the words aloud, everything made sense. That is exactly what the Drew Forsyth I knew would do. Did I believe what he was telling me about the phone call? I did, so much so that I wanted to kick myself for not talking to him sooner. If he was fooling me, he was doing it perfectly and completely. "Your mission is really dangerous?"

"Very. Most of them are. That's why, originally, I wanted Linda and me to get married before I go."

"You might not come back?"

"I plan on coming back and living a wonderful life with the woman I love, but there's always the possibility that something could go wrong. Please do your best to understand my situation, and try not to judge me too harshly."

I sighed heavily and, frankly, wanted to cry at the tragedy of it all. Drew's mother had died a horrible death. He was now facing a terribly dangerous military mission. He loved my friend and my friend loved him and they should be together, but that could all be for naught if something horrible were to happen to him.

"Did you tell Sam about the situation with your commanding officer?" I asked.

"Why would I? It has nothing to do with my mother."

I nodded. "Does Linda know? I mean, that you might not come back."

"Becca, this is a conversation I had with her on our first date. I appreciate your concern, I really do, but though most of what I do has to remain a secret, I want the people in my life not to be too surprised by potential outcomes."

"I see."

"I didn't have anything to do with my mother's death. Our relationship was complicated at best, but I never would have killed her. I realize you're here because you care so much for Linda, and I get that, and believe it or not, I appreciate your concern. I'm pleased that when I'm not here, Linda will have friends who care enough about her to make sure she's being taken care of. I know that you and I haven't spent a lot of time together, but I really hope we can be friends—when I come back, I want to make that a priority. Okay?"

"I think that's more than possible." Ian smiled.

Drew was right—he and I didn't know each other very well. I acknowledged that I'd probably been intimidated by his persona—gorgeous, secretive military man. He was the stuff of romance and adventure novels. For so long, he'd seemed larger than life. But as we sat around the kitchen island, sipping water, he suddenly seemed normal. I didn't think he had anything to do with his mother's death.

I scooted off the stool and hugged his rock-hard body, my head hitting his firm chest. "I believe you, but if you do anything to break my best friend's heart, I'll have to find a way to hurt you. It won't be easy, but I'll find a way."

Drew laughed and gently hugged back.

"I think I like that trait in a . . . Number One. You're in charge of making sure she's fine while I'm gone. When I get back, the wedding will be handled quickly."

"I plan on it," I said. For an instant I thought of telling him about the potential surprise wedding, but it didn't seem to be either appropriate or necessary. If it happened, it happened. It seemed close to impossible at this point, anyway. Why throw another thing in the mix for him to think about?

It seemed to be the right time for an exit, so Ian and I made our way back down the hallway.

"Drew," I said as we reached the front door, "is Alan staying with you?"

"Yes, but he's not here at the moment. Do you need to talk to him, too?"

"Not really," I said. I wanted to talk to him, but I wasn't sure about what. "Is he working?"

Drew laughed. "Alan's always working in one way or another, but none of us has ever been sure of what he does. He's a mystery, and I'll admit he's odd, but he isn't a killer, Becca. I promise you."

"Do you know where he was the day Madeline was killed?" I couldn't help asking.

"He and I were together the morning my mother was killed. He forced me to tag along with him to look at some properties."

"Were you with Linda during the afternoon?"

"Yes," he said hesitantly, "but I know Alan didn't kill my mother."

"How do you know?"

"My mother was very good to Alan. He would have had no reason."

"But you don't know where he was during the afternoon?" I couldn't resist. I thought Ian might be giving me another impatient look, but out of the corner of my eye I saw that he was looking at Drew for the answer.

"He said he was here," Drew said. "I was at Linda's house."

"I see," I said, sounding much snottier than I intended. I didn't like Alan, but I needed to be careful about sounding like I thought he killed his aunt.

"Becca, Alan would never kill my mother, I promise you."

I kept my mouth tightly shut as I nodded. I didn't want my future hindsight further compromised.

"Thanks for letting us drop by, Drew. We're very sorry about your mother, and we only want what's best for you and Linda. May your travels be safe. Don't hesitate to call either of us—ever, for anything." Ian extended his hand.

"Thank you." Drew and Ian shook hands, and I hugged him one more time, though his arms weren't as welcoming this time around.

"Feel better?" Ian asked as we made our way to my truck.

"Yeah, sort of. I don't think Drew killed his mother or had any part in the murder, at least."

"Me either."

"But I'm not so sure about Alan."

"Me either, but I'm glad you didn't push it further. Let's leave that one to Sam. I do think you should let him know about what you overheard in the men's bathroom. I think you should also let him know about this visit, too."

"I agree."

Ian's eyebrows rose. "Really? Good. That's good."

I called Sam on the way back to my house. As expected, he wasn't thrilled I hadn't told him earlier about the call I'd overheard. Plus, since I'd snuck into the men's bathroom, he wasn't sure what he could legally use for the investigation, but I also told him how strongly I felt that Drew was innocent. He remained uncommitted, but I thought he appreciated my input.

My head swam after the call. I really wanted to make

some notes, but there wasn't time. The presentation had to become top priority for at least one night.

I allowed my mind to let go of Madeline's murder and hold on to things like wholesale and retail prices. It was a good diversion. By the end of the evening, I hoped I'd make a good impression on the Maytabee's managers. I had one thing up my sleeve that would both surprise and impress Ian.

Hopefully, it would do the same for the Maytabee's managers and owner.

Nineteen

I kept telling myself that there was no need to be nervous, that I'd prepared as well as I could. Besides, I was going to talk about some of my favorite things—my jams and preserves. How hard could it be?

I couldn't remember the last time I stood in front of a group of people and wanted to make a good impression. It must have been in college.

I'd had customers who told me they thought I had an easy job, that maybe I'd taken the easy way out of really having a career. I worked in a farmers' market, how hard could it be?

I never explained how full-time and physically challenging my job was because, secretly, sometimes I thought they were correct. No matter that I was almost always working in one way or another, I loved what I did so much that it never felt like real work.

Today, I wore the same clothes I wore to the fateful dinner—after having them one-day dry-cleaned. I put on a little makeup and forced some earrings into the holes in my ears that frequently were forgotten because of more important things on my to-do lists. I was, in my way, dressed up.

And the moment after I was introduced to the owner of Maytabee's, Clarissa O'Bannon, I spilled some coffee on my blouse. She pretended not to notice, but it would have been difficult to miss.

Clarissa, dressed in casual but comfortable clothes, was all business. She greeted me with a firm handshake followed by a cup of steaming coffee. Her thick black hair was pulled back in a ponytail, Allison's favorite style, but Clarissa's dark features were severe and serious compared to my sister's serious but softer look.

She told me and Ian to make ourselves at home at a table in the corner and that her managers would be there shortly, and then she disappeared to take a call on the cell phone that was clipped to her belt.

I took a deep breath as Ian and I sat down.

"You're nervous?" he asked.

"A little. This is the first time I've done something like this. I'm afraid I'll stumble over my words." I looked at the spot of coffee on my blouse. "Or that no one will be able to pay attention to what I'm saying because of this distraction." The spot was in about the worst place it could be, and would have made junior high boys giggle.

"Run to the bathroom and try to get it out," Ian said.

"I'd just end up making the wet area larger."

"Good point." Ian looked around. "Hey, I have a plan." He stood up and went to a low set of shelves on the other side of the room. He rummaged around a moment and then pulled something from the bottom shelf. He took it to the counter, paid for it, and brought it to me.

"This might work." He handed me a T-shirt.

I unfolded it and laughed. Printed on it was: Maytabee I Just Need Some Coffee. Now Would Be Good.

"That's perfect. Thanks, Ian." I could have run to the bathroom and changed into the shirt, but I slipped it over the one I already had on, instead. It covered the inconvenient spot.

Soon, the other managers filed into the store. They were a young group, probably none of them over twenty-five. Most of them looked like they could use their coffee, so Clarissa passed cups all around and then turned a couch just enough that they could sit on it and look at me.

Maytabee's was comfortable, just like most coffee shops I'd been to. It had plush chairs, a couple of couches, plenty of work space, and good lighting. Maytabee's was different in one important way, though. It was very affordable. It didn't charge the arm and leg for a latte that other, bigger chains did. I remembered reading a story in the *Monson Gazette* about the shop's lower prices and how the owner was causing trouble in the coffee shop community because she kept her prices too low. At the time, I didn't know who the owner was, but I remembered something the paper had quoted her as saying.

"My number one goal at Maytabee's is customer service. I'm a businesswoman, of course, but if I'm ripping off the customers every time they come into my store, I can't see how that's good customer service."

Two men and two women were facing me from the couch and a chair that had been pulled up. Clarissa stood next to the couch, and I stood up as she introduced me. Ian moved away from our table and sat in a chair behind the couch. From there, he could send confident smiles in my direction and no one would notice.

"Becca Robins is a local farmer," Clarissa began. "She grows her own strawberries and pumpkins. With her own fruit and some from other farms, she creates jams and preserves. I've asked her here this morning for you to consider a couple of ways we could incorporate her products into our stores' offerings. I think her jams would make a great topping for the English muffin breakfasts we're introducing next month." The four managers looked at her and nodded. I was impressed at how much she knew about me, but she was stealing my opening lines. There wasn't much more about me, other than my two divorces and my amazing dog, that I could share. "And I'd like for you to consider giving her shelf space to sell jars of her products. Becca, do you have some samples?"

"Yes, I do."

"Great, let's pass around some jars. I'd like for everyone to look at your labels. I think they're brilliant and perfect."

I passed around some jars. My labels weren't fancy. In fact, I thought they were too simple, but I'd used them for so long that I didn't want to confuse my customers by changing them. On a white background, the top of the label said, "Becca's Berries." And in a smaller font and on the next line, it said, "Home-Made Berry Jams and Preserves." Then there was a hand-sketched picture of whichever fruit was inside. I'd done the sketches when I started my business. At the time, I couldn't find clip art I liked, and I didn't want to pay someone else, so I sat down and created them. I liked how they'd turned out, but they were meant to be temporary, something I could use until I knew if the business was going to be successful or not. The last line on the front of the label said, "a product of South Carolina."

"You've already added an ingredient list and nutritional information on the back," one of the female managers said. She was tall, with short brown hair and big green eyes. Her name was Mary, and her skin was perfect.

"Yes, I did that a couple of years ago. At the time it wasn't a requirement, but with so many allergies out there, I thought I should list the ingredients. The nutritional information seemed like the only thing missing, so I added it, too."

"The pictures of the fruit are wonderful!" Kyle said. He had dreadlocks underneath a blue scarf. "They scream 'homemade' and 'country' and . . . well, 'yummy.' "

"Thanks," I said. I didn't want to tell them I'd drawn them. I wasn't an artist, but it hadn't been difficult to draw some pictures of fruit. "How about a taste test?"

Ian and I spread preserves on some English muffins that we'd brought. We also topped some crackers and bagels, and passed the food all around.

"I'm including a new product for you to consider. I haven't begun selling it yet, because . . . well, frankly, I haven't made a lot of it, but I can. It seems like a pretty good fit for a coffee shop. It's chocolate strawberry jam."

The *ooooh*s and *ahhh*s for the chocolate strawberry jam were exactly what I was hoping for, and were the same response I'd received from Ian the night before. I'd been experimenting with chocolate strawberry, and I thought I'd mastered the recipe, but since my winter supply of strawberries had dwindled to almost nothing, I was holding off introducing it until fall. It was unique and would probably sell well, but only time would tell.

"This is so good," Mary said. "It's the most amazing jelly I've ever had. Both the stuff with the chocolate and without it. How do you do it?"

"Thanks," I said, not pointing out that she was currently testing some preserves, not jelly. "I don't know, really. I have a way with strawberries, I think. My farm has the perfect growing conditions for berries that are very sweet. From experience, I know exactly when to pick them, and I've made so many jars that my process is automatic. Plus, I inherited the farm from my aunt and uncle when they died. I like to think that in their way and wherever they are, they're helping." It was honest, if not flashy, and hopefully somewhat humble.

My presentation had turned into more of a taste test than a presentation, and that was fine. Ian and I had worked up something the night before on his laptop, but we thought it would be too boring to talk about my products with a computer attached. I'd planned on just talking to the managers and then offering the samples. As it was, Clarissa had done most of the talking and I'd just passed around the food.

"How much?" Jarad asked. He was young but balding, and wore slacks, a dress shirt, and a tie.

"I've written it all out for you." I passed around the papers that listed the wholesale and recommended retail prices. I used the same font on them that I used on the front of the labels, so the information almost looked like it was handwritten. It wasn't a big deal, but a detail I hoped made the right impression.

The managers read the papers. Jarad and Mary pulled out pocket calculators and punched buttons. Olivia, the manager who hadn't yet spoken, studied the sheet closely, her long blonde hair cascading over her shoulders. She looked up, put her hair behind her ears, and asked, "How much can you handle?"

This was the most important question of all. Ian and I had done our own calculations, and we thought I could handle the five Maytabee's stores if I purchased extra fruit during the summer.

"I've written that up, too." I handed out another set of papers that listed what I thought was a reasonable output from me. I wasn't ready to hire employees, so if I couldn't handle the Maytabee's business on my own, I didn't want either of us to commit to anything. "Please look at the numbers and let me know if you have any questions. This is a reasonable expectation."

Again, the managers peered at the papers. Clarissa's phone buzzed loudly, interrupting her study. She didn't hide her exasperation as she pulled the phone from the clip on her belt.

"Excuse me, Becca," she said.

I nodded as she walked to the other side of the store, where she could have a mostly private conversation.

I answered a few more questions, and the managers answered some of mine. We chatted easily, and they asked for more samples. I happily obliged.

"Okay," Clarissa said as she joined the crowd again. "Anyone have any more questions for Becca? No? Okay, we'll let her get back to her real job and we'll continue our meeting. Get your sales numbers ready while I walk them out."

And just like that, the presentation was over. It had been painless. Clarissa led the way out of the store.

"Ian, thanks for introducing me to Becca's products," she said as she shook his hand. She turned to me. "I'm sure we'll do business together in one form or another. Give me some time to talk to the managers and look at the numbers. I'll get back to you no later than next week."

"I appreciate your time. You've created a great business," I said, though I was afraid it sounded like I was sucking up. I wasn't.

"Well, it's a passion, but I don't think I need to explain passions to you. I apologize for the phone interruption. I've been dealing with some silly bank issues."

"Really? Me, too," I lied. Chances were, considering the small community, she was talking about Madeline's bank. "I bank at Central, and something weird must be happening over there, because they've sent me some questionable paperwork lately." They hadn't, of course. I was still lying, but I couldn't resist seeing if there was a bigger pattern emerging at Central Savings and Loan.

"Well, I suppose this is a terrible thing to say, but I'm pleased to hear it isn't just me. I bank at Central, too, and . . ." She didn't want to share what the issue was, and I didn't blame her. She didn't want to spread her own bad rumors. "Anyway, I hope you're getting yours straightened out. We're almost there, I think, but I have to answer whenever they call, or the phone tag can go on forever."

"I know. Gosh, I can't think of the name of the person I'm working with." I looked at Ian, who was playing along well.

"I'm working with a Sarah Nelson, but she just told me that someone else would be calling. They all seem to want to pass off the work. Well, sorry about that. I shouldn't complain if they're fixing it," Clarissa said.

Sarah Nelson. The one person who wouldn't talk to me about anything.

"Well, thanks again, Becca, and good job covering the coffee spot," Clarissa continued. She turned and went back into her store.

"Great job, Becca," Ian said. "You're a natural."

"Thanks," I replied absently. I was pleased with the presentation, but my mind was already rummaging through the new information about the bank. What was going on there that was causing so much false information to be disseminated? There must be legal issues involved, but I didn't have any idea what they might possibly be.

"Do you know who Bud Morris is working with at the bank?" I asked.

"Someone named Addison Something . . ."

"You have time for a trip to Central?" I said to Ian.

"Why did I know you were going to say that?"

Twenty

Sarah Nelson wasn't anywhere to be seen. Either she wasn't working or she was on a break. Unfortunately, no one else could offer much help.

Our first stop was the teller line. Ian remembered that Bud's bank contact was named Addison Stinson, but two youngish male tellers said they were new to the bank and they had no idea who that was.

And there seemed to be no manager on duty. The tellers told us all the managers had been called to a meeting out of the building. They admitted it was strange, but considering the bank president had recently been murdered, everything at the bank had seemed strange lately.

We sat in the lobby for ten minutes, hoping someone, even Sarah Nelson, might show up to give us more substantial answers. Every second seemed too precious to wait, though, so I came up with another plan.

"Come on." I got up and led the way outside. I said, "Ian, I'd love to meet Bud Morris."

"Right now?"

"Yes."

"Why?"

"Something tells me that Bud's issue is tied to Clarissa's. Something really odd is going on. You said he received a foreclosure letter from Central. Did you see it?" I was also adding Jeanine's issue into the mix, but I continued to keep my promise not to tell, which was becoming very tedious. I almost wished Allison hadn't shared.

"Yes, I did. It was just a letter notifying him that he was going to be foreclosed on within the month if he didn't pay some seemingly random amount. But . . . Becca, that's a pretty big leap—tying Bud's and Clarissa's issues together. Bud is a residential property owner, and Clarissa is a business owner. Whatever their issues are, real or not, they're worlds apart."

"Probably, but it's all very coincidental, don't you think?"

"Yes. Coincidental, but that's probably all."

"Maybe. But what would it hurt? Do you think he'd show me the letter?"

Ian squinted. "You feel pretty strongly about this, don't you?"

"Yes."

"I suppose you should meet Bud anyway. Let's go." Ian maneuvered the truck back to the world of my childhood, but this time I was so focused on getting to the shack that I didn't even glance at my old house as we passed it.

Bud Morris was exactly as Ian had described him: old and unable to move well.

His shack was as clean as could be expected under the circumstances. It consisted of two rooms: the main room and the bathroom. He didn't have a kitchen, but there was one burner on a counter next to a small refrigerator. The rest of the furnishings consisted of a small table, three chairs, and a bed. He didn't have any family left. In fact, he didn't have much of anything at all. His circumstances broke my heart, but he seemed content and happy.

"Ian, how wonderful to see you," he said as he opened the front door. He was a smallish man, his bent-over stance making him seem even smaller than he really was. He had a few strands of gray hair left on his head, and his eyes were as bright a blue as I'd seen on anyone, young or old. He used a cane, but every movement seemed a challenge. "Did we have an appointment today?"

"No, this is a surprise visit," Ian said.

"Well, come in, come in. And who's your friend?"

Ian introduced me as we occupied the chairs. The space was crowded but not unpleasantly so. It wasn't really clean, but it wasn't really dirty. Ian had explained to me that Bud's wife had died twenty-some years ago. When his unmarried son died ten years later in a tragic car accident, Bud had left his home in Monson and moved out to the shack. He'd owned the land for decades but hadn't ever tried to grow anything on it. It had always been his plan to sell it when he needed the money. His career as a farm equipment salesperson had been successful enough that he'd never needed anything extra. According to Ian, Bud didn't look at his living circumstances as dire. When he lost his family, he moved away from other people because he wanted to. According to Bud, his retirement income had been enough. Until recently.

Though he owned the land outright, yearly property taxes were still due, and he was finally beginning to run out of money. He wanted to sell the land to Ian, but shortly after they began talking, Bud received the foreclosure notice.

"Can I get the two of you some tea?" he asked. He turned over a notebook that had curled edges and small torn pieces in the spiral binding.

"No, thanks, Bud. I drove Becca by here the other night, but I wanted her to see what it looks like in the daytime. Plus, I wanted her to meet you."

"He's something, isn't he?" Bud mused as his bushy eyebrows rose. "He's brilliant. Lavender! Makes sense, and I think he'll do well when we can get those bas . . . oh, sorry, those bank people . . . to stop their shenanigans."

"I think it's a good plan," I said. "Sorry about the bank, though. I bet it'll get worked out."

"Yes, I think so. I had my cab driver stop by there Saturday morning." Bud looked at Ian, who nodded that he was listening.

"They talked to you then?" Ian asked.

Saturday had been the day after Madeline's murder. The bank was normally open for a couple of hours Saturday morning, so they must have stuck to their schedule.

"Yes, sir. They said to give them just a little longer to figure things out. The gentleman I met with said there might be some sort of mistake. Some—oh, what was the word he used?—some sort of *glitch* in the system."

"Did you meet with Addison?" Ian asked.

"Nope, he wasn't in when I got there. Let's see . . . who did I talk to? Darn it, I can't remember. Some new fella, but . . . oh, give me a minute, maybe I'll remember it. He was in a tizzy, I'll tell you. He seemed nervous and upset, but calmed down enough to look at my letter. He took it from me and told me not to worry for the time being. I think we're going to be fine, Ian."

My stomach fell. "Did you keep a copy of the letter, Bud?"

"No ma'am, didn't think I needed that nasty thing hanging around."

The person at the bank probably didn't think so either. I would have put money on Bud's letter disappearing into thin air. Yes, there was most definitely something going on at the bank.

I didn't want to point out that Bud might have given away evidence, so I said, "It might not have been valid—that's what he said?"

Bud shook his head. "The gentleman wouldn't commit to anything, but it'll be fine, I know. I can prove I own the land. I'd just like to move things along."

I hoped Sam was looking at the bank employees along with its customers. Something fishy was going on there. A *glitch* in the system? False foreclosure notices were lots bigger than glitches. The word "fraud" came to my mind, and though I knew little about the details of the law, I knew that fraud, when combined with banking, was a big deal.

"I do have a bit of good news," Bud said. "I've found exactly where I want to live if we get this deal done. There's an old person's—well, that's what I call it—apartment complex right in Monson. I can have my own apartment with two bedrooms, of which I'll only need one, but two is as small as they come: a living room, a bathroom, and a kitchen. Part of the deal is that they take care of the whole shebang. They come in and clean, help with cooking if I need it. I'm not a fancy eater or anything, so I won't need that. But they help with medications if I ever need them." He looked at me. "I haven't taken so much as an aspirin in over thirty years. What do you think of that?"

I smiled. "I think you must be very healthy, and I wish I could say the same for myself." I'd been known to pop an aspirin or two after a long day in my fields. The older I got, the more frequently it happened.

"Weeeell, I guess I'm healthy except for not being able to straighten up, but it only hurts when I try." Bud smiled, more with his eyes than his dentures.

"You know what they say don't you?" I asked.

"Then don't stand up straight!" Bud laughed.

We chatted a little longer before Bud seemed to get tired. He gave us his blessing to walk over his land whenever we wanted. He promised he'd neither call the police nor shoot at us for trespassing.

"Darn," I said after Ian and I left the shack and ventured up a small slope of the rocky land. "I can't believe the bank took back the letter."

"Yeah. I wish I'd insisted that he make a copy of it, but I had no idea he'd go in on Saturday. I do think you're right, Becca, there's something going on at that bank, and I wouldn't be surprised if figuring it out will lead to Madeline's killer."

"I'll call Sam this afternoon and tell him about Bud. But what else about him? Does he need groceries or something? Does he need rides, or does he use cabs all the time?" I asked.

"I've offered, but he won't take me up on it. A cab stops by three mornings a week and takes him into town.

He buys groceries and runs other errands. I think he was offended when I offered to help, so I haven't brought it up again."

"What else does he do with his time?" I looked back at his old shack. I didn't want to feel sorry for him, because he didn't want people's pity, that was clear. But I couldn't help it.

"He writes poetry."

"What?"

"Well, that's what he told me. That notebook he turned over when we went in—he says he spends most of his free time writing poetry."

"Is it any good?"

"I don't know. He wouldn't let me read it."

"He doesn't seem lonely."

Ian shrugged. "I hope not. He's been through a lot. He strikes me as someone who likes his alone time. Life just doesn't always turn out the way we plan."

"That's for sure."

We made it to the top slope of the property. There was a patch of trees bordering Bud's land, but the land itself was true to my earlier impression of being—what had Ian called it—gritty? It also seemed more fertile than I'd originally thought. I didn't understand my connection with such things—more instinct, I guessed. But there was something about the feel and smell of the earth that spoke to me. Again, it was probably a feeling that was courtesy of having hippie parents, but I couldn't deny that it existed, and that my sense of these sorts of things was usually on target.

It was another perfect South Carolina spring day. The sun was warm, but the air was cool enough that the sun didn't feel too hot. There wasn't much humidity, and I wished we'd packed a picnic lunch.

"What do you think? Really, Becca, I want to know what you think about all this." Ian gestured at the land.

"I think it sounds like lots of hard work. I think it's a beautiful place. And I think you'll be successful."

"No reservations?"

"Not really. You can afford it?"

"Yes, more easily by the day. My business is growing steadily."

"Then I hope you and Bud can do business. Besides, I think he likes the apartment idea."

Ian laughed. "Me, too."

We walked around the rest of the property, dug our fingers into the soil, tentatively planned where Ian would put his warehouse, and discussed layouts for the lavender plants. It was the most relaxing couple of hours I'd had since the moment before Linda had asked me to be her Number One. It was about the land, the soil, the air, and working to create something that not only would, hopefully, give Ian a great living, but also would be something beautiful.

That was the best part, the real payoff; the cycle of life, the beauty of that cycle, through the earth. I loved the time we spent on the property, and by the time we drove away, I felt rejuvenated. Enjoying the brief respite, I hadn't intended to put my thoughts back to who killed Madeline Forsyth so quickly, but something occurred to me as we drove again down the old road in front of my childhood home.

And then it passed right through my mind, too quickly to be stopped.

"Ian, stop the truck," I said urgently.

"'K." He pulled to the side of the road and followed my glance. "What's up?"

"I thought . . . I'm not sure. It was something from my childhood that I think may have had something to do with Madeline's murder."

"Really? What's that?"

I thought a minute more, then decided I was probably searching for something that wasn't there. I so desperately wanted Madeline's killer found that I was finding answers where there couldn't possibly be any.

"I don't know. Sorry about that. We can go."

I craned my neck to look at the house as we drove away, but whatever spark might have been there a few minutes before was now completely gone.

Twenty-one

I woke early the next morning and decided to call off the rehearsal. I didn't see any way Madeline's murder was going to be solved before tomorrow. I was going to give it another half hour before I called everyone. I hoped Mamma Maria hadn't already made the peach delight.

But then Allison called. "Why aren't you here?"

I looked at the clock beside my bed and confirmed that it was still way before the crack of dawn.

"What do you mean?"

"Well, we're all still hoping that the wedding will happen. We're rehearsing."

"Who's rehearsing? And why so early?"

"The only ones not here are you, Linda, Drew, and Alan. Your surprise wedding has us all on the edges of our seats, and we thought we should have a rehearsal breakfast just to be safe."

"Before breakfast and without the wedding party?"

Allison paused. "If that's what it takes."

I hesitated as my gears started to mesh. "Okay, Hobbit and I will be right there."

I'd all but given up on the wedding, since it didn't seem anyone was much closer to finding the killer. I'd talked to Sam the day before, and told him about Bud Morris and Clarissa O'Bannon. He told me he'd look into it. He also told me that the police had investigated the bank employees, but hadn't yet been able to find anything substantial.

But leave it to Bailey's vendors to want to make sure everything was just right, especially for one of their own, another vendor and friend.

I got dressed in my cleanest overall shorts and loaded Hobbit into the truck. She was thrilled to be getting some extra attention, even if it did take away from her sleeping time.

When I got to Bailey's, I made my way to the area Allison had said would be perfect for the wedding. And she had been right. As I walked into the large tent, she was rearranging chairs and had somehow folded the canvas walls so that the entire back wall, the wall that the guests would be facing, was open to the rolling South Carolina countryside; a countryside that was just beginning to see the light of day.

"Allison, this is perfect," I said as I jumped in and joined in her arranging efforts.

"I thought it might work." Not one strand of hair was loose from her ponytail, and there wasn't a single bag under her eyes. She had the energy of ten toddlers. "You just missed everyone else. They ran to their stalls to make sure they were ready for the day, but said they'd be back to show you what they'd come up with."

I shouldn't have wasted one moment worrying about my duties as Linda's Number One. Once everyone heard about the wedding, they took on their jobs with vigor. Actually, I was suddenly concerned that I should have reined them in. The wedding was far from a sure thing.

"Great. Thanks. I hope we get to have it," I said, hoping I didn't sound as doubtful as I felt.

Allison stopped arranging. "We're prepared, and it didn't take much to get there. We discussed it and decided that we didn't want to be caught off guard, so with each of us doing our part, there really wasn't much to it."

"Okay."

As we continued to set up the white plastic chairs, I thought I'd see if our twin psychic connection was in working condition.

"Al, think about our childhood a minute."

"Okay. Sure."

"Ian and I drove by our old house yesterday, the one on Rural Route 6, and something seemed to flash at me from our childhood. I couldn't pinpoint it, but it seemed to have something to do with Madeline Forsyth. Did Mom and Dad know her when we were kids?"

"Gosh, I have no idea. I don't remember knowing her at all. I'd heard of her, but until last Friday, when you told me that she was Drew's mother, I had no idea."

"*Hmm*."

"What do you think you remembered?"

"I don't know. I wish I did. It was a flash—literally a flash of something in my mind's eye, but I lost it as quickly as it came."

"Quit trying so hard to think about it. It'll probably come back to you on its own. Have something handy so you can write down your impressions. If you remember something substantial, I bet I could expand on it."

It wasn't easy to let go of the inkling that I was almost on to something, but there was plenty to keep me busy.

Just as Allison and I finished placing the chairs, Abner Justen joined us. When I'd first started my farmers' market business, he'd been the one to teach me the finer points of creating and growing a successful market stall. He'd been like a father to me for a long time, but that didn't change the facts that he was old and cranky and was bound to do things his way. I was shocked when he showed up with a handful of pictures and wanted input.

"Becca, here are some sample bouquets I created. Look at them and tell me which ones you and Linda might want." He handed me the pictures and rubbed a finger under his nose.

There were an all-white bouquet, a multicolored bouquet, some small bouquets, and some large bouquets, all of them done with the wildflowers that Abner grew in a science fiction–like greenhouse on his property. They were all gorgeous.

"Thanks, Abner." Picking Linda's bouquet felt too personal but, like everyone else, I thought it would be better to be safe than sorry. I decided she'd like something with lots of color, so I picked a medium-sized bouquet of soft pastel colors. "This one looks perfect."

"Very good. I'll decorate in here, too, if we have the wedding." Abner smiled. I'd never seen him so happy about doing something.

"That's a great idea," I said as he turned and walked around to study the rest of the tent space.

"You know, weddings and babies bring out the best in everyone," Allison commented as she noticed Abner's excitement. "Come help me with this." She was maneuvering the white arbor that Linda's pastor would stand under as he joined the happy couple in marriage. "I'm trying to find just the right spot."

"You need to move it about two feet to your right," Abner said before he left the tent.

"He was right," Allison admitted after we moved the arbor. "It really balances the entire space."

"Has Sam given you any indication that the murder will be solved in the next twenty-four hours or so?" Allison asked.

"No. Of course, he'd like it solved right this minute, but I don't think he has one lead stronger than any others."

"As far as you know, Drew is definitely leaving for duty?"

"Yes. No question. Ian and I talked to him about it, and he feels it's his duty, and his alone."

"I guess I understand that, but . . ."

"I know."

"Yeah."

"Have you thought of telling Sam about Jeanine's letter?" I asked quietly after making sure no one else was around.

"I don't know, Becca. I've had a hard time with that one. I think I probably should. I don't think she's the killer, and I don't think she's in danger. I think she's just being Jeanine—paranoid about something—and I want to respect her privacy. But I do wish she'd let someone know she was leaving."

"That would've been helpful. I've come across a couple of other seemingly related incidents involving the bank. I told Sam about them. It might help if you tell him about Jeanine."

"Really? What else have you heard?"

I told her about Bud and Clarissa. She was impressed that I'd made a presentation to Maytabee's, and convinced she should talk to Sam. In fact, she seemed relieved to have a good reason to break Jeanine's confidence.

Soon, Barry, of Barry Good Corn, joined Allison and me, wrangling his large body to the best of his ability. He wore overalls with a clean T-shirt underneath. He'd brushed his hair and had shaved with care. His outfit was almost as formal as Barry ever dressed. Linda had asked him to give her away.

"Becca, I promise I'll wear something nicer if we have the wedding." He patted his hair to make sure it was in place.

I was touched. "You look great," I said. "Linda will be pleased no matter what you wear."

"Well . . . shoot." Barry's cheeks reddened. I was often surprised at the tender heart he carried beneath his large exterior.

"Have a seat, Barry," Allison said. "We'll go through everything once the pastor gets here."

"You even invited him?" I asked.

"Yes. We want to make sure everything goes well." Allison looked at me like I was crazy for thinking otherwise.

"Got it," I said a second later. I should have known. Allison didn't improvise anything.

All the market vendors were invited to the wedding, but for the rehearsal Abner, Carl Monroe, his girlfriend, Mamma Maria, Don, and Ian served as the guests. I was surveying the sparse group when Reverend O'Reilly, I presumed, joined us.

He wore a simple button-down shirt and khaki slacks. He had a ready smile, and his hair was so red and unruly that I thought it might ignite at any second.

"And where's the lovely couple?" he asked after I introduced the rest of us.

"They're not here," I replied.

"Well, not to worry. I can wait a little while."

"They won't be at the rehearsal."

"Oh, dear, are they having issues?"

"No, this is the rehearsal for a surprise wedding."

Reverend O'Reilly blinked. "That's . . . interesting. I've never presided over a surprise wedding. Are you sure it will be a happy surprise?"

"Yes, positive. That is, if it happens at all." In summary and without mentioning the murder, I explained that there were some extenuating circumstances, but the ultimate goal of the couple was indeed to be married even though their schedules had become an issue.

Reverend O'Reilly, being the ultimate good sport and probably suspecting there was more to the story but not needing to pry for answers, agreed to pretend along with the rest of us.

"We need a bride, a groom, and a best man," I said as I surveyed the smallish group of onlookers. "Carl and

Mamma, will you be the bride and groom, and Ian, how about taking over the role of best man?"

Their romance going well, Carl and Mamma agreed easily, and Ian sent me a sly smile as he stood and took his place next to the arbor. Carl stood next to him and did his best to look both excited and scared to death, like any groom.

The reports I'd heard about Herb's abilities with the violin had not been overstated. He was fabulous, and I took a slow saunter, as maid of honor, down the aisle just so everyone could enjoy the music longer. It was difficult not to watch Ian watching me. Neither of us would have fit the fairy-tale description of a bride and groom, but his glance might have been the most romantic thing I'd ever seen. It was difficult to keep my eyes on his without blushing—I adored him as much as I thought he adored me, but I wasn't sure we needed to be sharing that with the rest of the world just yet. Fortunately, Allison interrupted and saved us from a further awkward public display of affection.

"Bec, you're supposed to walk slowly like that, but with more even steps. And don't jaunt so much. Try it again," Allison suggested.

I went back to the starting place and waited until Allison cued me to begin. Herb was well into a song before she sent me off.

"Okay, Herb, once Becca gets to the end of the aisle, stop a moment and then begin the Wedding March. Mamma, be ready."

Though Mamma was tall, thin, busty, blonde, and beautiful, she didn't necessarily fit the description of a fairy-tale bride. She had an over-the-top-ness about her, and I doubted there was a wedding dress in existence that was cut as low or showed as much cleavage as the shirt she was wearing. She was also one of the sweetest people I knew. The glance she shared with Carl was just as personal as the one between me and Ian. Ian must have noticed, too, because he raised his eyebrows conspiratorially at me. I just smiled.

"Ian and Becca, both of you take one step backward," Allison ordered as Mamma joined us at the arbor. "Good. Okay, now the vows, I suppose."

Reverend O'Reilly went through a quick version of the vows. Carl and Mamma were perfect in their roles, and something told me we'd be hearing about another wedding soon. I told myself not to be overly friendly with Mamma, just in case she found herself in search of a Number One.

All in all, though we did it without the main participants, the rehearsal was a resounding success, in my opinion. And to top it off, Mamma had brought the peach delight.

The coffee and yummy food made a perfect end to the short rehearsal. Reverend O'Reilly stayed and joined the breakfast.

As I was conferring with Stella on just exactly how much time she would need to frost the cake she'd already baked, Sam walked into the tent, his expression serious and concerned.

"Sam, what's up?" Allison asked as she greeted him. I tried to excuse myself from the conversation with Stella so I could join them, but Sam took Allison's arm and led her out of the tent.

Allison came back shortly. She acted like there was

nothing wrong, but I knew something wasn't quite right. She stood to the side of the group and casually kept glancing at her phone.

"What's up?" I asked as I sidled next to her.

She kept her head down, pretended to look at her phone, and said quietly, "Sam found Jeanine. *Shhh.* We'll talk about it later."

Later? I wanted to exclaim. This was not something that I wanted to put off. I immediately had a million questions, but there were too many people around, and Allison soon disappeared to attend to other market business. One of Ian's customers was talking to him, so he wasn't available for commiseration.

It was a miracle I didn't abandon my duties as Number One and chase either my sister or Sam Brion to find out more. Instead, I made small talk with my other friends and then patiently helped clean up before I searched for Allison.

Of course, I couldn't find her. *Why aren't people where I need them to be?*

I escaped to my truck and called Sam.

Twenty-two

"Brion," he answered on the first ring. "Hey, Becca, I had a feeling you'd be calling."

"You found Jeanine?" I asked.

"Yes. She's home and she's fine."

"Where was she?"

"Let's just say I don't think she had anything to do with Madeline's murder."

"Why?"

"A credit card record and some surveillance tapes. I might not know exactly where she was the whole time she was gone, but at the time of Madeline's murder she was in Charleston, filling her van with gas. I just confirmed it this morning. I drove by her farm to check on the chickens and that damn . . . that cat, and found she was home."

"And she wouldn't tell you what she'd been up to?"

"Not completely, no, and legally I have no right to pry,

since she couldn't have committed the murder. Taking a trip to Charleston or taking some time off isn't a crime."

"But . . ." I protested. There was still something strange about her disappearance. Had Allison told him about the letter yet? I didn't know, and I couldn't find my sister, so I didn't bring it up. "I still wonder, don't you, Sam?"

"Sure, but again, *I* have no legal authority to question her further."

Bing! I got what he was saying, and I was caught between glee and disbelief. He wanted me to talk to Jeanine—as a friend and Bailey's co-vendor. Sam had told me that he thought I had good instincts. He trusted me in ways law enforcement officers probably shouldn't trust civilians. I would have hugged him if I could've reached through the phone.

I cleared my throat. "Do you mind if I give it a try?"

"I don't see why having a friend stop by to inquire about her well-being would hurt anything."

"On my way."

"Call me if you learn anything."

I hung up and steered my truck to Jeanine's house. I had no idea what she could tell me that would help solve the murder of Madeline Forsyth, but talking to Jeanine was a piece of the puzzle that I couldn't let go of. Even though she hadn't killed Madeline, had she perhaps confronted her regarding the foreclosure letter? Again, a letter I wasn't supposed to know anything about. Keeping secrets was rough.

Solving Madeline's murder before tomorrow was looking less and less realistic, but what if Jeanine knew something? I'd get whatever I could from her.

I parked in front of her small house and made my way to the front door. As I knocked, I pasted a friendly smile on my face. We'd always gotten along, but Jeanine would still find my visit far from ordinary.

"Becca?" Jeanine said as she opened the door. "Hi." She stepped onto the small front porch and looked around. "What are you doing here?"

"I . . . well, I was worried about you. You disappeared, and I thought I'd just come see if you were doing okay." So much for easing into anything.

"I was only gone for a couple days." Jeanine folded her arms in front of her chest. She continued to look around as if we were being watched.

"Barry didn't know you were leaving, and he said that the two of you always stay in touch." As I often noted to myself, I wasn't good at subtle.

She looked up at me. It was rare that anyone other than Hobbit had to look up to address me. Jeanine was so little that in the rare moments I stood close to her, I had a surge of self-assured bigness. But this time it was different. She was suspicious of my motives because she was suspicious of everyone's motives, and I was sounding accusatory instead of friendly. I smiled again, but it felt forced and I thought I might be about to lose her.

"I talked to Barry a few minutes ago. I apologized to him. He would have wanted to come with . . . Becca, what do you really want?"

I sighed. "Can I come in?"

She thought about it a few seconds. Her suspiciousness made me feel guilty.

"Sure, come on in," she finally said.

She led the way and directed me to the couch. I sat,

nursing a silent hope that Sam would never tell her about our excursion. We had done it out of concern for her safety, but she would never forgive such an intrusion, that much I knew.

She sat down in the rocking chair but didn't start rocking.

"What's up, Becca?"

"Jeanine, have you heard about Madeline Forsyth?" I began, because I didn't know where else to begin.

"Yes, I have. I'm not surprised. She was an awful lady. Someone was bound to kill her," she said bluntly. I looked for some sign of paranoia in her statement, but nothing showed. On the way from the porch to the rocking chair, her demeanor had changed. She suddenly seemed calm and comfortable. I wondered if the only place she felt totally safe and unobserved was in her house. I suddenly realized how much pain her paranoia caused her, and I was sorry that I hadn't been more sensitive.

"Why did you dislike her so much? How well did you know her?" I asked.

"I knew her better than I ever wanted to, I can tell you that much."

"Oh?"

"Yes, well, I knew *of* her, at first. And I bank—used to bank—at Central Savings and Loan until a few days ago. I'd see her there, through the glass wall, talking on the phone, or with someone who looked scared of her. I wasn't scared of her, and that's probably why she did what she did."

I was sure that Jeanine was petrified of Madeline Forsyth, but I didn't say as much.

"What did she do?" I asked.

"She sent me a letter of foreclosure on my farm. Well, it wasn't an official notice or anything. It was just a letter—a threat."

"Oh, I'm sorry, Jeanine." I tried to act surprised, not relieved. Finally, I could "know" about the damn letter.

"Like I said, it wasn't real," she said. She leaned toward me. "It was 'a mistake,' according to the man I met with at the bank. Said there was some sort of glitch in their system, and that he'd make sure it was taken care of. I didn't believe him, though. I think it was something personal."

I had to remember that Jeanine would think that way. She would always lean toward a conspiracy theory.

"*Hmm*, that's both bizarre and interesting," I said.

"I know. And I did something about it, let me tell you."

"What did you do?"

"That's why I left town. I went to Charleston, found a new bank to put my money in, and I reported Central Savings and Loan."

"You reported them? To who?"

"My new bank man." She stood and walked to her desk. She lifted a business card off the top of one of the stacks I'd previously looked through. "His name is Frederick Austin. He said he'd take care of reporting Central Savings and Loan to the proper authorities."

"I see." I didn't know what would happen because of Jeanine's report, but it wouldn't be good for Central Savings and Loan. "What day did you do all this?"

"I got my money Friday afternoon and then drove to Charleston. I had to wait until yesterday, Monday, to open my new accounts."

I could picture Jeanine hiding in a hotel with her

money. Though it was most likely in bank check form, she probably spent the time afraid that someone would steal it from her. She didn't answer her cell phone because she didn't want anyone to know what she was doing, including Barry. If they knew, they might take her money from her.

Most people would have taken their foreclosure letter to the bank and asked for an explanation. Some might have moved their money in a fit of anger, but very few would have been so secretive about it.

"You have to watch everyone all the time, Becca. Really, it makes me tired, but whenever I let down my guard, I find someone is out to take something away from me."

"I'm sorry you had to deal with something like that," I said. I was. I was also sorry for Bud Morris and Clarissa O'Bannon. Something was terribly wrong at Central Savings and Loan.

The black cat I'd become too acquainted with sauntered into the room from the kitchen. It looked at me, and I was certain a flash of fear widened its green eyes.

I stared at the cat, hoping it sensed my animosity toward it.

"Hey, Buster, come here, boy," Jeanine coaxed.

The cat lifted its nose in my direction and pranced to Jeanine. He jumped up on her lap and stared at me with the confidence of a creature who knew Jeanine would protect him from evildoers such as the likes of me.

"How do you manage to have both a cat and so many chickens?" I asked.

"I have to have a cat. Keeps the rodents away from the chickens. And Buster here is scared enough of the chickens that he never bothers them. In fact, they've put him at the bottom of their pecking order. He's mostly inside with me unless he's after a mouse or something."

Or just wants to cause a state of panic among two police officers and a jam and preserve maker.

"Well, Buster sure looks like a fine cat," I said. Jeanine didn't catch the sarcasm, but I thought Buster did, which made me happy.

"He's my buddy. Well, he and the chickens are my buddies," Jeanine said as she scratched behind his ear.

I sighed silently. "I'm glad you're home safe and sound, Jeanine."

"Thanks, Becca. Really, I'm sorry I worried everyone. It wasn't my intention."

"Everyone understands," I said. "Hey, can I ask you one more question?"

"Sure." Jeanine stood, holding on to Buster.

"Did Madeline call you on the day she was killed?"

"Yes, actually she did," she replied cautiously. "It was soon after she was at Bailey's. She was finally returning my messages. She wanted me to come to the bank, and she'd get everything straightened out. I went, but she wasn't there—that was the final straw. That's when I decided to take my money to Charleston."

"Was Madeline kind to you during the call?"

"She was fine. Not kind, but not rude, I would have to say."

"I'm sorry I keep asking questions, but do you remember the name of the man at Central who helped you?" I was hoping to get Bud Morris in to see him.

"Let me think. Yes, his name was Alan something. Alan Cummings."

I was so stunned at the news that I went silent and

my jaw dropped. *Alan worked at Central Savings and Loan?* I didn't think anyone knew this. Sam hadn't said anything, and Drew hadn't mentioned it when we talked about what Alan did for a living.

"Becca, you okay?" Jeanine finally asked.

"Uh, yes. Fine. Thanks for your time," I said. I stood and made my way out of the house.

I would never remember the drive back downtown, but I would always remember the thoughts that jumbled through my mind. Alan, who was supposedly "between things" at the moment; Alan, who was creepy when he stared at Linda, when he showed up at my house and then at Jeanine's house; Alan, who just plain rubbed me the wrong way—Alan worked at Madeline's bank? What was he up to, and why didn't he admit to working there?

Suddenly, amid my turning and questioning thoughts, I was pulling into the Central Savings and Loan parking lot.

I'd call Sam soon enough, but not before I got a few more answers.

Twenty-three

I sat in the parking lot for a moment and stared at Central Savings and Loan. The building was round and brown and unattractive, but easy to get in and out of because of entrances and exits on the intersecting streets. There were a few other cars in the small lot, but I didn't recognize any of them, nor did I recognize anyone entering or exiting the bank. It was rare to have a moment of anonymity in a town as small as Monson, but I hoped to get into the bank, talk to Alan, and then leave without anyone I knew seeing me. My bright orange truck wouldn't help in that mission, but I still hoped. I didn't want to have to explain myself to Sam, Ian, Allison, or anyone else. I hadn't called anyone. I would, but I wanted some answers of my own before I handed this new discovery over to the police. Alan had bugged me more than he'd bugged anyone else. I was determined to find some good reasons before I tried to again convince someone that something was off with him.

The complete opposite of yesterday, the bank was full of employees. I saw Alan immediately after I went through the main doors. He was sitting at a desk next to Madeline's glass-walled office, talking on the phone, and his expression was serious. There were three customers in the teller line. I felt safe; I could talk to Alan with a good-sized audience whose members might not know me. If he had any dangerous intentions for me, they'd be thwarted inside the bank walls.

I walked toward him. As he looked up, he did a double take, folded a piece of paper he was looking at, put it in the top drawer of the desk, and then smiled. He waved at me and seemed to tell the person he was talking to on the phone that he'd call them later.

"Becca, hello. Please have a seat." He stood. "Can I get you something? Coffee? Water?"

"No, thanks." I sat across from him, noting that there was nothing but a phone on his desk. "I didn't know you worked here," I said.

"Oh, I don't. Not really. I'm just . . . well, I suppose I'm just helping out a bit."

"Really? How are you helping out a bank? Specifically, the bank that was run by your aunt, who was murdered Friday?"

Alan sighed, then sat back in the chair. He looked both angry and intrigued. I'd caught him—in what, I wasn't sure. Had he killed Madeline? Sitting at an empty desk in the middle of the bank she used to be president of was not evidence of murder. But he was up to something, up to no good, I knew that much.

"Come on." He stood and waved me to go with him.

"Where?"

"Conference room. We need privacy." The conference room was next to Madeline's office's glass walls, but it had solid walls and a solid door. We would be hidden, and my sense of security fizzled. It wasn't smart to close myself in such a room with him, I knew. But I was just curious enough to swallow my discomfort.

I stood, then hesitated. I fake-sneezed loudly and made sure that a woman with short, jet-black hair who was working on the other side of the bank noticed me. I smiled, excused myself, and then followed Alan. The woman smiled and mouthed "Bless you" in my direction. At least someone saw me enter the room with Alan. If I didn't make it out of my own accord, at least the woman would know who to talk to first.

"Have a seat," Alan said after he closed the door.

The conference room was done in shades of gray. Even the long oval table had a gray top. I sat in the chair closest to the door, and Alan sat next to me, so close that I moved my chair slightly.

"Why do we need privacy, Alan?"

"Becca, someone was trying to ruin my Aunt Madeline."

"Someone killed her. I'd say that's as ruined as someone can get."

"Of course," he said, "but there was more to it. Something was going on before she was killed, and I'm trying to figure out who was after her."

"What was going on?" He had my attention, and I stopped gripping the arms of the chair so tightly. He wasn't acting murderous.

"I suppose it's much more complicated than I'm going to make it sound, but simply, someone got hold of some of the bank's letterhead and was sending out fraudulent letters."

"Really?" I sounded surprised. "How would that destroy her? It seems she could have explained it as a mistake, as someone else getting hold of the letterhead. She didn't do it, did she?"

"No." Alan paused and ran his hand through his hair. "She could have explained it, and she was going to do just that. The day she was killed, she told me she was going to have to call the SEC the next day, but nonetheless, Becca, you have to understand that Madeline's reputation was integral to her business. At first, she thought she could handle the situation herself, but it got too big very quickly, and she waited too long to make an official report. Yes, she was going to do that, but since she'd waited so long, she knew she'd probably lose her job."

For a long moment I thought about what he was saying. If I was jumping to the correct conclusion, it sounded as if Madeline had made a huge mistake. She knew something fraudulent was happening at her bank, and her ego made her slow to report it to the proper authorities. She was such a professional that I questioned whether or not that behavior fit with what I knew about her. It did, in that her ego was involved. She'd ruled the roost for a long time. She would never have wanted to admit failure, and her ego was big enough to talk her out of doing the right thing if it meant she'd look the fool.

"Not to speak ill of the dead, Alan, but her reputation was that she was brutal and mean and horrible. There wasn't much there to ruin."

"Yes, she knew that, and don't get me wrong—that reputation was well earned, but she never foreclosed on someone who didn't . . . well, *deserve* is a juvenile word for such a thing. If someone didn't pay their mortgage payments, she foreclosed on them, yes. But I'm also speaking about her reputation in the banking industry. She was hugely successful—this little bank in Monson, South Carolina, was . . . is a big moneymaker, and in banking that's what it's all about. The fact that the letterhead was taken was beyond a rookie mistake."

"Do the police know this?"

"Not from me, no. I've been here since a few days before Madeline was killed. She called me to ask for help. She knew I wasn't currently employed, and she wanted to give me something temporary. I'm a numbers person, Becca. Madeline thought that might help. When the police—Officer Brion—interviewed me, I didn't tell him I was working here because I'm not, not really. I'm not on the payroll. I wanted to help him, but I was still concerned about keeping the bank issues hidden. I didn't want Madeline's reputation to worsen after her death."

I didn't know if he was telling the truth. I didn't know if he really had arrived here a few days before Madeline's death. I didn't know if she'd really asked for his help. And I had no way of finding out.

"Who else knew what you were doing?" I asked.

Alan's face fell. "That's just it. Nobody. Madeline introduced me as a temporary consultant but didn't tell anyone what I was doing. They"—Alan motioned to the building beyond the conference room door—"still don't know what I'm doing. Until today, no one has really questioned me, but they've got to put someone into Madeline's place quickly. Suddenly, and rightfully so, they're all interested in how I'm spending my time. I doubt they want me around much longer."

"I still don't understand why you didn't tell this to the police when Madeline was killed."

Alan's face fell further. "Two reasons. When this comes out, Madeline's hard work will have been for naught. She'll be looked at as not only wicked, but stupid. Even though she's dead, I felt I owed her—maybe I could figure out a way to make her look less . . . well, incompetent."

"Second reason?"

"Think about how guilty I might look. I started here a few days before Madeline was killed. I'm the mystery man looking into a mystery that Madeline was attempting to keep hidden. I have no alibi, Becca. I was by myself all afternoon on Friday. But I did not kill my aunt. I adored her."

I had no way to prove otherwise.

"I'll go to the police if I can't get to the bottom of what was going on here," he continued. "Actually, I think I might be on to something." Alan's eye twitched. He looked away from my glance, and my gut twirled uneasily again. Was he lying?

"You need to talk to Officer Brion today."

Alan nodded. "I understand. The new bank management will be in place tomorrow, and I'm sure I'll be asked to leave the premises. I just need a little more time. I promise you this, Becca: if I can figure this out in the next couple of hours, I can probably point the police to Madeline's killer. If I don't try, we might not find that person at all."

A part of me wanted to offer to help him, but a bigger part wanted to be far away from him.

"I'm going to call Sam—Officer Brion—in two hours and tell him what you've told me, Alan. That's the best I can do."

"Thank you. I think that'll be good enough."

"Why were you really at Jeanine Baker's?"

"I wanted to talk to her in person again. She took her money out of the bank and was very angry at Madeline. I thought maybe she had something to do with her death. I was . . . I was investigating on my own, I suppose. When I saw you and the police there, I thought maybe they had something on her, but I never heard that she was arrested. I'm sorry I lied about having met her."

Who was I to criticize him for conducting his own investigation?

"She was out of town. She had nothing to do with Madeline's murder," I said.

"You sure?"

"Positive."

Alan's eye twitched again and he ran his hand through his disheveled hair. It was obvious that he was stressed; I just couldn't be sure about what.

"Why did you ask about the availability of my land? Why did you ask Herb and Don at Bailey's about other land available?"

"I really am looking for some land. I need to invest a chunk of money, and this is a beautiful area. I'm sorry if I was pushy," Alan said, defeated.

I nodded, but I didn't say anything.

"I'd, uh, I'd like to get back to work now," Alan said as he stood.

He still gave me the creeps, perpetually. That wasn't fair, because though he was odd, I wasn't sure he deserved the title of creepy. Nonetheless, I was happy to leave the conference room.

Once back in the lobby, I turned to Alan. "Does the name Bud Morris sound familiar?"

"Yes. He came in Saturday morning, early. It was before the bank opened, and I was the only one here. I came here right after I went to your house with the pies. I met with him and told him he didn't need to worry about the letter he'd received."

"I'd like to get that in writing," I said.

"Why?"

"You took the only evidence that the original letter existed. You're lucky I'm not asking for that back, too. Before I leave, I want something in writing that I can give to Mr. Morris that clears him from any sort of threat of foreclosure, real or not."

You could almost hear the standoff Old West whistle in the background as Alan and I stared at each other. I wasn't going to blink, and he was in a hurry to get back to work. I would break my promise and call Sam immediately if he didn't give me what I wanted. I was in a position of power like I'd never been in before, and I was going to get something out of it.

"How do you know Bud Morris?" Alan finally asked.

"Let's just say I think your problem is more widespread than you know. It's a small town." I didn't mention Clarissa because I wasn't sure of her specific issue, and she would easily be able to take care of herself.

In truth, this sort of synchronicity occurred in Monson all the time. It was bound to in a small town. Plus, lots of people banked at Central Savings and Loan—

probably the majority of the local population, and we all talked.

"Give me a minute," Alan said as he disappeared through another door.

"Thank you," I said quietly.

I sat in the chair in front of Alan's empty desk and looked around. The bank was decorated in bland and boring. The good stuff was locked up—except, apparently, the letterhead.

Either gaining access to the letterhead was easy or stealing it had been an inside job. I stood, tried to look like I wasn't going to snoop, and walked to the other side of Alan's desk. I opened the file drawers and peered into nothing but emptiness. If the letterhead was stored in desk drawers, it was probably only in the desks that were more permanently occupied. This desk must have been available to anyone who just needed to use the phone. Or to store a mystery piece of paper.

I opened the top drawer, the one where, if I had such a desk, I would store pens, pencils, and other small stuff that didn't have another place. The paper that Alan had been looking at was there, folded into thirds. I reached for the open top flap.

"Becca," Alan said behind me, "what are you doing?"

I slammed the drawer shut, garnering the attention of everyone in the bank.

"I, uh, well, I was seeing if there was letterhead in the desk. I wanted to see how easy it was to steal."

"I see." Alan glared. "Well, it isn't easy at all, especially now. We have it locked up, and only certain people have access to it."

"It looks like you've taken care of that, then."

"Yes, Becca, we have."

"Is that my letter?" I pointed to the piece of paper in Alan's hand.

Alan handed me a simple letter of apology that was written on the bank's letterhead.

"Thank you," I said.

Alan nodded, turned, and walked away.

Once in my truck, I looked at the time on my cell phone. I was going to do as I said, and give Alan two hours before I called Sam. I set the alarm.

Two hours not only gave Alan some time, it gave me some, too.

Why wouldn't Madeline call the police, or the "proper authorities," whoever they were, when she found out someone was messing with her bank?

Despite what Alan had said, there was no reasonable excuse for her not to have called someone. I might not have known her well, but I knew she was the picture of pure professionalism. Given normal circumstances, she would have contacted the authorities before taking her next breath. Therefore, her excuse must have been unreasonable, the circumstances abnormal.

I had two hours to think about about what motivated Madeline to do what she had done, and not done. If I figured how and why, I knew that would lead me to who—who killed her.

Twenty-four

I could drive and think at the same time. I had Bud's letter, and a great way to make the time pass would be to make sure he had it in his hands.

I hadn't driven by my childhood home three times in the last ten years. As I drove past it for the third time in a week, once again a stab of something melancholy rolled through my gut. Or was it something else? I shrugged off the feeling and continued on to Bud's.

Ian would be successful, I knew that. Bud's land was beautiful and wide open. It was like a canvas just waiting for the right artist. I envisioned it all in purple, and realized just how much Ian was the right artist.

I parked the truck and made my way to Bud's shack. I knocked but received no answer. The door wasn't locked, so I opened it just a bit and peered in. There was no sign of Bud anywhere.

I grabbed some paper from my truck and wrote him a quick note, put it and the letter from the bank between the door and the frame, and got back on the road. I stopped in front of my childhood home again.

"What is it?" I asked aloud. That returning inkling made me want to remember . . . something.

The house was in great shape, well taken care of and loved. Nothing needed painting, nothing needed extra attention. It looked perfect.

I got out of the truck and stood on the road, staring at it. If someone was home, I was sure to cause suspicion, but I'd explain myself if I had to.

I stared at the windows, at the front door, at the welcome mat, at the walkway leading to the front door. Nothing, and yet something. I couldn't help taking a few steps toward the front door.

And it took only a few steps to realize what I'd been trying to remember. The scene was specific as it played in my mind's eye. I stood still so as not to disturb its flow.

When Allison and I had been young—very young, actually—we'd had a twice weekly ritual with our father. We would each try to be the first one out of bed on those days, even attempting to beat our early bird father. We never did. He was always up before the two of us, and on the front porch in his blue robe, waiting for his little girls.

"I didn't think you'd make it this morning," he'd say as we hurried out to the porch, afraid we'd missed the big event.

"I was up first," I lied.

"You were not." Allison rolled her eyes.

I remembered catching my reflection in the glass in

the front door, noticing how wild my hair was and how neat Allison's was. I remembered punching her in the arm that day, and our father being angry at me.

Soon, the real adventure began. We always heard the truck before we saw it. It rumbled down the dirt road and stopped in front of the house.

It was the Loder Dairy truck, white with black lettering and a black-and-white smiling cow. But for us children, it was more than the dairy delivery. Our father had turned it into an adventure. The driver/delivery person knew our names, and he always played a game with us.

"Heads or tails? It's your turn, Becca."

"Heads," I said as he flipped a coin that magically seemed to alternate wins between me and my sister.

"Heads it is. Do you want to carry the milk or the butter?"

"The butter!" It was always the butter. Whoever got to carry the butter got some extra time to feel the stamp impression underneath the wax paper, and whoever guessed the stamp impression correctly got to butter her toast first. Yep, it was always the butter.

But it wasn't our father, Allison, the milk, or the butter that made this memory so important. It was the deliveryman. I couldn't remember his name—any of their names over the years. But I suddenly remembered something else. All of the trucks were identical, and so was what the delivery people wore—they all, without fail, wore black-and-white checkered shirts. I'd seen the "scarf" around Madeline's neck but hadn't made the connection until that moment. Sam had told me it was not a scarf but a T-shirt. That's what had choked her.

"Oh. My. God," I said aloud.

"Can I help you?" A young woman with a long brown braid peered out the door.

"Sorry. No. I apologize for disturbing you."

I hurried back to my truck and waved to the woman as I pulled back onto the road and fumbled for my cell phone.

"Hey, Becca, what's up?" Allison answered after the first ring. Thankfully, she was where I needed her to be.

"Al, what happened to the Loder Dairy trucks?"

"What?"

"The trucks. I haven't seen them for years. Why haven't I seen them for years?"

"Becca, I have no idea. But you're right. I haven't seen them for years either. Huh, I wonder what happened."

"Can you do me a favor?" I asked.

"Sure."

"Can you find out, somehow, some way, in the next five minutes?"

Allison laughed. "I might need a little more time. What's going on?"

"It's important."

She was silent as she processed the tone of my voice and my words.

"I'll do my best. You'll be by your phone?"

"I won't make another call until I hear from you."

We disconnected, and my thoughts turned as I drove toward town. I was certain that the shirt used to choke Madeline was a Loder Dairy deliveryman's shirt. The more I thought about it, the more I was certain. But why, and who had used it? I had some strong suspicions, but Allison would have to help confirm them.

The phone rang six minutes later.

"Al?"

"Becca, I have some information, not much but some."

"Good. I'm ready."

"Loder Dairy hasn't used delivery trucks for about ten years. Apparently, about then the dairy ownership switched hands, though I don't know who and how." I didn't interrupt her to tell her that Loder Dairy had been in Madeline's family and that those new owners were Mid and Shawn McNeil. "Anyway, apparently when the new owners took it over, it had been losing money. It lost even more with the new ownership. They had to get rid of their home delivery trucks and work only wholesale. They have products in some local grocery stores, but that aspect of the business is small. Why do you need to know this?"

I told her what I knew about the ownership of the Loder Dairy.

"I had no idea," she said. "I can't believe I didn't notice that the trucks weren't around."

"Where did you get this information?" I asked.

"I called Jeanine. I remembered her telling me a few years ago that when her parents ran the egg farm, they supplied a dairy with eggs for fresh delivery. What other dairy could it have been except Loder? She said that when Loder quit the home deliveries, her family had to rebuild that part of their business. She knew the date they stopped almost exactly."

"Do you think she'd know anything about Loder's current financial situation?"

"Do you want me to ask?" Allison said.

I thought a minute. "No, I think I already know."

"Becca, what's going on?"

"Al, I need to call Sam. I promise I'll tell you all about it after I talk to him, okay?" I felt kind of awful for not sharing as nicely as she had shared with me, but there was only so much to tell, and after Alan had seen me looking at the letter in his desk drawer, there might not be time to tell enough of the story for it to make sense.

"Okay, but don't you dare forget to call me."

"I'll call in a couple of hours. Thanks for your help."

I wasn't going out to Loder Dairy by myself. When Abner had been suspected of killing Matt Simonsen, I'd taken on the killer without much thought for my safety. I still didn't know precisely who killed Madeline, but things were becoming clearer, and I didn't think I'd ever take such a chance again. Fortunately, Sam answered on the first ring.

"Hello, Becca."

"Sam, listen. You need to question Drew's cousins Shawn and Mid more closely."

"Why?"

The two hours I'd given Alan weren't up, but I didn't care. I told Sam that I'd snuck into Loder Dairy and what I'd overheard, but that it was more than that. I told him I wasn't sure, but I suspected that the business was in financial trouble because of the empty house and the small number of people working at the dairy. I told him about what had been happening at the bank and how Alan had been trying to solve the problem, but seemed torn between wanting it fixed and wanting it hidden. And I told him about the checkered shirts the delivery people wore when they brought milk and butter in their delivery trucks that weren't around any longer. Most of what I said was an information dump. I wasn't as coherent as I wanted to be, and I couldn't seem to find the words I needed: *So somehow this all has to tie together, doesn't it?*

But my recognition of the shirt did it for him. I told him I didn't know exactly who killed Madeline, but I suspected that at least one of Drew's cousins was somehow involved. I hoped he'd be able to take all I'd said and see the same thing.

"I'll go out to the dairy right away. I'll send Norton and Sanford to the bank. And listen to me, Becca, let us do our jobs. Go home or go back to Bailey's or to Allison's or Ian's. I'll call you when we're done. Okay?"

"Sam, one more thing," I said, ignoring his demand.

"What?"

"Look at the butter stamps."

"What?"

"Look at the edges of the butter stamps. I think they might have been what made the defensive wounds on Madeline's hands."

He was silent long enough that I knew he was processing what I said. It suddenly seemed so obvious.

"Thank you, Becca. I'll call you."

We hung up, and I steered my orange truck on the proper course. I wouldn't go to the dairy by myself, but I sure wasn't *not* going to go. If Sam was there with me, everything would be just fine.

Twenty-five

I parked my truck in the gully down the road from the dairy. I didn't want Shawn, Mid, or Sam to see me, but I wouldn't be able to hide my orange truck completely. Sam's police cruiser wasn't at the dairy yet, and I wasn't going in until he arrived. The only drawback to where I situated myself was that some passing drivers thought I needed assistance. I smiled and gave the thumbs-up many times.

Where was Sam? By my calculations, he should already be at the diary. After twenty more impatient minutes passed, I began to think that he'd gone to the bank first, and was on to something there. I didn't leave, though; he still could be on his way.

I tried to call him but he didn't answer, his voice mail greeting message coming up after four rings. It was probably a good thing he hadn't answered; I wasn't supposed to be where I was, and he'd wonder how I knew he wasn't there yet.

For ten more minutes, I watched traffic. Finally, I decided I was tired of being patient. Sam would be there eventually, I was certain of that, unless he'd caught the killer at the bank. In that case, I wasn't putting myself in harm's way by visiting Shawn and Mid.

The mind is an amazing thing when it comes to justifying less-than-intelligent acts.

I drove the truck out of the gully and bravely parked it in the dairy's long driveway. There were cows in the pasture, but I didn't spy my new friend the calf, although I wasn't sure I'd be able to tell the difference between her and any other black-and-white calf. As on my first visit, there wasn't anyone else around. But if my hunch was right, there weren't many people to *be* around. Somewhere business had gone bad for Loder Dairy, and Shawn and Mid had to run the place with a skeleton crew.

I'd noticed it when I snuck in previously, but I hadn't known what I was noticing. With the information that Allison had supplied and the realization that I hadn't seen the delivery trucks for a long time, the pieces fit together: the Loder Dairy of my childhood no longer existed. Now there was a sense of emptiness, even a sense of abandonment, all around, and it went far beyond the empty house.

I didn't know why the financial situation of the dairy might have caused Shawn and Mid to kill their aunt, but I was certain that money or issues regarding money were behind Madeline's untimely and horrible death. It wouldn't be the first time money was a motive for murder. And, I told myself, though I still didn't really know who the killer was, George was right; the murder was personal. I guessed a family member or members were involved.

Who, or which ones, though? I hoped Drew had nothing to do with it, and I didn't see Sally being involved. That left Alan, Shawn, and Mid. I suspected that in some way all three of them were involved, but which one tied the shirt around Madeline's neck?

I stopped on the wide porch at the front of the house.

I swallowed hard and hesitated. *Okay*, I told myself, *don't be stupid. Don't be confrontational. Just say you're here for a tour. Just tell them about the tour you took when you were a child and how much you enjoyed it and how much you'd love to look around the dairy again. Besides, Sam should be here any minute.*

It was a formality, because as I climbed the porch steps, I knew no one was inside the house. I forced my knuckles to knock on the front door. The sound echoed in the emptiness behind the door. But in case I was being watched, I had to do what would be expected of the casual visitor. I made a show of shrugging my shoulders and then moved to the side of the house to make my way back to the dairy.

"Hello, anyone home?" I called as I stepped into the open area in the middle of the buildings.

Maybe Sam had already been at the dairy and found what I seemed to be finding: no one and nothing around but the cows in the pasture.

But a moment later, the door to the hay barn opened a crack and Shawn made his way out. He closed the door behind him and brushed his thinning hair back. I remembered thinking how much his face was transformed when he smiled. He wasn't smiling now, and he looked older than he probably was. He wore faded jeans and a faded red T-shirt. He waved hesitantly.

"Becca, right? Hello." He extended his hand as he reached me. He was surprised, but cleared his throat and said in a friendly tone, "What can I do for you?"

Play it cool. Play it cool. "Hi, Shawn. I know it's short notice, but I had the afternoon off and I was thinking about the dairy and how much I enjoyed touring it as a child. I was wondering if I could request another tour—the grown-up version." I laughed.

"Oh?" It wasn't a good time, I could tell, but I didn't want to give up.

"I can show myself around if you're busy and you don't mind me peeking at all your dairy farm secrets." I smiled again, but with less enthusiasm.

"Uh, no, I guess I don't mind at all. I, uh, well, I am kind of busy at the moment. Why don't you start over in the milking barn"—he pointed—"and I'll catch up to you in the butter barn." He pointed again. I hoped he didn't notice that my eyes landed on the buildings easily, as though I knew exactly which ones he was talking about.

"Thanks," I said cheerily.

Shawn nodded, turned, and hurried back to the barn he'd come from. I wanted to follow him and see what was keeping him so busy, but I'd catch up to him soon enough.

I sauntered to the milking barn, keeping my eyes toward the road. I wanted to intercept Sam if I could. He wouldn't be happy I was there, and I'd try to ease his anger before he talked to Shawn and Mid.

Instead of going into the milking barn, I walked around it and stood at the fence. Shawn knew I was there, so I could openly admire the pasture. There weren't many living creatures I wasn't fond of in one way or another, and though cows might not be the most amazing species, I found the pasture a beautiful sight. The black-and-white animals looked healthy and well-fed, so if Loder Dairy was having financial problems, at least they'd made sure to take care of their animals. Could people who made sure their animals were taken care of kill a human being? I knew a few people who thought animals were much better company than humans. In fact, my relationship with my dog was far more enjoyable than either of my two marriages. But I chose divorce over murder.

Moo. My friend, or another calf that looked just like my friend, was approaching the fence. It must have been the same one, because how many calves had it in them to be so engaging? This one must have been unique.

"Hello. You're doing whatever you can to get me to quit eating hamburger, aren't you?" I said as I reached through the fence to pet its nose.

But this time, the calf wasn't being friendly. She seemed agitated, as though there was something she really wanted to communicate. She was almost twitchy; her short legs couldn't stop moving even if she'd wanted them to. I couldn't get my hand to her nose because she kept pulling it away from my grasp, as though she was trying to tell me to follow her, which couldn't be possible. Could it?

"What? I'm afraid I don't have a clue what you're talking about."

The calf mooed and walked a few steps down the fence line, toward the butter and hay barns. She turned around, walked back to me, and mooed again.

"Do you want me to follow you?" I knew how ridiculous my attempt at human/bovine communication was, but the calf really did seem to want to tell me something. "Are you that smart?"

It didn't seem possible, but I didn't want to discount the moment. Okay, maybe the calf was just being a calf, but I was curious enough to jump over the fence and join her on the pasture side.

At first, I froze and looked around. I'd just invaded alien territory, and I didn't know how the native population would react. Fortunately, most of the cows were too concerned with their own activities to pay me any attention, but a few of them did glance in my direction and twitch their ears before ignoring me again. I looked around for anything that looked like a bull; even a female digging her hoof in the ground in attack mode would have scared me back to the other side of the fence. But it seemed I was safe.

Moo! my friend exclaimed

"Okay, okay, I'm coming." I stepped lightly and cautiously. I knew enough about cow pastures to know that the cow pies weren't scooped away on a regular basis. I was close enough to the fence, though, that the path was pretty clear.

We passed the butter barn and moved toward the hay barn. The first time I'd been at the dairy, the doors on both sides of the hay barn had been opened wide. Today, they were closed.

The calf stopped at the doors of the hay barn and looked at me as if to say our journey was done. I looked around, wondering who had trained this animal and how hard they were laughing at my willing participation. The other cows couldn't have cared less what I was up to, and there were still no people anywhere. No one. I hadn't checked the butter barn, but it seemed empty, too.

And Sam still wasn't there.

The sense that something wasn't right hit my gut with a thud. Not only was something not right, something was really wrong. I just didn't know what it was. I had a strong urge go back the way I'd come, and leave the dairy and go home before Sam knew I'd been there. Just as I turned around, the calf mooed again, but more quietly this time, as though she didn't want to be heard.

"Impossible! You can't be communicating with me," I said just as quietly. She looked at me plaintively. "Do you want me to look in there?"

The good news was that the calf didn't nod or say anything more. She just stood and looked at me, her big eyes blinking and her baby legs wavering slightly.

"Damn." I wiped my sweaty palms on my thighs and then stepped to the side of one of the huge doors. I tugged gently on the handle. It didn't yield easily, but I managed to open it a small crack.

I had to shove the side of my head against the door to be able to peer into the barn. At first all I saw was hay—more of the bales I'd seen and hidden behind earlier. But when I twisted my neck and pushed my head in deeper, I thought I saw something silver—no, it wasn't silver, it was chrome. I thought I was seeing the back of a car.

That might not be too odd. I knew lots of people who sometimes kept their cars in a barn. But there was something off about a car in this particular barn. When I'd been in it earlier, the barn had looked like it was specifically and only for hay. In fact, so much so that it seemed it would be off limits to a car, perhaps a pollutant of animal feed.

I pulled my head back and thought a second. Should I open the door further and look? Should I run back to my truck? If I was caught, I could just say I'd finished looking in the other buildings. Finally it came down to this: I knew I wasn't going to leave the dairy without knowing more about the car in the hay barn.

I didn't want to get caught, though, so I reached for the handle again and opened the door just a little more. I crouched down to my knees, so if someone looked at eye level, they wouldn't see me. I froze in that position for a second before leaning my head against the door again.

It was most definitely a car. In fact, it was a police car. And if I needed evidence as to just whose police car it was, I only had to look next to it. Officer Sam Brion had in fact made it to the dairy before me. And now, he was a bloody mess tied to a chair with his hands cuffed behind his back, and his head hanging down.

I had to put my hand over my mouth so I wouldn't scream. It looked as if Sam wasn't breathing. He wasn't moving at all. Was he dead? I had to stifle another scream.

With a zip of adrenaline-induced fear, I stood and turned to run to find help. But my escape was thwarted by something hard and metallic; something flat and steely pounded on my face.

I was aware enough for a brief second that I knew my body swung around like a stunt person in a movie fight. I fell and hit the ground, and sank into a dark world.

I'm sure the calf tried to tell me she was sorry.

Twenty-six

It wasn't easy, but I finally opened my eyes. I was inside the hay barn, and someone had tied me to a chair and then tied my wrists behind my back. The position stretched my shoulders to the point of burning pain, but they didn't hurt as much as my head did. I couldn't see straight and I couldn't think straight, but the pain told me I was still alive, though for how much longer I wasn't sure.

I thought I was going to throw up. I wanted to lean forward so I wouldn't throw up all over myself, but my neck wobbled and I couldn't move in any direction without some sort of support.

"Becca," a voice next to me said.

A wave of nausea spun the room as I tried to make my blurry eyes see who was talking to me.

"Becca," the voice said again.

I blinked hard. Why was I seeing only light and fuzzy shapes? Oh, yeah, I'd been hit in the face.

"Who's there?" I slurred.

"It's Shawn."

"What's going on, Shawn?" I asked.

"Why did you have to come out here today?" he responded in a childlike tone.

"I wanted a tour," I lied after a long second of attempting to put some thoughts together coherently.

"Bad timing."

And then I remembered Sam. I sucked in a gasp and thought about standing, but nothing moved. I blinked even harder and told my eyes to clear up, dammit!

"Sam? Sam!" Where was he? I could see a shape next to me. "Sam?"

"Won't do you any good," Shawn said. "He's dead."

"You killed him? You killed a police officer? You killed Sam?" Somehow, panic caused my vision to clear slightly and make the pain less noticeable. *Sam was dead?!*

Shawn crouched down in front of me. "I'm sorry. We had no choice."

"What do you mean, you had no choice?" Horror bubbled in my chest and up my throat. Tears started to flow down my cheeks and I wanted to scream, but didn't think I would be able to.

"He must have figured out what we'd done."

"What did you do?" I screamed, though I knew perfectly well.

"Her truck's in the garage," Mid said as he slipped into the barn through a small opening in the front doors. "Damn, she's awake."

"Yes," Shawn said. "Now what?"

"Why didn't you hit her harder?" Mid asked, as though he wanted to know why Shawn hadn't put out the cat.

Shawn shrugged. "I, uh, I thought I did, I guess."

Even with the panic and horror I felt, I was suddenly aware that Shawn wasn't happy with what was going on. In fact, as my now teary eyes turned to him, I thought he looked green around the gills. His face was drawn; Mid's face was rosy and his eyes were bright behind their professor-type glasses, as though he was relishing the adventure. I have no idea why I noticed these things, except that somewhere deep inside I must have been trying to figure out how to get out of my current predicament alive, and I was looking for the person I might best be able to reason with—and then perhaps kill. They'd killed Sam, and I knew if there was any way I could get free of the ropes, I'd would take out these two men. And wasn't it only a few moments ago I was wondering how someone could possibly kill another human being? I didn't take the time to acknowledge that the universe had sent me the answer in a speedy fashion.

"We've got to kill her," Mid said.

I looked at Sam's slumped and bloody body, and the tears started to fall harder. They probably thought I was crying in fear of my own death, but killing me seemed much less important than the fact that they'd already killed Sam. *How could he be gone?*

"Hang on, Mid. Let's talk about this," Shawn said.

"Talk about what? She can't live. She knows too much."

"She knows about the police officer, but she doesn't know everything; she doesn't know all the details of *that*, anyway. Maybe we could just get out of here. Leave her tied up, and by the time someone finds her, we'll be long gone. Everything else can remain a secret."

"Alan said she saw the letter," Mid said.

"Alan said he *thought* she saw the letter. He wasn't sure," Shawn corrected him.

They both looked at me as if I'd tell them what I knew and what I didn't know. I didn't say anything because I was choking on sobs. I wasn't scared, I wasn't even sad; I was angry, and I wanted my anger to burn through the ropes that held me in the chair. I wanted to hurt these two brothers. Badly.

"Here, use this," Mid said as he reached to the back of his waistband. He pulled out a gun and held it out to Shawn. "It's his." He nodded at Sam's body.

Shawn took the gun but pointed it toward the ground. "Mid, I just don't know."

The sound of a vehicle quieted the brothers. Was it another police officer?

"It's Alan," Mid said as he peered though the space between the doors. "I'll go talk to him. You stay here."

Shawn looked at me. "No, she's not going anywhere. I'll come with you."

Once they were gone, the barn filled up with Sam's death, and I started to cry even harder.

"Sam, Sam, Sam," I wailed loudly. I didn't think Alan would be on my side, but perhaps someone in the vicinity would hear me and offer help.

"Hush, Becca. Come on," a voice said from Sam's direction.

I gurgled and gasped and stopped mid-sob. I looked at him. His eyes were open, and he was peering over at me.

"Oh, my God, you're alive?!"

"Yes, but come on, I need you to focus here. I'm hurt—I think they broke my ankle, and at least one of my shoulders is dislocated, so I can't get to you. You've got to get yourself over to me, get the knife that's in my side pocket, and we'll cut you free. And then we'll get out of here."

I was frozen. He was only three feet away, but I looked at him hard. I wanted to make sure I wasn't hallucinating or having some weird hopeful vision. Not only had they hurt him in the ways he'd mentioned, but he had a huge gash on his head that had bled heavily, covering his head and face in a gory mask. If he really was alive, he might be close to being dead.

"Becca, come on, kiddo, you can do it. We don't have much time." Sam smiled, his teeth bright against the background of the blood. It was the best smile I'd ever seen.

"I'm so glad you're alive," I said.

"Me, too, but let's both get out of this alive. Get moving."

At first, I couldn't make anything move, but I gritted my teeth and placed my feet flat on the ground. Somehow, I'll never understand how, I hopped the chair toward Sam. Pain burned in my head, but it was almost as if it was a separate part of me. I had often noted that there was a separate compartment in my stomach just for dessert. The pain was kind of like that—there, but not a part of my main self.

"Good," Sam said. "Now, you need to try to turn about ninety degrees and get your fingers to my belt. My knife is in the pocket right there."

"They took your gun but let you keep the knife?" I hopped the chair to my left.

"Shawn did. I don't think he wants to be as much a part of this as Mid wants him to be. He was supposed to kill me, but he didn't hit me hard enough. I wasn't out for long, and was conscious when he told Mid I was dead. Now you need to back up just a little . . . without knocking us both over."

I dug my foot into the ground and tried to move only a little bit.

"One more time," Sam said.

I did as he said.

"You're there. Your fingers are only about an inch away from my pocket. Reach. Come on, Becca, really reach."

My fingers cramped from the awkward position, but a long moment later, I felt the solid metal of the knife.

"Good. Yes, that's it. Can you pull the handle of the knife up and out of the pocket?"

"I don't know," I said, my teeth still clenched. I took a deep breath and put two fingers around the handle. I pulled, and the knife dropped back into the pocket. "Damn, my fingers don't want to move that way."

"Try again."

I pulled on the ropes around my wrists, trying to loosen them a little. Then I reached my right hand and put my fingers more firmly around the knife handle and pulled. Suddenly I had it, though my grasp was precarious.

"Okay, don't drop it. Hang on. Listen to me. You need to pull out the blade. It's folded into the handle. And then you need to move around me now so you can either cut my ropes or you can give me the knife and I can cut your ropes."

Since I had to get my fingertips to pull out blade, I had

to get the knife into my hand better. Surprisingly, that was the easy part. I had a grip on the knife and pulled the blade out quickly.

"Okay, which one of us is going to cut?" I asked.

"Just move first, and we'll see which one works better. Don't drop the knife, okay?"

I dug my feet into the ground again and moved. It wasn't as easy as it should have been. My ankles weren't tied together and neither of them was hurt, so I didn't understand why moving the chair was so tricky. I wasn't looking at Sam and was moving around him as I held the knife—barely held it. I could easily either drop the knife or stab him in a kidney.

"Just about a half inch more. No, stop. Back a little. There you go. I think you're at my hands. Do you want to try to cut the ropes or give me the knife?"

"How tight is the rope around your wrists?"

"Tight, but loose enough that I can move them."

"I'm going to give you the knife, then. I've loosened my ropes as much as I can. Here. Got it?"

"Almost. Yes. Good. We're running out of time, but I'm going to try to place the blade on your ropes. Tell me quickly if I'm on your skin."

"'K."

I held still as I Sam struggled to do whatever it was he was doing. I felt pressure on my wrists, but no blade.

"Go, Sam. Cut quickly. Do whatever you have to do."

With surprising strength, Sam sliced through the ropes. My hands flew apart.

"Hurry, get the knife from my hands, Becca. I'm about to drop it."

I caught it just as it came out of his grasp. I hurried through the ropes around my chest.

"Good. Now, Becca, get out of here and get some help. I'm not sure I can walk. Hurry."

"Not a chance in hell I'm leaving this barn without you." I cut the ropes around his wrists and his chest. I hadn't noticed it before, but his ankle was swollen to about three times its normal size, and his right arm hung limp once he was free.

"Really, Becca, this isn't a good idea. You can't carry me."

"If I have to, I will. Shut up and do what you can to help me. Can you move your left arm?"

"Yes."

"Put it around me, and I'll lift you up."

He did as I commanded, and somehow I got him to a sort of standing position. His legs buckled once, but then he stabilized.

"I can't go far with this ankle. Get out of here. Get some help."

"Your ankle just needs to hold long enough to get us out to the road," I said.

We were both silent for a moment. The road might as well have been a million miles away. It was going to be a long journey, but we didn't have a choice.

"Come on, Sam," I said.

We didn't have time to waste, but suddenly, we were both caught in the moment. With his good arm around my shoulder, he pulled me close and kissed the top of my head. There was nothing romantic about the gesture, but there was something that seemed bigger than that—

stronger, perhaps. I couldn't define why, but I didn't want him ever to let go.

"You're okay, Becca. We're okay. Let's get out of here."

We hobbled toward the back doors of the hay barn. On the other side were the pasture, the cows, and the road; the world and safety.

But we weren't quick enough.

A noise sounded from the front of the barn.

I turned just as Alan flew through the doors. He landed on his gut and rolled as though he'd rehearsed the move. In the next instant, he noticed us and his eyes widened.

"Run if you can," he said, just before the boom of the gunshot rattled my teeth and all the bales of hay, and I dropped the knife into a small pile of straw.

Twenty-seven

We tried to do as Alan said, but didn't get far. We didn't even make it to the back doors before Mid stopped us. He pointed Sam's gun at us. "Get back here," he said calmly.

I looked at Sam's face. Blood had dried and crusted thickly on the right side of his forehead and his cheek. He was unrecognizable except for his blue eyes that could be friendly one moment and iced with anger the next. I was now scared, but one look at his icy blues told me that he wasn't scared. He was angry, to the point that I was worried he'd do something stupid, like put himself in the line of fire. I placed my hand on his arm and hoped my expression told him not to be rash.

We turned and hobbled toward Mid, Sam making sure he was slightly in front of me, his body protecting mine.

"Mid, put the gun down. You haven't done anything

yet that we can't work out," Sam said. I was surprised at the evenness of his voice.

Mid laughed. "Right. We've assaulted a police officer. Thought you were dead, but I guess not"—he looked at Shawn—"and my brother coldcocked her." He flicked the gun. Sam leaned even more in front of me.

"We're okay. Alan's okay. Let us go, and we'll get you some help," Sam said.

"Help? You want to get me some help?" Mid laughed. The maniacal tone in his voice made me swallow hard.

"Maybe they're right," Shawn said as he came through the opening. "We've caused enough harm. Let's talk about this, Mid."

"You killed our aunt. I don't think you'll get off that easily," Alan said. He was still on his side on the ground. I cringed at his timing. Even though he'd told us to run, I still didn't like him.

Mid walked over to Alan and kicked him hard in his back, probably right on a kidney. Alan made a horrible noise that sounded like an exhale mixed with a groan, and then curled into the fetal position.

"Mid, stop," Shawn said. He looked at Sam, and his expression seemed to plead for help or mercy. Sam couldn't do much, but I didn't point that out.

Clearly, it was all of us against Mid. Even Shawn wanted his brother to stop, but Mid had the gun and that made him more powerful than the rest of us combined, unless we could come up with a way to get it away from him. And that didn't seem very likely. Sam, Alan, and I were addled, and Shawn didn't seem to the have the guts or influence of a goldfish.

"You could have helped, Alan," Mid said, but Alan

was in too much pain to care what Mid said. "You didn't have to let her see the letter. We should have killed you, too."

"No more killing, Mid," Sam said. "Listen to me—no more killing. We can still work all of this out. If you kill anyone else, we won't be able to help you. Okay?"

Mid looked at Sam, and though he held the gun and had pretty much admitted to murder and to wanting to kill again, a wave of sorrow rolled through my gut. It mixed with fear and anger, and again I wanted to throw up. I tried to swallow the huge lump in the back of my throat.

"Mid," I said, surprised my voice still worked. "What happened? Why did you have to kill your aunt?"

For a moment it seemed as if he wasn't going to answer. He moved into his own thoughts, and his eyes became glazed and distant. I thought he might actually be tearing up. He lowered the gun.

Shawn noticed, and stepped toward him as though he might try to take the gun. But Mid recovered too quickly, as if remembering where he was and what was going on. His eyes cleared, he took a step away from Shawn, and raised the gun again.

"She set us up. She gave us the dairy and made sure we'd fail."

"No, Mid, she didn't make sure you'd fail, she just knew you would," Alan said.

"Same thing, isn't it?" Mid spit out the words. "Then she wouldn't help us. We'd lost almost everything, had been losing so much for years. She could have given us money, but she refused—said that we should have run the business better, said that the family had run it successfully for years and that we should have been able to handle it. She gave us the dairy and made it so we'd fail. She did it because we didn't 'appreciate' or love her enough. She admitted as much right before I . . ."

"Why didn't you just sell the farm?" I asked.

Mid laughed. "She'd have bought it and given it to Drew or someone else in the family, and then given them the help to make it work. If she'd just given us a little money, if she'd just helped us . . ."

"Why didn't you go to another bank?" I asked. How had Madeline's hold been so strong on these men?

Mid laughed and then wiped at the spit at on the corner of his mouth. "She had us blackballed. Even Sally, our own sister, couldn't get her bank to help us."

I wanted to ask why they didn't just walk away from the dairy and their family, but somehow I already knew the answer—that just wasn't an option. Somehow the hold that Madeline had on them was strong, too strong. It came from their childhood when she "rescued" them. In her mind, they hadn't treated her as she deserved to be treated, so she punished them with the full force of her power. Sally had worshipped Madeline, and she was now an emotional wreck. Shawn and Mid hadn't worshipped her, and they had become homicidal. "Dysfunctional" only scratched the surface when describing this family.

"I don't get it, Mid. Why the fake foreclosure letters?" I asked.

"We wanted to ruin her. When she wouldn't help us— her own family, for God's sake—we knew we had to ruin her. I stole the stationery from her desk. It was so easy, too easy." Mid laughed and then sobered as he looked down at Alan. "And then he figured it out. He figured out we were doing it."

"I wasn't going to tell anyone, Mid. I just wanted the two of you to stop. Even when I thought you'd killed Madeline, I wasn't going to tell anyone. I just wanted you to stop," Alan repeated.

Mid looked at Shawn. "You told me Alan was talking to the authorities."

"I told you they'd contacted him," Shawn said, anger now beginning to thicken his voice. "I was concerned that he'd have to talk to them. I didn't ever say that he had. You haven't really been listening, Mid. Come on, listen to me now. Put the gun down."

Mid looked at me. "Alan called today and told us you'd seen the letter in his desk. We knew we'd been caught. We were going to just leave, but you showed up." Mid looked at Sam.

"But I didn't, Mid. I didn't see the letter. I have no idea what it said. Alan came back to the desk too quickly." I shifted my weight and Sam's weight to my other foot. We were both becoming increasingly heavier. I wouldn't be able to prop us up much longer.

"I told you she might not have seen it," Alan said.

Suddenly, regret filled the barn. Whatever was in that letter must have been the final straw, so to speak. It was clear that if Mid and Shawn hadn't thought I'd seen its contents, none of what was happening would be happening.

Mid looked at Shawn, who ran his fingers through his hair and then looked away.

"Idiots," Alan said. His timing once again made me question his intelligence. Of course, Mid kicked him.

"Why did you kill your aunt, Mid?" Sam asked. "Sounds like she was doing everything she could to make your lives difficult, but why did you *have* to kill her?"

"I went to her house early to try one more time to see if she'd give us some money. I snuck in and went up to her room. She flew into a rage. She couldn't believe I had the gall to keep begging." Mid shook his head. "She was so arrogant and so self-righteous. She said that we'd ruined the family name, and probably her reputation. I just wanted her to shut up about it, but she wouldn't."

"So you choked her with an old shirt?" I asked, disgusted. I was getting more tired and aggravated by the second.

"It was a gift for her. I thought she'd be in a good mood. I took her one of our old delivery shirts and a stupid butter stamp. I wanted her to reminisce about the old days, I wanted her to remember the good times.

"But she was so angry. So very angry. I had no choice, don't you see? She was going to take everything from us."

"I understand," Sam said. "You were pushed to kill her. You had no choice." His voice was slurring. He was getting too heavy, and if he passed out, I'd drop him.

Shawn took another brave step toward his brother.

"Oh, no, step back. I need to think," Mid said. Shawn stepped back and to the side.

"It's all right, Mid, we understand," Sam continued.

"No." Mid raised the gun and aimed directly at Sam.

I tried to maneuver Sam backward, but I couldn't move either of us.

"Mid, come on, put the gun down. Let's talk about this some more," Sam said.

Mid raised the gun and took perfect aim at Sam's head. I pulled my shoulder out from under Sam's arm, and he fell to the ground. I crouched next to him. I knew I'd hurt him. Mid, now even angrier, aimed the gun at Sam again. There was nowhere for us to go, unless the earth could open and swallow us to safety.

I paid attention to my breathing because I thought I was about to take my last pulls of oxygen, ever. Mid would shoot Sam and then me. No one would stop him, and because they were cousins, together they'd figure out how to cover up their crimes.

"Becca," Sam said, "please try to run."

"No way."

Sometimes things just don't work out.

But sometimes they do.

We'd managed to calm Mid's anger just long enough. Suddenly, one of the barn doors swung open and hit him in the back. The force of the blow caused him to fire the gun, but his aim was directed away from Sam. Later, I would swear that I didn't hear the gunfire until *after* I felt the searing pain hit my arm. After the pain and the noise, I was flat on my back, wondering what I'd missed.

A scuffle must have ensued, because I heard yelling and confusion as I stared up at the rafters and tried to guess how many pieces my arm must be in.

"She's going to be okay." Sam was sitting up next to me. "We need to try to stop the bleeding and get her to the hospital. Put some pressure on the wound." He looked at the person who was on my other side. I turned my head slightly and focused my eyes.

"Allison?" I either thought or said aloud, I wasn't sure which.

"Hey, Sis." Her brown eyes were wide, and her olive complexion had gone green. "You didn't call me back. I called Vivienne Norton. Every police officer from Monson and the surrounding counties is here. I'm sorry I got you shot, though."

I knew she was, and I knew that if she was there, I'd probably be okay. Probably.

Twenty-eight

I was down an arm and loaded with painkillers, but there were enough helping hands to compensate.

It was only a suface flesh wound, even though it hurt like more. It would leave an interesting scar, but no real damage. My arm was in a sling, but I wasn't going to let something like a little gunshot wound ruin a perfectly good wedding. Plus, apparently it had once again been medically confirmed that I have a hard head. I had no concussion to go along with the lovely bruise on the side of my face. I'd covered facial injuries with makeup before, though, so I'd been able to handle the task.

"How about these, Becca?" Abner asked as he held two of the most colorful and beautiful bouquets I'd ever seen.

"Perfect. She'll love them."

"Good. I'll take care of them until she gets here."

"Thanks, Abner."

Hobbit stood at my side as I looked around the tent.

"Looks good, huh?" I asked her.

She nudged my leg in agreement. She sensed I was hurt, and I knew she wouldn't leave my side until she knew I'd be okay.

Everyone had their game faces on and were busy doing their parts to make Linda and Drew's wedding memorable. Abner had decorated the tent and the arbor with hundreds of his wildflowers. I was sure that Stella had been up all night frosting the Navy-themed wedding cake. She was still fussing over the ribbon topper. Allison was everywhere, making sure everything looked perfect. Herb was practicing his violin. His face was pinched, and little beads of nervous perspiration had popped out on his temples, but he sounded great.

Barry, decked out in a suit, was beginning to guide guests and vendors to their seats.

"Second time I've seen you in a dress," a voice said from behind me.

I turned. "Sam! They let you out of the hospital?"

Sam's ankle was a "mess," according to the same doctor who took care of my arm. One shoulder had been dislocated, and that arm was now in a sling that matched mine. His head was wrapped like a mummy's, leaving him no opportunity to slick back his hair. He was in a wheelchair being pushed by the biggest muscles in town.

"No, we escaped," Officer Norton said. "Sam wasn't going to miss the wedding."

"We didn't escape. I got permission, but I have to go back to the hospital right after the wedding," Sam corrected her.

"I'm glad you're here," I said.

We looked at each other for a long moment.

"I'm sorry I was so careless," Sam apologized. "I should never have gone to the dairy alone. If I'd taken someone, another officer, I doubt either of us would have been hurt."

So that's why he came. For some reason I'd never completely understand, Sam felt guilty for putting me in the line of fire of a maniacal killer.

I bent down and kissed his cheek gently. "We're both alive and we're both going to be fine. I know I'd be dead if you hadn't brought yourself back to life. Thanks for doing that."

We were interrupted by other vendors who wanted to talk to Sam. I stepped carefully away from the growing crowd.

It wasn't until long after I'd been taken to the hospital that Allison told me what Sam told her. Sam was searching the dairy when he was hit in the head from behind. He didn't see who'd done it, but Shawn confessed to being the one. Sam was glad he was the one who'd done it. He probably saved Sam's life by telling Mid that he was dead.

Shawn had hit me, too, but not hard enough to cause permanent damage. Oddly, I felt gratitude for what had happened. Other than hitting Sam and me, Shawn hadn't done anything very criminal. Mid had stolen the letterhead, written and mailed the letters, and killed Madeline by himself. But Shawn and Alan were both being charged with aiding and abetting. Sally had done nothing criminal, but she wouldn't be at the surprise wedding; she was with her brothers in their "time of need." She was a mess, and it wasn't going to be an easy road for her. I promised myself to check in with her every now and then.

Oh, and Shawn had done one other thing.

He'd written a note to Alan. Shawn knew that Mid had killed Madeline and that Mid was losing whatever was left of his sanity. The failing business had taken Mid to dark places that scared the entire family. Shawn hand-wrote the note that Alan put in his desk the day I was at the bank. It said simply: *If something happens to me, Mid was involved. He's out of control.*

He didn't say that he knew Mid had killed Madeline. He didn't mention anything else, but it was enough for Alan to know—know who'd killed Madeline, know who'd been sending out the fraudulent letters. When Alan thought I'd seen the note, he called his cousins to tell them. Shawn told Mid that he written the note. After the two hours passed, Alan thought I'd probably call the police if I hadn't already. He felt he should drive out to the dairy to make sure Shawn and Mid were okay. Plus, he hoped to get the full story about what happened with his aunt. He never expected to see me there.

"Hey," Allison said as she moved next to me, "you okay?"

"Yeah. I'm glad Sam's here."

"Me, too, but he should be in his hospital bed eating Jell-O and watching bad television."

I nodded.

"Are they on their way?" Allison asked.

"Yep. Ian called a few minutes ago. They're almost here."

I'd wanted to be the one to pick them up and explain

the wedding surprise, but the chauffeuring task had understandably been passed off to Ian.

Drew and Linda had been told the details of the murder the night before. It had been rough on them both, but knowing the truth had been a relief of sorts. At first they argued with Ian about going ahead with the wedding plans, but he'd managed to talk them into being ready to be picked up. They thought they were going to meet me at the justice of the peace's office. I hoped they were ready for the surprise when Ian brought them to Bailey's. It was a risk—Drew's family had been completely torn apart in the last week. But when he married Linda, he would be well on the way to a new family. He was leaving Friday, no matter what. It was time to make things better, and a wedding would surely do the trick. Right?

"Hey, Al, thanks for saving our lives," I said.

"You're welcome." Allison smiled. "I'm glad you're still here."

Ian walked through the tent opening with Drew and Linda. Though the surprised looks on the bride's and groom's faces needed my immediate attention, I took a moment to fully appreciate my adorable boyfriend.

Ian, having been promoted to the position of best man since Alan was in jail, was decked out in a suit—one he must have purchased recently, because I was pretty sure I knew every piece of clothing in his closet and I'd never seen it before. The gray suit, white shirt, and blue tie wasn't a normal ensemble for him, but it worked very well. His ponytail was smooth and perfect.

He'd made it to the hospital in record time the day before, and hadn't stopped attending to me until I sent him to get Linda and Drew a couple hours ago. He caught my glance and smiled. He subtly raised his fingers to his lips and blew me a kiss. I didn't know it was possible to fall in love over and over again with the same person, but he kept busting any myth that falling in love was all done in one swoop. That morning, I'd told him that I couldn't wait to go to Iowa with him. He told me he wouldn't accept that answer until I said it to him while I wasn't in a pain medication-induced state. I wouldn't change my mind, but I got his point.

I approached the bride and groom. "Linda, Drew, I see you're surprised." Linda's eyes were tearing, and Drew put his arm around her shoulders. "I know it's been a rough time, and this isn't exactly what you envisioned, but we wanted you to have a real wedding, not just a trip to the justice of the peace. I hope you don't mind."

They were both struggling. It might have been too much for them to process, so I slipped my good arm through Ian's and we gave them a moment.

"It probably isn't appropriate, I know that," I said. "But we thought, maybe Drew could leave on a happy note."

"You okay with this?" Linda finally asked Drew.

"What about you?" Drew replied.

"I think it's lovely."

"Then I think it's perfect. Thank you, Becca." Drew smiled.

At that moment, I didn't think I'd ever admired someone more than I did Drew. He'd lost his mother, his family had betrayed him, he was about to leave on some top-secret and dangerous mission, and he still wanted Linda to be happy. Maybe he *was* perfect, or maybe he was just a good guy and he and Linda were as lucky to have each other as I was to have Ian.

Though I'd been married twice, I'd never officially walked down an aisle. You know, it wasn't so bad after all. It was simply one step after the other.

Linda and Drew's wedding was beautiful. We all ignored the bad things and focused on the good things and a hopeful future.

Despite everything else—the murder, the craziness, and the injuries—when it was spring in South Carolina, and friends and family were all around, and there was a wedding to witness, it was hard not to call it a pretty good day.

Recipes

Mamma Maria's Simple and Quick Mini Banana Cream Pies

6 mini piecrusts—Mamma uses the graham
   cracker crusts, but some people claim that
   chocolate is good, too.
1 box banana cream instant pudding
2 cups whole or 2 percent milk (for the pudding)
2 medium bananas, sliced
¼ to ½ cup toffee pieces—Mamma uses the Heath
   English toffee bits found in the grocery store by
   the chocolate chips.
Whipped cream—Mamma likes heavy cream, but
   if you prefer the taste of nondairy whipped topping, that's okay, too.

Make pudding according to package directions.

Slice bananas and place 2–3 slices in the bottom of each mini piecrust.

When the pudding is ready, whisk a big dollop (½ to 1 cup) of whipped cream into it. Mix until combined.

Fill the piecrusts with the pudding mixture and top the pudding with remaining banana slices.

Place pies in the refrigerator to cool.

Once the pies are cool, sprinkle them with toffee bits. Don't be shy with the toffee. It adds a great crunchy flavor.

Right before you serve the pies, top them with more whipped cream. Of course, Mamma piles it high!

Dan's Lavender Cookies

⅝ cup butter
½ cup white sugar
½ teaspoon vanilla extract
1 large egg
1½ cups all-purpose flour
1 teaspoon lavender flowers, crushed with a mortar and pestle *

Preheat the oven to 350 degrees F. Grease one regular sized cookie sheet.

Cream together the butter, sugar, and vanilla.

Beat the egg, and blend into the butter mixture.

Mix in the flour and the lavender flowers.

Drop batter by teaspoonfuls onto cookie sheets.

Bake 15 to 20 minutes, until golden. Remove the cookies and cool them on racks. Makes eighteen cookies.

*When you're baking or cooking with lavender flowers, make sure you purchase culinary lavender. Culinary lavender is grown without herbicides or pesticides. Some lavender is better in savory dishes, some better in sweet dishes. Royal Velvet lavender works well with sweets such as cookies.

Mamma Maria's Peach Delight

Given to her from Mamma Marilyn

FILLING

1 (21 ounce) can peach pie filling
1 (16 ounce) can peach slices in light syrup, well
     drained

TOPPING

1 cup firmly packed light brown sugar
1 cup all-purpose flour
½ cup quick-cooking oatmeal
½ cup butter, softened

CAKE

1 cup sugar
1 cup butter, softened
2 large eggs, slightly beaten
1¼ cups light or nonfat sour cream
1 tablespon vanilla extract
3 cups all-purpose flour
1 teaspoon baking powder
1 teaspoon baking soda
½ teaspoon salt

GLAZE

1 cup confectioner's sugar
1–2 tablespoons skim milk

Preheat the oven to 350 degrees F.

Stir together filling ingredients, then set them aside.

Stir together all topping ingredients until crumbly; set the mixture aside.

In a large mixer bowl, beat sugar and 1 cup butter at medium speed, scraping bowl often, until light and fluffy (1–2 minutes).

Add eggs, sour cream, and vanilla; continue beating, scraping bowl often, until smooth (1–2 minutes).

Add all remaining cake ingredients and continue beating, scraping bowl often, until smooth (1–2 minutes).

Spread half of batter in greased 9 x 13-inch baking pan. Spread peach filling over batter. Drop spoonfuls of remaining batter over filling. (Do not spread it.) Sprinkle with topping.

Bake for 60–70 minutes, or until a toothpick inserted in the center comes out clean. Cool at least 15 minutes. Meanwhile, in small bowl stir together glaze ingredients until smooth; drizzle the glaze over the cooled cake.

Makes 15 servings.

After a weekend together full of farmers' market shopping and cooking, this recipe was given to Mamma by the amazing and wonderful Marilyn Peterson. Thanks, Marilyn!

George's Quiche Jeanine

George makes quiche using only Jeanine's farm-fresh eggs. He makes many variations, but everyone's favorite is his version of quiche Lorraine: quiche Jeanine.

1 9-inch pastry piecrust
8 slices bacon
4 large eggs, slightly beaten
½ cup sliced onion
1 cup sliced mushrooms
1½ cups light cream or half-and-half
¼ teaspoon salt
1½ cups shredded Swiss cheese
1 tablespoon all-purpose flour

Preheat the oven to 450 degrees F.

Place the pastry crust in a 9-inch pie pan and bake the crust for 8 minutes or until lightly browned. Remove it from oven and reduce temperature to 325 degrees F.

In a large skillet, cook the bacon until it's crisp. Drain it, but save 3 tablespoons of the grease. Crumble the bacon and set it aside. Sauté the onion and mushrooms in the reserved grease until the onion is tender. Drain the vegetables.

In a large bowl, mix together the cream, salt, and eggs. Stir in the bacon, mushrooms, and onion. In a separate bowl, toss the cheese and flour together, then add to the egg mixture. Be sure to mix well. Pour the egg mixture into the piecrust.

Bake in a preheated oven for 40 to 45 minutes, or until a knife inserted in the center of the quiche comes out clean. If necessary, cover the edge of the crust with foil while baking, to prevent burning or overbrowning. Let stand for 10 minutes before serving.

Serve with a salad and the yummy bread of your choice!

Becca's Strawberry Chocolate Preserves

This new flavor was as easy as adding the chocolate to Becca's original strawberry preserves recipe. I've repeated the original recipe below, adding the chocolate changes in boldface type.

> *4 pints strawberries, to yield 4 cups crushed*
> *berries*
> *7 cups sugar*
> *3 ounces liquid pectin*
> *Strawberry huller (if you don't have a huller, you*
> *can use a small knife,or even a paperclip)*

1½ cups of grated bittersweet chocolate
12 8-fluid-ounce canning jars
Baking sheets
Jar lids
Colander
Food processor
Big saucepan
*Boiling water canner (some people use a pressure
    canner, but I prefer the boiling water method)*
Tongs

Boil jars (at least 5 minutes). My dishwasher has a fancy-schmancy Sterilize mode, but that feature is still rare.

Remove the jars with tongs and place them on a cookie sheet to dry and cool.

Prepare lids by placing them in a saucepan of gently boiling water. I never use the dishwasher for the lids.

Prepare the strawberries by dipping them in a sink of cold water and immediately lifting them into a colander to drain.

Hull the strawberries. Place half the strawberries at a time into a food processor and process them for 10 to 15 seconds; they should still be slightly chunky. This step becomes intuitive over time. Some people like larger chunks of fruit in their preserves, but I prefer uniform pieces that make an even "spread." (Hint: the chunks of fruit are what make the preserves. Jams are made with totally crushed fruit and, typically, less sugar.)

Place the strawberries into a 6- or 8-quart pot. Stir the sugar into the fruit and mix well. Bring the mixture to a full, rolling boil over high heat, stirring constantly.

Add the pectin and return the preserves to a full, rolling boil. Boil hard for 1 minute, stirring constantly to prevent scorching.

Remove the preserves from the heat and skim off and discard any foam, using a metal spoon. **Stir in the chocolate.**

Cover and refrigerate the mixture overnight.

The next day, bring the preserves to a boil again; boil hard for 1 minute, stirring constantly.

Remove the preserves from the heat and discard any foam, using a metal spoon.

Ladle the preserves into a liquid measuring cup and immediately fill the jars to within 1/8 inch of the top.

Wipe the jar rims and threads with a clean, damp cloth.

Place the lids on the jars and screw them on tightly.

Fill the canner half full of water; then cover and heat the water to boiling.

Using a jar lifter, place the jars filled with preserves on the rack in the canner. If necessary, add boiling water to bring the water to 1 to 2 inches above the tops of the jars. Do not pour boiling water directly on the jars. Cover the canner.

Boil the jars for at least 5 minutes, and longer at higher altitudes. (Check the recipe on the package of pectin.)

As soon as the processing time is up, use a jar lifter to remove the jars from canner. If liquid has boiled out of the jars during processing, do not open them to add more. Do not retighten the screw bands, even if they are noticeably loose.

Check the seals after one hour, to make sure the lids are curving down. If the seals are not tight, refrigerate the jars and use the preserves as soon as possible.

WELL-CRAFTED MYSTERIES
FROM BERKLEY PRIME CRIME

- **Earlene Fowler** Don't miss these Agatha Award–winning quilting mysteries featuring Benni Harper.

- **Monica Ferris** These *USA Today* bestselling Needlecraft Mysteries include free knitting patterns.

- **Laura Childs** Her Scrapbooking Mysteries offer tips to satisfy the most die-hard crafters.

- **Maggie Sefton** These popular Knitting Mysteries come with knitting patterns and recipes.

- **Lucy Lawrence** These brilliant Decoupage Mysteries involve cutouts, glue, and varnish.

- **Elizabeth Lynn Casey** The Southern Sewing Circle Mysteries are filled with friends, southern charm—and murder.

penguin.com